Magnificent Devices

A steampunk adventure novel

Magnificent Devices, Book Three

Shelley Adina

Moonshell Books

Cover design by Ann Bui Nguyen.
Cover art by Phat Puppy Art, used under license.

Discover other titles by Shelley Adina at www.shelleyadina.com.

Copyright © 2012 Shelley Adina Bates
All rights reserved.
ISBN-13: 978-1-939087-02-7
ISBN-10: 1939087023

For every young lady and gentleman
who ever looked to the horizon
and wondered what was on the other side

Chapter 1

Somewhere over the Atlantic, late September 1889

The man's eyes bulged in his final moments and he glared with brutal accusation. "You—" he choked. "You did it ... and you'll regret it ..."

She faltered back, but her feet tangled in her apple-green skirts and she couldn't run. Still he staggered toward her.

"You—" Those eyes, filling her vision. Hazel eyes under auburn hair. James's eyes in another man's face. And then they boiled over, sizzling like bacon on a griddle, and popped and she screamed—

—and woke herself up. The breath left her lungs and Lady Claire Trevelyan flopped back on the bunk with a gasp. Sweat trickled down her temple.

Breathe. You must breathe.

Lightning Luke had met his Maker several weeks ago at her hands, and while he might have found some measure of peace, she had not. Most of the time she was able to tamp down the guilt at having ended the life of another human being. It had been an accident. But in the midnight hours, there was his face again, contorted and boiling and accusing her until his last breath.

It was always so real, even if she had never actually seen his eyes. Her mind had put those of another in that face, one she had wronged, as if he—

Something rustled in the dark.

Claire sucked in a breath. It was not Lightning Luke. He was in a watery grave, to the best of her knowledge. It was not even Lord James Selwyn, who was in London. She was safe aboard the *Lady Lucy*, the luxury airship belonging to John, Earl Dunsmuir, and his wife Davina, to whom she had restored Willie, their son, not a week past.

Her cabin, while comfortably appointed with a velvet coverlet on a bed set into a kind of curved cupboard, and gleaming paneling that set off the visiting chairs, was not large. She could cross it in six steps, and by now, the third night of their voyage, she knew its topography by heart.

"Maggie?" she whispered. Perhaps one of the Mopsies had awakened in the night and needed her. "Lizzie?"

A thump, followed by scratching that somehow communicated agitation. This time, she could pinpoint its location: above, in the brass piping that ran along the floors and ceilings conveying heat, gas, and various other necessities in an airship this size.

She reached for a moonglobe. That was what the countess called them, she being of a gentle and fanciful turn of mind. Claire had inquired of the chief steward what they were, and he had launched into such an enthusiastic explanation of its properties ("One cannot have lamps and flames on an airship, my lady —only think of the gas fuselage above our heads!") that even she had been astonished that so much clever chemistry could be cupped in her hand. She shook the globe and it lit from within as the chemicals combined, illuminating the entire room.

No one was there.

But something was. Something that scratched, and clinked, and—was that a flutter? Good heavens, did *bats* lodge in the high ceilings of the passenger deck?

She lifted the globe and peered upward, and an enormous winged shadow leaped down upon her head.

She choked down a second scream that wanted to rattle the pipes, and grabbed for the shadow. It fought back, a limbless fighting ball of claws and feathers that—

Feathers?

Claire pounced on the moonglobe she'd dropped and held it up.

The fighting claws and feathers landed on the nightstand and resolved themselves into a small red hen, who shook her plumage into order and glared at her with offended dignity.

"Rosie?" Claire's knees gave out and she sat in the opening to her bunk rather suddenly. This couldn't be Rosie, the alpha hen of the flock of rescued chickens at the cottage in Vauxhall. The Dunsmuirs must have a small flock aboard for eggs, though with the powers of modern refrigeration, this seemed rather bucolic and unnecessary.

The hen stepped daintily off the nightstand and onto her knee, settling there as if she meant to spend the night.

She always did this. And it never worked.

"Rosie, for goodness sake. How on earth did you come to be on the *Lady Lucy* when I thought you were safe at home?" She petted the hen, speaking softly. "Lewis is going to be frantic, to say nothing of your flock. You will be supplanted by that rooster, my girl, and there will be no going back."

The door cracked open and in the greenish-white light of the moonglobe, Claire could see a two-inch-wide sliver of white batiste nightie. "Come in, Maggie."

"I 'eard a noise, Lady. All right?"

"Yes, quite all right. Come and see who has taken ship with us."

If she had expected Maggie to fall on Rosie's neck rejoicing, she was sadly disappointed. She looked almost … guilty. "Hullo, Rosie." She stroked the gleaming feathers with gentle fingers, and Claire put two and two together.

"Maggie, did you know Rosie had stowed away?"

Maggie chewed on her lower lip. "She ent no trouble, Lady. She's bunked wiv us before."

"True on both counts. But that does not answer my question."

The ten-year-old's eyes filled with pleading. "She wanted to come, Lady. So I tucked 'er in my kit and she were quiet as the grave ... 'til she found out she could roost up there." When she lifted her eyes to the pipes, a tear escaped down her cheek. "She's been up in the pipes a day and a half and I couldn't get 'er down."

"She'll be hungry, then."

"Aye. And thirsty."

"Then we will nip along to the dining saloon. You know Mr. Skully keeps a cold collation on the sideboard in case the family wishes a snack in the night."

"I know. Me and Lizzie, we found Willie an' Tigg in there two nights in a row. Willie can't keep out of the trifle. Nor can Lizzie, except when she's underfoot in the guardsroom and the gondola."

The little monkeys. "Is there anywhere on this ship you haven't gone? Captain Hollys gave me a tour of the gondola, but I couldn't tell you where the guardsroom is."

"Below and aft," Maggie said. "Just forward of the storage bay where the landaus are."

"Goodness." Claire slid a hand under Rosie's feet and carried her out into the corridor, closing the door behind them. "You sound like a proper airman."

"Only 'cos Willie laughed at me when I called the bow the front." She kept pace with Claire without effort. Regular meals, exercise, and hope were causing her to grow. Soon she would be past Claire's elbow and asking to have her skirts let down. "He's got nuffink to be proud of—a month ago he couldn't've said nor bow nor front."

"Wouldn't, Maggie. You know why."

"I know. Still. He oughtn't to've laughed and called me a silly gumpus."

They passed into the dining saloon and closed the door behind them. Ship's rule—doors left open tended to swing to and fro and smash walls and people when wind gusts affected their trim. At the sideboard were two little nightgown-clad figures, and a taller one with his nightshirt tucked into his pants. Willie turned at the sound of the door and a smile broke out that was brighter even than the moonglobe on the rail above the dishes of food.

"Lady! I saved you some trifle."

"You did not." Lizzie tolerated fibs in others about as often as she told them herself. "You'd 'ave eaten that quick enough if she 'adn't come in."

"You're too kind, Lord Wilberforce." As the son of an earl, Willie outranked her, even if he was only five. "But I must see to Rosie here first."

"You found 'er." Lizzie smiled at her twin. "I was that worried we wouldn't."

"She found her way to my cabin like the lady of resources she is," Claire said fondly, crumbling a blueberry scone into a Spode saucer and sprinkling a palmful of tiny red grapes on it. Rosie fell upon the food, and Claire filled a second saucer with water from a cut crystal carafe. "Now that I know she is traveling with us, I shall mention it to Mr. Skully. He will see that the crew knows she is one of our party and not a future meal."

Willie gasped. "No one will eat Rothie, will they? Papa will throw them overboard if they do."

His charming lisp was fading, only cropping up now in moments of stress. "It shall not come to that, my lord."

"My lord," Lizzie mimicked in her best private-school voice, and nudged Willie so hard in the ribs that the whipped cream wobbled on top of his trifle and the blackberry he'd so carefully placed at the summit rolled off onto the floor.

Rosie dispatched it with the speed of a striking cobra.

His face crumpled and Claire replaced the blackberry with another, and a second for Rosie, before the storm broke. "Rosie says thank you for the berry, your lordship," she said. "And for being a gentleman who always puts a lady before himself."

The skies cleared and Claire did not point out that he had already eaten half the trifle he had offered her. She cut a slice of apple pie instead, and poured cream over it.

Even now, she could not quite believe that the food would not disappear as magically as it came. As the daughter of a viscount, she had grown up eating mounds of food in multiple courses—so much that it regularly went back to the kitchen uneaten, to be made into something else or distributed to the poor. But in those dark days between being forced out of her home in Wilton Crescent and taking up residence in the river cottage in Vauxhall, she had gone hungry for days at a time. She had been reduced to foraging for the scraps that had once been thrown away, and she never forgot it.

She would never take food, shelter, and companionship for granted again.

The closing of the door signaled the arrival of yet another midnight marauder. Jake joined them and began piling cold meat and cheese on a thick slice of bread.

"Couldn't you sleep, Jake?" Claire cut a slice of beef into beak-sized bits, then put them in Rosie's saucer.

His gaze followed. "Found 'er, did you?"

Clearly she was the only one who had not been permitted knowledge of the stowaway. "She came along the piping to my cabin."

He nodded, mouth full. "Told 'em she'd come down when she got hungry. Bird's not stupid."

"She didn't feel safe," Maggie informed him. "I think she's clever for finding the Lady all her own self."

"Not feelin' so safe neither," Jake mumbled around the beef. "How much longer we goin' to be floatin' around under this big gasbag?"

"Why, Jake," Claire said in surprise. "I thought you were enjoying your duties in the gondola with Captain Hollys."

"I'd enjoy 'em more if I couldn't see out." He began to build another sandwich. "Gondola's mostly glass held together with strips of brass an' curly bits of wood. Makes a fellow woozy."

"Hard to steer if you can't see out," Tigg observed.

Jake cuffed him on the shoulder, but since the sandwich was in that hand, it wasn't much of a blow. "I'd like to see you up there wi' the navigation charts an' nowt but stars and waves to go by."

"Not me," Tigg said, apparently unmoved. "I'm 'appy in t'aft gondola, wi' little windows and big engines. Mr. Yau—he's the chief engineer—he says I'm a dab hand wiv 'em."

"Hard to be a dab hand at anyfink after only three days." Jake wiped the crumbs off his face with his sleeve and eyed the pie.

"Jake, that weren't kind," Maggie said. "Who was it told me the captain let him take the rudder wheel for ten minutes? You got no call to talk to Tigg so, when from accounts he's as good as you."

"Three days is enough to show you everyfink you don't know." Jake cut the pie with the knife he kept at his belt, and wolfed it down without benefit of a plate.

"I don't know anything, that's wot I know," Tigg said bravely. "But I'm workin' on it, not complainin' about it."

When Jake stabbed the pie again, Claire opened her mouth to remonstrate about both greed and unkindness. But when he offered the second slice to Tigg, and the latter took it, she turned her attention to Rosie, whose appetite was finally satisfied. An apology had been given and accepted, and it was a foolish woman who would intrude on affairs of honor between gentlemen.

She hoped they would become gentlemen, in any event.

Some day.

Even Jake.

Chapter 2

If owning a private airship like the *Lady Lucy* was a measure of wealth, then the Dunsmuirs were wealthy indeed. For the most part, the family passed the voyage on the A deck, where the staterooms, reception lounge, smoking lounge, and dining saloon were laid out with every attention to luxury and good taste. Claire had packed only one evening gown, but when the countess came in to dinner the first evening in the family diamonds and the last word in Paris décolletage and trained bustles, she realized she would not be wearing anything less than silk to the table.

Even if it was the same silk for seven nights running.

On the B deck, however, one could wear one's raiding rig and striped stockings, for all the attention the crew paid to such things. There, everyone had his job, from Captain Hollys at the helm to Tigg in one of the two engine cars on either side of the treated-canvas fuselage, watching over the great Daimler steam engines as though his personal attention were all that kept them running.

"*Lady Lucy* is one of the original Zeppelin passenger airships," Captain Hollys told her proudly, one hand resting gently on the wheel that controlled the enormous rudder far to the stern. "Even *Persephone* isn't as fine a design, though of course she's bigger."

Ian Hollys was a former pilot of Her Majesty's fleet, invalided out after an injury in the war, much to his vigorous indignation. He and the earl had served together briefly, and when the *Lady Lucy* needed a man at the helm, John Dunsmuir had turned to his dashing companion-at-arms to offer him the position. Claire suspected there was much more to the story than Lady Dunsmuir had told her, but there was no arguing that both men had an air of command that was most attractive.

Most attractive indeed.

"Have you met Count Zeppelin?" she inquired, forcing her gaze to the vast wrinkled sheet of the Atlantic two thousand feet below. "I have recently bought stock in his company. I do hope that was wise."

"Very wise. I congratulate you on your perspicacity, Lady Claire."

Oh dear. It would not do to blush at a compliment. One should save one's blushes for those one has kissed.

"I have met him, at a gathering of pilots in Paris one winter. He is a force to be reckoned with, and anyone who doubts he will lock up the transatlantic shipping lanes for himself is going to be sadly left behind."

"Even the businessmen of the Americas?"

"Particularly those. Oh, they have ships, for what that's worth. But they're the inferior French design, and the engines simply aren't up to the rigors of the crossing. Too many accidents, too much hemming and hawing and not facing up to the fact that German engineering is superior."

"Which manly British opinion has nothing to do with Her Majesty's family connections, of course," Claire said slyly.

"I am a loyalist, it's true. But I'm also a realist. As are you, I suspect." He took his gaze from the course ahead and she met it with only a tiny blush. At least she did not blotch. The heat in her cheeks was not from humiliation; it was merely the acknowledgement of the presence of a companionable mind.

"Sir, we have a pigeon incoming."

Captain Hollys turned to the young man whose collar insignia would have told Claire he was in charge of communications, if his duties as they left the airfield at Southampton had not already demonstrated it. "Let the aft control room know to open the stern hatch."

"A pigeon, captain?" They were four days out on either side. How could a bird have flown this far without dying of exhaustion?

"Not a real one," he assured her with a smile. "It's simply what we call them for the sake of convenience. Would you like to go aft and see?"

"I would indeed. And I'd like to pay a visit to Tigg in the engine room. I've barely seen him the whole voyage."

"From what I hear, we'd better keep you out of there, or you'll be tinkering with the engines yourself." He gave the helm to the first officer, and accompanied her to the ladderlike stair from the gondola beneath the fuselage up to the B deck. "After you, my lady."

Claire hitched up her workaday blue wool skirts and climbed the ladder nearly one-handed. The captain, gentleman that he was, may have had more of a view of her ankles and calves than she might have intended, but he said not a word. Instead, he guided her up a second stair and onto a catwalk as delicate as a spiderweb, though it appeared to be made of some metal. "This is the main coaxial corridor that traverses the length of the ship," he said.

"Corridor?" Claire hesitated the briefest of moments, then bravely stepped out onto the catwalk. Below was the network of piping and the thin partial ceilings of the A deck, where Rosie had been trapped. Above were the huge bags of gas, separate from each other but still bigger than any building Claire had ever been in with the exception of Parliament.

"A practical design," she said, to keep her mind off the space around her.

"It is indeed. If one bag should get into trouble, there are still five to do the work."

"And if all five get into trouble?"

"We do not like to think of such things, but each member of the crew is trained in what to do."

"And what should the passengers do?" Dear me. This was no way to keep one's mind off the two thousand feet of space beneath one's feet. Perhaps she should change the subject.

"Each member of the crew is assigned a passenger, my lady. I, of course, am assigned to his lordship, the chief steward to her ladyship and Lord Will."

"And I?"

"You are under the care of the chief engineer, which I believe to be singularly appropriate."

"The children?"

"It is unlikely the girls will be separated from you, so I have assigned Mr. Yau to them as well. Young Mr. Terwilliger is unlikely to be separated from him, so you make a party of four. The lad Jake will go with my communications officer."

"And Rosie?"

Behind her, the captain's step hitched. "Rosie? Is there another in your party of whom I am unaware?"

"Rosie was spirited aboard the vessel by the twins. She is a red hen of singular ability. Though she can fly, I fear two thousand feet may prove too much even for her."

"You don't say." The captain took a moment to absorb this information. "A hen."

"She is not to be eaten."

"Of course not. I will inform Mr. Yau that he is responsible for a party of five, then."

"And what do these responsibilities include, if I may ask?" If one were falling out of the sky at some horrific rate, she did not see that any action on the part of the crew would help the situation.

She had counted five gas bags. The sixth loomed ahead, so they were nearly to the stern. She turned to get her answer.

Captain Hollys practically ran into her. "I do beg your pardon, my lady." Now it was his turn to be flustered, as he set her away from him on the narrow catwalk and stepped back a respectable distance. His cheeks were ruddy, but whether it was because she had embarrassed him or because he was used to standing in rushing wind and sunshine, she did not know. "What was your question?"

She had nearly forgotten herself. Dear, dear. "The responsibilities of each crew member," she finally recalled. "What are they, if we are falling into the sea?"

"Ah. Firstly, you will not fall. Even if all six gas bags come to grief, enough gas will remain to make it more of a long glide, with a gentle landing."

She frowned at him. "This seems difficult to imagine." Anyone who read a newspaper knew of the fatal mishaps that balloonists sometimes experienced. Gentle gliding did not seem to be a feature of such stories.

"You are thinking of balloons, I see." He had regained his composure, and indicated that she should precede him down the ladder. The engine noise was much louder here, and he raised his voice. "The physics are quite different with a zeppelin. It is merely a matter of collecting one's valuables, strapping on a small rocket pack, and leaping to safety once the ground is within a one-hundred-foot range."

"Good heavens. Are we permitted to practice with these devices?"

"The *Lady Lucy* has never gone down in a decade of flight," he said as he jumped the last of the steps and showed her into the engine gondola. "I do not expect that record to change this week. The rocket packs are merely a precaution. They are tested periodically by the middies, but no one has ever actually had to use one."

Claire fervently hoped that this was not a case of famous last words.

Mr. Yau, who wore his dress blue uniform with an interesting sash of intricate knots worked in red silk cord, looked up and straightened into a salute as they stepped into the gondola. It was smaller than the control gondola forward, but still held a dizzying array of equipment, including the controls for both engines and all six gas bags within the fuselage.

Captain Hollys returned the salute. "I have brought Lady Claire to see the pigeon and Mr. Terwilliger, Jack."

Mr. Yau nodded. "I sent one of the midshipmen to fetch it. Tigg?"

A black curly head popped out of the space behind a console. "Sir?"

"Is that pulley assembly fixed?"

"Yes, sir. Good as new."

"You have visitors."

Claire smiled at him, conscious of his pleasure at this attention to his duties. "I will not keep you from your work, Tigg. But I hear good reports of you from Captain Hollys."

His coffee-colored skin suffused with a blush and he ducked his head wordlessly. With a mumble, he vanished through a door. The sound of engines increased and softened as the door closed behind him.

"A good little chap, that," Mr. Yau said, as a boy in a sailor collar scrambled down the ladder with a device under his arm. "I'd be tempted to offer him a job if he wanted one."

"He acted as a laboratory assistant until very recently," Claire said. "I would be loath to lose him, but of course a man must forge his own career." In point of fact, an opportunity to learn his trade under the care of one of the most powerful families in the land—in the world, if one counted their holdings in the Canadas—merited careful consideration. "If you are serious, I could have a word with him."

"I'm quite serious," Mr. Yau said. "All the middies up to the age of sixteen receive instruction in reading, penmanship, navigation, and mathematics from Mr. Skully. His education would not go a-begging because of his duties here. Isn't that right, Mr. Colley?"

"Yes sir," the boy piped. "Here's the pigeon, sir."

Claire examined the device with interest. A combination of propellers and articulated wings for gliding made up most of it, with a cell on top that in some ways resembled the power cell in her own lightning rifle. "It is not propelled by steam?"

"No, ma'am," the boy said, evidently under the impression she was asking him. "It's a sun cell." At her raised eyebrows, he explained, "It gets its power from the sun, and when it's cloudy, there's enough stored to make the props and wings go. The mail's in here."

He flipped it over and opened a compartment emblazoned with the emblem of the Royal Mail, now filled with rolls of paper.

"How on earth did it find us?"

"Magnetic signal, same as the land post," the boy said. "Milady, there's something here for you."

"For me?" She unrolled it eagerly. "Poor Lewis has no doubt written to tell me Rosie is missing." But it was not from Lewis. It was from Andrew, and the news it held made the blood drain from her head.

"Lady Claire!"

The captain, ever gallant, caught her just in time.

Chapter 3

"In the Texican Territory." Lady Dunsmuir could not seem to wrap her mind around the astounding news as she pressed the smelling salts into Claire's hand yet again. "Lord James Selwyn is pursuing you to the Americas to press his suit? I cannot comprehend it. It is either utter devotion or sheer madness."

Claire put the smelling salts firmly on the table. She was quite recovered. Embarrassed, yes. Determined not to lace her corset quite so tightly in future, yes. But quite recovered physically, thank you very much.

Mentally, she was struggling with how much of the truth she should reveal to Lady Dunsmuir. For Andrew's message had told her that James had reneged on his agreement with Ross Stephenson and his railroad, absconding instead with the Selwyn Kinetick Carbonator they had invented, with plans to sell it to a Texican consortium.

It was the act of a scoundrel, not a gentleman. But though she trusted Andrew's word, she could not condemn a baronet in the eyes of his peers without physical proof. And how she was to lay hands upon that in all this vast country was a conundrum.

"It is not solely devotion that has brought him so far. Andrew Malvern—my erstwhile employer in the laboratory—was Lord James's partner in his railroad ventures. James was in the midst of negotiations with the Midlands Railway Company, but it appears he has broken those off to come here with a group of Texican railway barons. Andrew has—has set out to bring him back. But my goodness, the Americas are enormous. How will he discover them?"

Dear me. She was skating dangerously close to the shameful truth. In a moment she was going to trip over her own tale. Because really, James did not deserve her protection. He had acted like a criminal, so he should face up to the consequences. It was a dreadful pity her upbringing would not allow her to be the instrument of it.

Because what if Andrew was wrong, or had misunderstood? Then she would have shamed a baronet publicly in error, and the consequences would be on her own head.

"If he does not find you in New York, I imagine his business will take him to Santa Fe." The earl shook a map out of a brass tube and unrolled it on the low table in front of the sofa. "New York and Philadelphia—" He pointed to the two largest cities of the Fifteen Colonies on the eastern seaboard. "—are where the railroad barons have begun building mansions, but if this is a group of Texicans interested in a business arrangement with a man of vision such as James, they'll be in Santa Fe." He indicated a dot in the middle of a large area marked TEXICAN TERRITORY and colored a faded red. "That's the capital of a territory that runs from the border of the Canadas all the way down to Texico City." His finger slid from one edge of the map to the other.

"But we will no doubt meet in New York," Lady Dunsmuir said. "That is the entry point for the Americas—not to mention the only airfield on the entire coast capable of handling the traffic. They must receive traveling papers for these skies. And of course they must take on kerosene for their engines, and supplies and the like."

Claire fingered the letter in the pocket of her skirt. "Andrew's message was dated the day we left London. Do you suppose we shall arrive at the same time?" What a joy it would be to see his familiar face—and to find out if, perhaps, she might assist him in his mission. After all, as he had said, that power cell was hers and the children's, no matter whose name was on the patent. If anyone was going to profit by the sale of it, it should be them, not James.

On the other hand, she had gone to great lengths to remove herself from James's orbit, where he could not touch her or force her to be his wife. She must continue on with the Dunsmuirs to the Canadas, as planned, far from Santa Fe. Andrew Malvern was perfectly capable of managing on his own.

"No telling if we'll arrive before or after *Persephone*," his lordship said. "We haven't been pushing the ship or attempting any speed records. Captain Hollys has been holding us back because of the hurricane."

All four children looked up. "Hurricane?" Lizzie said. "Wot's that?"

"You know how the water behaves when you pull the drain plug in the tub?" Lady Dunsmuir asked. When Lizzie nodded, she said, "Imagine the water is air and we a very tiny rubber duck, and you have a hurricane, more or less. It's an enormous storm that spells disaster for any zeppelin. We are forced to stay well clear of it."

"This rubber duck is going to stay far north of their brewing grounds in the Bermudas and the southernmost of the Fifteen, you may be assured of that," said Captain Hollys, entering the room in time to hear. "My lord, might I have a word?"

"What is it, Ian?"

The captain kept his gaze on his employer. "In private."

"Good heavens. If you and Jack have been gambling again, I'm not advancing your wages."

"It's not that, sir." The gravity of his tone and the absence of a smile caused a flicker of unease to dart through Claire's stomach. The two men stepped into the corridor and Lady Dunsmuir distracted the children by pulling out the Chinese checkerboard and a fat bag of marbles.

Most of the children. Not all.

Claire caught Lizzie's eye and glanced toward the door. Lizzie got up and drifted toward the serving pantry, aimless as a cloud and harmless as a dove.

They had already discovered the pantry contained three doors, one of which led into the corridor. There was even a dumb waiter apparatus to transport food from the galley below on B deck to the dining saloon. The fact that it transmitted sound as efficiently as it did filet of sole and steamed vegetables was an advantage, if you had an interest in gathering as much information about the goings-on among the crew as you could.

Lizzie, Claire knew, had quite an interest.

In fact, she must ask her to find out about these rocket packs as soon as possible.

When Lady Dunsmuir and Willie later retired to their cabin for afternoon naps, Lizzie and Maggie appeared in Claire's own doorway with eyes that told her they had news. Claire ushered them in and removed Rosie from Maggie's shoulder, setting her on the nightstand with a saucer of water.

"Well?"

"I didn't understand most of it, Lady." She exchanged a wordless glance with her sister. "Wot's *diversionary tactic* and *circumnavigate?*"

"The first is a dodge and the second a runaround."

"Ah. Then that's wot Cap'n Hollys wants to do."

"Why? Is he dodging the storm?"

"Not only. Seems there's a ship off our stern that's been behavin' bad. Captain don't like it."

"They're probably doing the same as we are—avoiding the storm."

"That's wot 'is lordship said. But Cap'n don't think so. 'E thinks it's pirates, Lady."

"Pirates!" She had heard of them, of course. Wherever there was wealth in transit, it seemed, there were those who wanted to skim off a little for themselves. To take rather than earn. But the *Lady Lucy* had been plying the skies for years. Surely Captain Hollys knew what to do.

"So 'e says, Lady. We ent near so high as we were off the Seychelles—an we'll make landfall tonight, 'e says. Just not in New York."

"How did we not know of this?"

"They think we're just girls," Maggie said with scorn. "Ent no pirate 'alf as nasty as the Cudgel, I'll bet—you put paid to 'im an' you're a girl."

"But Maggie, that was with the assistance of the lightning rifle. I can't use that aboard ship. An inch too close to the fuselage and we'll go up in an explosion they'll see all the way to New York."

Lizzie sat on Claire's bunk and tucked her feet up under her dress. "I knew I should've stayed wiv Lewis and the others."

"We must consult with Jake tonight when the family is asleep," Claire said after a moment's thought. "He's been in the gondola, so he must know what's going on. In the meantime, pack your kit and let Tigg know, too."

"Pack?" Maggie repeated. "Wot for?"

"Just in case."

"Lady, you don't think t'ship'll go down?" Lizzie's eyes grew huge.

"Of course not. Captain Hollys is an experienced airman and our waiters in white gloves have an air of competence that suggests they know more than merely which side to serve on. But it does not hurt to be prepared."

Lizzie looked as though she wanted to ask what she was to be prepared for, but she did not.

When they found him in the dining saloon some hours later, Jake did not have much more to tell them. "We're way north of New York now," he reported, wolfing down a cream-filled biscuit. "Dodgin' that ship and waitin' for t'storm to pass over New York. Can't moor till it blows itself out."

"I saw the cloud bank as the sun went down," Claire said. "I've never been in the sky to see a storm before. It's much more frightening up here than it would be tucked up in a warm library."

"Captain plans to circle around and come at New York from the west." Jake mumbled something else and stuffed a plum in his mouth whole.

"What was that, Jake?"

"Nuffink."

"I quite distinctly heard you say something about fuel."

"We'd 'ave enough if we'd just quit this dodgin' and back-trackin' and fire something at those rascals."

Claire's stomach did a dip and twirl that had nothing to do with the ship's trim. "So let me understand you correctly. We are not only illegally flying in American air space, we are the target of sky pirates and are running out of fuel. Would you say that was accurate?"

"Lady Claire."

She choked on a scone covered in cream and turned to see the earl not six feet away. "Your lordship," she said when she could speak. "What are you doing here?"

"I hope you do not expect me to sleep when my family and guests are in—" He stopped.

"Danger?"

"We are in no danger at present."

"But we could be, if that ship gets down to business and our engines give out."

He eyed her. "You are singularly well informed, though I would appreciate it if you would not say such things in front of the children."

"The children are my source of information."

He selected a scone and slathered cream on it while he recovered. "They are mistaken."

"Aren't!" Lizzie lifted her chin, affronted. "I 'eard the captain tell you so meself."

"Then you should know that eavesdropping is most unlady-like."

"So is takin' a stone to a knife fight." Her tone dripped with scorn. "I don't aim to carry stones if I c'n 'elp it. I aim to be pre-pared."

He regarded her with raised brows. "I see I have underesti-mated you, young lady."

"If I were to wager who would succeed in a *contretemps* with sky pirates, my lord, I would put my money on Lizzie," Claire told him. "We do not mean to displease you, but any of these children will tell you that the secret to beating a bully is to be ready for him. That is all we are trying to do."

"I hope it does not come to that. Both vessels are struggling with the storm, which has pushed us far off our course. We have evaded miscreants before with success, and shall do so again, I trust."

It was a thin comfort, but it was all she had to keep warm with during that fitful night.

That and her raiding rig. If one were to face danger, it would certainly not be in a nightgown.

Chapter 4

Claire woke to a crack like a buggy whip, and the sound of feet pounding down the corridor. Her internal clock told her it was past dawn, but the gloom outside the porthole cast her cabin in darkness.

Something was missing.

A moment later, when she heard Rosie cluck a sleepy inquiry from the back of the guest chair, she realized what it was.

The engines had stopped.

She leaped for the porthole and looked out into the slashing silver of rain. Lightning flashed in the belly of a cloud—they were surrounded by clouds—buffeted to and fro at the whim of the weather. She could no longer see the ground.

What was going on? They were to have avoided the storm, not sailed smack into the middle of it! And where were the pirates? Were they at the mercy of the winds, too, or were they using them to their advantage while *Lady Lucy* wallowed, helpless without her engines?

"Go back to sleep, Rosie," she said, pocketing a moonglobe. "I'm going to find out what has happened."

Another crack of thunder shook the ship—at least, she hoped it was thunder. Claire ran down the corridor and was forced to use the moonglobe. All the lamps were out. At the door to the main saloon, she found Tigg.

"What has happened?"

He turned, his eyes wide with distress. "I can't tell, Lady. They locked us in."

She tried the handle. Stupid. Of course he was correct. She peered through the circular window, trying to see through the gloom. "This is maddening. Where are the Dunsmuirs?"

The family had its own set of staterooms further aft. A dash to the other end of the corridor ended in a locked door as well. Claire set her teeth.

"If we cannot go out, we must go up. Tigg, if I give you a boost to the top of the wall, can you remove the paneling and go through to the catwalk?"

"Quicker'n you can think of it, Lady."

It took a moment and some unbalanced staggering to find a loose enough panel, but once through, Tigg's feet disappeared and Claire was left to wait. She went to Jake's room.

"Jake, I fear we must—" The room was empty, the bed mussed as if he'd just climbed out of it. "Jake?" He had not been in the corridor. Maybe he had gone to wake the girls.

"Mopsies?" The twins peered down from the top bunk, where it was clear they'd gone to sleep together fully dressed, with only a heavy tartan blanket over them. Clutched in Lizzie's hand was the heavy silver carving fork that usually attended the roast at dinner. "Good heavens, Lizzie. You might have put an eye out while you slept."

"Not likely." Lizzie slid to the floor and jammed the fork in her sash. "Are we boarded?"

"I cannot tell. I don't think so. We are, however, locked in. Tigg has climbed up to the catwalk to reconnoiter. Have you seen Jake?" They shook their heads. "That's a puzzle. Perhaps he had the same idea."

"Perhaps we all ought to go up an' out," Maggie suggested. "Why'd they locked us in?"

"Don't much like that," Lizzie said. "I'm for up an' out."

The words were barely out of her mouth when the floor jerked out from under them as though it had been a rug yanked by a giant. All three landed in a heap next to the wall.

"What was that?" Claire said on a gasp.

"We're goin' down." Lizzie's face held all the conviction of one who has long known men were not meant to fly.

"If we were going down, we should know it by the angle of the floor and the weightless feeling in our stomachs." Claire struggled to her feet, rubbing the bruise that was surely forming on her hip. "Come, we must—"

Another jerk of the fuselage sent them to the floor a second time.

"Either the wind has risen, or we've just been bumped by something." With caution, Claire got up, hanging on to the wood opening of the double-decker bed, and peered out the porthole.

"Oh, dear."

They had indeed been bumped by something. A ship rode the air currents next to them—a ship with dual fuselages, one of which had clearly struck their own, considering its close proximity. Between the fuselages like the downstroke of a letter Y hung a gondola, with a spiderweb of catwalks and ropes that at present were swarming with men.

Armed men. Men with ropes over their shoulders, and dangling from those were large versions of the grappling hooks she had used herself.

"We are being boarded. In midair. By sky pirates."

The thing his lordship had assured her would not happen.

Where in the name of heaven was the family? Had she and the children been locked behind sturdy teak doors for their own safety? Or had everyone fled in the equivalent of a dinghy and left them to fend for themselves?

The floor jerked again as the two ships collided, but it was gentler this time—as though the *Lady Lucy* were snugging herself up to a dock. Claire came out of her horror-filled trance with a jolt.

"I don't know what is going on, but we must prepare to defend ourselves. Maggie, find a weapon. I'm going back to my cabin for the lightning rifle."

"But you said—"

"I would rather an explosion and a long glide to earth because of a ruptured gas bag than to be taken and held for ransom by a pirate. I'll be back in a moment. Keep an eye out for Tigg."

In her cabin, she filled her pockets and pouches with every device she had brought with her. Her notebook went down the front of her leather corselet, her grandmother's emerald ring on an ivory pick slid into a hastily assembled chignon. She rammed the lightning rifle into its holster on her back. She put Rosie on her shoulder and cast an affectionate glance at the evening gown hanging in the closet. It was not likely she would see it or her favorite blue hat again.

The twins met her in the corridor. "Now what, Lady?"

"We go topside. We must find the crew and make our stand with them."

A thump sounded above their heads and the panel in the ceiling wiggled back and forth.

"Tigg? Maggie, put your foot in my hands and help him move the panel."

Thump. Scratch. A small blond head popped out of the opening and Maggie reared back and practically fell to the floor. "Willie, you gumpy, you scairt me."

Above her, Willie's tear-filled gaze found Claire's.

"What is it, darling? Did Tigg send you?"

Wordlessly, he shook his head, and Claire's stomach sank. "Have you seen him?"

Another shake.

"Willie, it's safe to speak. You must tell us what has happened."

But it seemed he would or could not. Something had frightened him so badly that his recently regained powers of speech had deserted him, and he had reverted back to the condition in which she had found him.

A condition directly related to being forcibly removed from his mother and father.

"Darling, I fear we have been boarded by sky pirates. Have they taken mama and papa?"

His face crumpled and he nodded.

Nausea and fear rose in her stomach and she struggled for control. "Did they lock us in?"

A shrug.

"Do the pirates know we are here?"

Willie hesitated, then slowly shook his head.

"Well, that's something, at least. How did you escape?"

He withdrew into the opening, and motioned with one hand that someone should come up and join him. "Aha. Your papa had the same idea as we did. He stuffed you in the ceiling, did he, to—"

Willie's small hand appeared again, and from it dangled the countess's diamond parure, fully two feet long and worth the price of the *Lady Lucy* at least. Even the gloom in the corridor could not disguise its brilliance.

"Dear heaven." Claire struggled to reconstruct the scene through which they had all managed to sleep. "He stuffed you and the family collection in the ceiling. What quick thinking for a man under siege. We shall follow his excellent example immediately. Maggie, Lizzie, up you go."

"Are we going to find the crew?" Maggie hefted herself into the hole and turned to pull her sister up after her.

"If the earl has not been able to make a stand, it is not likely his crew has, either." At the far end of the corridor, she heard a shout. "He means us to stay hidden if we can. Here, take Rosie."

But Rosie did not want to be taken.

"Rosie, this is no time to give us trouble. Someone's coming!"

The bird flapped and fluttered and took off down the corridor. With a moan of frustration, Claire dashed into her cabin, snatched up the hatbox, dumped her beloved blue hat out of it, caught the hen and put her in. "You'll thank me when we get out of this." Slamming down the lid and tightening the cord, she passed the hatbox up to an anxious Maggie.

Someone kicked the door, and she heard a burst of raucous laughter.

There was no one here to give her a leg up. She would have to manage it herself, without benefit of rope or hook.

Using a candelabra on the wall, she pulled herself up on the railing.

Bang!

They were kicking in the locked door. Teak was a sturdy wood, but it would be no match for the combination of strength and greed.

She got both elbows inside the opening.

"We'll pull you, Lady." A twin knelt on either side.

Claire pushed off from the railing as hard as she could. She landed on her chest. With the girls pulling, and by bracing one knee on the next panel, she kicked her way up and through.

Another shout, this time of triumph, as the brass locking plate gave way.

Footsteps pounded down the corridor as Claire whisked her black skirts up after her, and together she and the girls slid the panel into place right over the heads of half a dozen pirates.

"Don't move," Claire whispered.

The children froze. The only sound was the *scritch* of Rosie's claws in the hatbox, but their pursuers couldn't hear it. They were too busy carousing through the cabins, exclaiming about bits of plunder.

Blankets. Pillows. Her hat.

Claire closed her eyes and wished it a fond farewell.

The pirates thundered back down the corridor and in a moment they could hear them clearly in the dining saloon. Up in the ceiling, sound seemed to distribute itself equally, as though there weren't much in the way of barriers to stop it.

"How many are there?" Lizzie whispered.

"Besides these? No telling," Maggie said.

"There were hundreds in the rigging of the other ship, it seemed," Claire added. "Shh. Let us listen. I believe they are arguing about my hat."

"That's all you found?" a deep voice roared—a voice that reminded her of the booming sea in the smugglers' caves, far below Gwyn Place. "A hat? Where's the girl?"

"There weren't nobody there, captain," said another voice. "Doors locked on both ends and not a soul to be found."

"They will be found, or it's a long step off a short board for the lot of you. Where's that kid? I want some answers."

The sounds of scuffling ended in a thud, as if someone had been tossed on the floor.

"You. Kid. You said the other lady was in the guest cabins. So where is she?"

"She's there. Where else would she be?"

Maggie gasped. Lizzie clapped a hand over her sister's mouth. They knew that voice well. Jake's voice.

"I locked the doors," the boy went on in a tone halfway between defiance and a sulk. "She's just hidin' is all."

"You two. Take our friend here back in there and don't show your windbitten faces unless you've got her. Why ransom two when you've got three?"

Claire and the children sat frozen in horror as they heard the footsteps return below them, and the systematic sounds of a search.

Jake had done what Claire had always secretly feared he would.

He had betrayed them all.

Chapter 5

Claire huddled in the crawl space with the children, thankful for one very small mercy—that the sounds of the search in the distance masked the sniffles of misery close by.

"I can't believe it of 'im," whispered Maggie, her voice clogged with tears. "Our Jake."

"'E ent our Jake no more." Lizzie's voice might have been barely audible, but her rage came through loud and clear. "It's every man for 'imself wi' that one, an' no mistake."

"Shhh." Claire sat up. "They're coming back."

"How many rooms does one nob need?" growled a voice directly below them—right outside her room, in fact. "Looks like she spent each night of the voyage in a different cabin."

"Who knows 'ow nobs fink," Jake said. "Wot're we gonna tell t'captain?"

"I'm gonna tell him she ain't here. And then you're gonna take whatever he dishes out, and hope it's not that long walk."

"But it ent my fault she scarpered."

Claire couldn't help it—Jake sounded so young and frightened that she could almost pity him.

Almost.

"It's your fault you didn't find out where she was first and save us all a bunch of time. Me, I'd send that pigeon pronto and get the Dunsmuir relatives coughing up the ransom. But the captain, he's a businessman. He's got other plans, and if you know what's good for you, you'll find that girl before you go back in there."

Other plans? For her? Claire's stomach did a dip and twist that had nothing to do with air currents.

But maddeningly, the pirates said nothing more, just hot-footed it out of the guest quarters, presumably to widen the search.

"I don't understand," Maggie whispered. "Why did he say you were sleeping in all those rooms?"

"Easy, silly billy," Lizzie said. "Jake squealed on t'Lady cos she's worth summat. But we ent. 'E's keepin' mum about us, for all the good it'll do us or him. We can't creep about up 'ere for-ever. They'll find us when we fall out of the ceiling from hun-ger."

"Then we must make them call off the search," Claire said with dawning realization. "If they don't know you're here, and they're not looking for you, maybe you can help us."

"Fine by me." Claire couldn't see her in the dark, but she could tell by the grimness in the girl's tone that she was already planning to start her help with Jake. "How you gonna get 'em to call it off?"

"By surrendering myself."

Maggie sucked in a breath, and behind her, a whimper es-caped Willie's throat. "Lady, you mustn't. We're a flock. We gots to stick together."

"It's the only way. The sooner they stop looking, the safer you and Willie and Tigg will be. And you will not starve up here. I'll find a way to get food to you, and if that fails, there is always thievery."

Dear me. If mama could only hear me now.

"I'll leave you the rifle," she went on. "If you're cornered, you must have a way to defend yourselves."

"Can't, Lady, beggin' yer pardon."

"Why not, Lizzie? I can't leave you with nothing."

"We ain't defenseless."

Claire was reminded again of how much she did not know about the twins' early years on the streets. How much, perhaps, she did not want to know.

"But Jake knows you got that gun, and he knows you always give it to yer second. If it don't show up wiv you, he'll make 'em keep up the search."

"Her second would've been him if he weren't such a blackguard."

Lizzie paused a second to acknowledge her twin's brokenhearted bitterness. "After 'im, it's Tigg. You got to take it or they'll hunt him sure. It's 'obson's choice, Lady, but you got to make it."

Claire swallowed the obstruction in her throat. "You will on no account allow yourselves to be captured," she said, her voice husky.

"No, Lady."

"You will protect Willie and Rosie at all costs. They are the least able to defend themselves."

"Yes, Lady."

"And if the opportunity arises to save them at the expense of the Dunsmuirs or me, you will take it as though it were an order."

A pause.

"Lizzie?"

"Yes, Lady," Lizzie said at last. "But it best not come to that."

Claire took this in the spirit in which it was meant. "I hope not. As Maggie says, we are a flock and I do not mean that we should be separated." She took a breath and willed herself not to cry. Then she took off the St. Ives pearls and wound them about Maggie's neck, under her voile blouse. The raja's emerald went on Lizzie's thumb by feel in the dark, and she replaced the sharpened ivory hair stick in her chignon. "Now, then. Let us move the panel. On three."

She slipped through the opening and dropped lightly to the Turkish carpet. Then she shook out her skirts, lifted her chin, and ...

... paused for a moment as an idea struck with the suddenness of lightning.

ॐॐ

Their hiding place had been just outside her cabin door. Through the porthole, she could see the pirate airship, riding easily next to them. Piled-up clouds formed a backdrop, and somewhere the sun was coming up, outlining them in a lurid glow of orange and red. Lightning flickered in their depths, and in the distance, thunder cracked. Not as close as it had been, but close enough to make her nerves jump.

The invaders did not yet know her location. She would give herself up, yes, but before she did, what damage could she inflict?

She opened the porthole and clutched its lower rim as she gazed out, cataloguing the parts of the ship and calculating distances.

The rightmost of the twin fuselages bumped gently against their own, which put the hanging gondola not thirty yards off. Most of the crew must be on the *Lady Lucy*, because the ladders and ropes had emptied, and men moved to and fro behind the glass of the gondola. Engineers, likely, and mechanics, though they were a motley lot with hardly a whole uniform among them.

Instead of engine cars flanking the fuselage, as on the *Lady Lucy*, though, this ship appeared to have some kind of external propelling assembly cobbled to the back of the gondola.

Inefficient. Ugly. A true engineer's nightmare, and quite likely the very devil to repair while under way.

Marvelous.

Claire unholstered the rifle with the ease of long familiarity and pushed the engagement lever forward.

It began to hum.

She did not have much time before someone decided that her disappearance was quite impossible and came back for a third search. At the moment when the rifle's pitch reached a working range, she hefted it onto the rim of the porthole and took careful aim.

A ragged beam of blue-white energy sizzled out of the barrel and arced across the space between the two ships. It hit the propeller assembly like a splash of wine in a man's face, and busy tendrils of light flickered over every surface, exploring and sizzling and frying every possible working component to a blackened mass.

Claire permitted herself a smile of satisfaction. It looked for all the world as though the pirate ship had been struck by lightning.

She pulled the rifle in. They would take it from her. But that didn't mean they could use it to threaten her or hers.

With quick fingers, she found a tiny brass coupling that formed part of the trigger assembly. Its removal would not be noticed unless the rifle was disassembled completely and the mechanic counted five instead of six. But neither would the rifle work without it.

She threaded the ivory hair stick through it and inserted it into her chignon.

Now then.

All she had to do was stay on the working ship. If they planned to take the *Lady Lucy* for salvage or sale, they would not harm it. In the wildly unlikely event that the Dunsmuirs and their crew could reclaim their vessel, their chances at an escape were marginally better now.

She hoped.

Her blue hat was not the best accessory for her raiding rig, but it made her look taller and gave her confidence. She collected it off the floor, punched the dents out of it with her fingers, put it on, and sallied forth to the dining saloon as though she had been invited to lunch.

All the food that had been on the sideboard had been commandeered to the family table. Behind a full plate lounged the largest man she had ever seen, with a wild mane of black hair. But it was not his size that made her steps falter.

It was the device set into his eye socket. As she advanced toward him and his table full of cronies, all eating and arguing and laughing at once, it swiveled toward her like a telescope, adjusting itself in and out until apparently it found a satisfactory focus.

And then as he raised a glass of the earl's good Madeira to his lips, she saw his left arm. It was mechanical also, a wonder of cogs and gears and pistons, each moving in smooth concert. Good heavens. The Texicans possessed technology the likes of which they had not even seen in London. What were they doing, masquerading as bumpkins and followers when they could be cornering the market on automatons?

"And what do we have here?"

She stopped, planting her feet as two miscreants leaped up and grabbed her arms as if she planned to escape, not come forward.

"If you don't mind," she snapped. "I am clearly not running away."

"This would be her," one of her captors said helpfully. "That girl you was looking for."

For answer, the mechanical arm flashed and the man on her right screeched as an apple bounced off his forehead. "I can see that myself, you dolt."

Hm. A little sensitive on the subject of his eyesight, was he? She made note, as well, of the accuracy of his mechanics.

"Do I have the pleasure of addressing Lady Claire Trevelyan?" he drawled.

There was nothing wrong with his mind, either. "You do," she replied. "But you have the advantage of me, sir."

"I do, at that." He grinned, and the men at the table laughed.

She waited, the very picture of icy dignity, and the laughter trickled off into grunts and grumbles as they returned to their food.

"Oh, let her go." He waved an irritated hand at the two men on either side, and reluctantly, the unhanded her. "I'm Ned Mose, captain of the *Stalwart Lass,* and I claim this vessel. And its occupants."

"By what right?"

"By right of arms, you little minx, and I'd watch my tone if I were you."

"Were you me, you would need a larger corset."

His nonmechanical eye bulged, and then he let out a bark of laughter. This time, the men shifted their feet and looked at one another, as if they hadn't gotten the joke and weren't sure whether to laugh anyway.

"There's nothing wrong with your tongue, at any rate. Where have you been hiding?"

"There are spare blankets in the cupboard in my room. I concealed myself behind them."

Without warning, he reached over and cuffed the man next to him. "Remember that next time, you idiot, so you don't spend an hour searching for a prisoner who isn't there."

"But—but—"

The man was perfectly justified in his confusion, since even Rosie would have difficulty concealing herself in that cupboard. But no one was listening.

One of her former captors yanked the lightning rifle out of its holster and tossed it in the captain's direction before she could pretend to protest. His hand ratcheted out at least an additional arm's length and snatched it out of midair, then the assembly clanked as it retracted to normal length again. "What's this? Some kind of gun?"

He examined it, and the hairs on the back of Claire's neck stood at attention as the telescopic eye swiveled to and fro. It was most unnerving. She had never been one to play with dolls as a child—any creation, in fact, that looked human but was not. She loathed the automatons that some families used as butlers. As a child, china faces of dolls with eyes that blinked had made her scream and run in the other direction ... and here was a face with practically the same effect.

But Ned Mose was human. Merely a man, and possessed of the same qualities all men possessed, including a sense of humor. She must remember that when the blank gaze of the telescopic eye passed over her once again.

"I asked you a question."

She collected herself. "Yes, it's a gun. But it no longer works. I don't know why."

If she had removed the power cell, Jake would have told them at once. But even he would be slowed down if he tried to repair the gun. The coupling was not the most obvious cause of its failure—in fact, it would charge perfectly well now that the captain had flicked the engagement lever forward.

The trigger would simply not release the charge.

And until this moment, she had never had reason to wonder what would happen if the charge was not released.

"I would not do that if I were you," she said pleasantly. "You might disengage the lever again."

"I might if I felt like listening to a slip of a girl." He heaved himself to his feet, brought the rifle to his shoulder, and aimed straight at her. "Enough conversation. You're coming with me."

If ever her life had depended on her own work, it was now. Stricken motionless, she gazed into the bell of the barrel, half expecting a bolt to sizzle out of it and fry her where she stood.

But it did not.

The captain waggled the trigger. Hefted the gun. Shook it. Pulled the trigger again while looking directly into the flared barrel.

Goodness. Here was something to know. In moments of frustration, logic forsook him. She might take it upon herself to engineer several more such moments, in hopes that she might find an advantage.

With a growl of frustration, he flung the gun at someone. "Fix that." The mechanical hand clamped her arm and she winced with pain. "You. Come with me."

He marched her down to the B deck and from thence into the gondola.

"Claire! Oh, thank God!" The countess flung herself across the bridge at the same time as the captain released her with a shove that told her just how much power that arm possessed. They crashed into each other in the middle of the deck, and Claire hugged Davina hard.

"Davina. John. I'm so glad you are all right."

"For now," the captain growled. "Long as I get what I want, I don't see the need for killing. But cross me and you won't get a second chance."

"You cannot kill an earl," Captain Hollys said stiffly. Blood had crusted in front of his ear and down the side of his neck, and one uniform sleeve was torn nearly off. A large bruise was forming on his right cheekbone. "You would be hunted from one end of the Empire to the other."

"Lucky job we ain't in the Empire, then, bucko." The arm ratcheted out and took a careless swipe at Hollys's head. He staggered back, but a fresh trickle welled on his cheek. "You're in the Texican Territory air space now, and nobody here cares if you're an earl or a girl, except if you've got money. And both earl and girl here do, if my information's right."

"You intend to ransom us?" John Dunsmuir asked, moving so that he stood between the pirate and Claire and the countess.

"Be pretty stupid of me not to, considering you're rich as Croesus." The telescopic eye looked him up and down, its assembly whining. "Everyone knows who you are, yer lordship. Be a fine feather in my hat to line my nest with."

Claire forebore to remark on this distressing mix of metaphors. The point was clear enough. And since he appeared unaware that the couple had a child, maybe he didn't know as much as he thought he did. Thank heaven for small mercies.

"My family does not negotiate with pirates."

"They'll negotiate for you. But I might be convinced to lower my asking price if your missus here will hand over the family hairlooms. I hear from a reliable source that she travels in style, diamonds and all."

"Your source is misinformed."

"Yeah?" He turned to holler up the gangway. "Jake! Get yer skinny carcass down here!"

In moments, Jake had tumbled down the ladder and fetched up at the bottom as though his toes hung over a precipice. The earl, his wife, and the crew stared at him with stony disbelief. But his panicked gaze went only to Claire.

"Jake," she said with the kind of politeness society matrons use to cut the unworthy to shreds in public, "I'm sorry to have missed you earlier."

"Lady, I c'n explain—"

"I am not interested, thank you. The flock has decreased by one, and you know what happens to birds left outside the coop at night."

"Quit yer babble." The captain, it seemed, did not appreciate metaphors correctly used. "Jake, tell us again about the countess's jewels."

"There's a big diamond necklace goes all the way to her waist," he said in a voice that cracked. "A couple ropes of pearls. Earrings and some other bits an' bobs I seen."

"Anything else?"

"A crown thing."

"She wears a crown?" This seemed to be more than he could believe. "You some kind of princess, lady?"

"Certainly not." Davina's voice was soft, but it held the same kind of society ice that Claire's had. Somehow its gentleness made it even more cutting. "He means a tiara."

"Ah. I got a woman who might like to see one of them. Maybe I'll give it to her for services rendered." He laughed raucously while Lady Dunsmuir's lips thinned—not, Claire suspected, because she was disgusted, but because it was that or cry. "So. Now that we have that cleared up, why don't you tell Jake here where the safe is, and he'll fetch them for us."

"The *Lady Lucy* does not have a safe," the earl said steadily. "Up until now, there has been no need."

"More fool you. Hoyt, take Jake here and a couple of others and have a look for the jewels. And to make you extra careful, Jake will take a long walk if you don't find them."

The blood drained out of the boy's face. "What?"

"You heard me."

Lady Dunsmuir paled even further, leaving her fine skin nearly grey. "You would not throw the boy overboard?"

Claire felt sick. Disgust and grief and dislike for his behavior was one thing. But no one deserved this. Not even a boy who had betrayed his closest companions for—for what? What had they offered him that meant more than his future? His very life?

"Just a little incentive to look harder, is all. Nothing personal."

No. Murder never was.

Chapter 6

Jake and his escort had barely cleared the ladder when a flat, tinny voice emanated from somewhere about the pirate's person. "Captain! You're needed urgently aboard ze *Lass*. Trouble in ze engine."

Ned Mose flicked a tiny brass lever on his shoulder. "Fix it, you dolt. Do I look like a mechanic?"

"*Oui, monsieur.* You're wasted as a captain. Ze assembly of ze arm proves it."

"I didn't yank you out of that Montreal prison to give me grief. You're aboard to see to the engine. Do yer job, Andre."

"Even I cannot fix what *le bon Dieu* has done. Ze engine, she is struck by lightning, *mon capitaine*. Wizzout ze *Lady Lucy*, we shall be adrift."

Mose slapped the lever the other way and roared like a frustrated beast. Then he glared at Ian Hollys. "You. Tell someone to go astern and prepare a tow line. If what he says is true, I'll command from here."

"Where do you plan to take us?" the earl asked.

"I'll take you where I take you and not after askin' your permission!" Mose snapped, and climbed the ladder. Moments later his bulky figure careened past on a zip line that had been rigged between the two vessels.

"Where is my crew?" Captain Hollys asked the two pirates left to guard them. "I must give your captain's orders."

"You're staying here. The crew's confined to quarters under guard. Zeb, you go."

"Me?" the other pirate said incredulously. "Why does it have to be me?"

"Because I'm senior. Do you want the captain to keelhaul you for not taking his orders astern?"

Evidently Zeb did not, for he slunk grumbling up the ladder and the sound of his boots receded in the distance.

"I'm going to get me some of that fine grub I've heard tell of." The second one climbed halfway up. "No funny business, you hear? I'm locking you hoity-toities in."

No sooner had the hatch clanged shut than Davina embraced Claire again. "Have you seen Will?" she asked urgently, as if the question had been blowing up inside her the whole time. "Is he all right?"

"Yes, he is perfectly well, as are the Dunsmuir diamonds."

"I don't care so much about those," said the earl. "We've been beside ourselves." He struck his forehead. "I don't know what I was thinking, putting him in the ceiling. What a mad idea. He'll probably fall and—"

"Willie is not in the least likely to fall," Claire said in bracing tones. "He found me and the girls, and it was such an excellent idea that I boosted them up there as well."

Lady Dunsmuir let out a breath as though she had been holding it all morning. "So he is well and as yet undiscovered. I feel as though I can go on now. Oh, Claire, you can only imagine my feelings. If he was snatched from me now that I have him back at last …"

"He will not be snatched from us, not in the near term, at least. I have made certain that we shall all stay on the *Lady Lucy* for now."

"Tell me you didn't have something to do with that lightning strike?" Lord John's face brightened even further.

"I did." She did not elaborate, merely smiled. "The *Stalwart Lass* must be docked somewhere for repairs. Our company will not be divided between two separate ships. At least now we have a chance to recover."

"But what do you make of Jake?" Captain Hollys touched his forehead and seemed surprised when his fingers came away smeared with blood. "I do not understand it."

"I do not know, nor do I wish to." The pain of betrayal and the loss of trust hurt her deep under her breastbone. "Captain Hollys, are you quite all right?"

He nodded. "Of course. These are scratches. Of no consequence. I have a ship to retake, and that fool thinks he has locked us in."

"Ian, you will not do anything brave," Lady Dunsmuir told him. "I could not bear it if something happened to you."

"It is my duty to see to the wellbeing of this family, my lady. Every man Jack aboard has the same duty, and we all know the contingency plans. It is simply a matter of putting them into action, now that we know everyone is accounted for."

"Tigg is not," Claire said. "I am hoping he is with the crew in Mr. Yau's care and will be considered necessary to the ship's operation. They would not harm him, I hope."

"Hope is well and good, but I prefer certainty." The captain crossed the gondola and cranked a wheel with a handle protruding from it. "This way, before those miscreants come back. If you have a fear of heights, I will assist you."

Claire had discovered there were many things in the world to fear, but heights, in her opinion, were among the more benign. That said, she still felt a sick swoop in her stomach when she realized that the captain meant them to climb out onto the roof of the gondola and into a hatch set in the fuselage of the ship. The curve of the great rigid structure did not conceal them entirely from the view of anyone in the pirate bridge. But there was no time to think of that.

The wind was like liquid ice this high above the earth, and as she tried to gasp for breath, it cut into her lungs as though it had actual physical form.

"Quickly." The captain lifted Lady Dunsmuir bodily through the hatch, and her husband pulled her through the rest of the way. "There is not enough oxygen in the air to sustain us long."

Claire scrambled through, and the captain closed both hatches behind him, spinning the wheels until they snugged tight. "That will keep them guessing for a few moments, at least, when they find a locked room with no one inside. Come."

Lady Dunsmuir was as white as her own Brussels lace waist. "Where are we going?"

"Our first task is to arm ourselves. Then free my crew. Then retake the ship and cut her free of the *Stalwart Lass*."

Such was the captain's confidence that Claire could almost believe it was possible.

Apparently the coaxial catwalk was not the only way to travel the length of the ship. "We are between the B and A decks now," Lord John said in a low voice, speaking over his shoulder to Claire, while Captain Hollys brought up the rear, herding them closely so no one fell behind. "The false ceilings were designed to lead up here so that if we were boarded, the family had a means of escape and concealment. I was not aware of the hatch out of the gondola. That anything escaped my brothers and me in our explorations quite surprises me." He touched a metal strut as he passed it. "I thought I knew the old girl inside and out."

"We could find William in here, then?" Hope had brought color back to the countess's face. "May I call him?"

"No!" both men said at once.

"The walls are thin," Lord John said more gently. "And he is in the A deck ceiling, a floor above."

"We must be quiet and take them by surprise," the captain added. "No more talking, now."

Moving swiftly, they reached the stern in a few minutes, evident by the narrowing of the fuselage and the increase in the sounds of men's voices. At a niche in the wall, the captain paused, selected a key on his ring, and turned it in a lock. "They must be under guard, or Jack and the other officers would already have been up here to retrieve these." He reached in and took a rifle, handing three of them back in rapid succession.

But it was not a rifle—at least, the kind that fired either bullets or current. There was no means of loading it. Claire turned it over. A trigger. Well, that was something.

"It is called an aural detonator. It fires sound waves," Lady Dunsmuir said, indicating the bell of the barrel. Suddenly Claire realized where the barrel of her own rifle might have originated. "We cannot use anything else aboard ship. Fired straight at a person, the wave it emits will knock a man senseless but will have no effect on the fuselage."

Clearly Lady Dunsmuir had not been as gently reared as one might have expected.

"Brilliant," Claire said.

"Here is our plan," the captain said. "We come out of the ceiling, we disable the guard, we release the crew and move forward. Questions?"

Claire needed clarification on one point. "Are we—Davina and I—to stay behind?"

Davina looked at her incredulously. "Certainly not. Can you fire a gun?"

"Yes."

"Then what purpose would it serve for you to stay up here?"

To which, of course, there was no answer.

Captain Hollys and the earl moved a panel aside, and then dropped to the carpet below. Davina went next, then Claire. As soon as possible, she was going to possess herself of a rope and grapple, if this climbing in and out of ceilings was going to become a regular practice.

The crew's quarters were guarded by two pirates, who whooped and raised their weapons. But the earl and Captain Hollys beat them to it. Claire felt a curious sensation, rather like the popping in one's ears when one descends to a landing field too quickly, and the pirates fell in a heap. A trickle of blood seeped from the ear of one of them.

The captain dragged them out of the way and pounded on the door. "Gentlemen! It is Hollys and the earl. We are coming in."

It was fortunate he had given a warning. As he opened the door, someone jumped down from a wardrobe pushed up next to it, and put away what appeared to be a candlestick. It was the first officer, looking enormously relieved. "Sir! Is the family all right?"

"Quite all right, thank you, Mr. Andersen," her ladyship said, stepping into view. "We must retake the ship and then locate Lord Will and the young ladies, who are in the A deck ceiling."

"Right ho. Middies, look sharp. First opportunity you get, scamper up into the A deck rafters and find his lordship and the girls."

The captain nodded. "The rest of you, arm yourselves. I want four men posted on the gangways to A deck. No one but our crew is to pass alive, is that clear? This is no time for Queensberry rules."

Claire had no time for more than a glance at the men in the room. Tigg did not seem to be with them—but she could be mistaken. Mr. Yau was not present, either, so perhaps they were still at the engines.

They divested the pirates of a considerable number of weapons and locked them in the wardrobe. Then they headed forward, to the closest gangway up to the A deck, which was between the galley and the crew's and officers' mess.

Two more pirates went down, a third caught halfway down the steep stair.

The first officer went up and kicked the unconscious body aside. Before he could clear the gangway, however, a pair of objects clanked onto the stairs and bounced down them two at a time.

They looked rather like pine cones, only made of metal. One rolled to a stop and the end of it popped open.

A wisp of green mist puffed out, then a stream, then a cloud.

"Gas!" the captain shouted. "Retreat!"

The first officer plummeted to the deck before he could finish the word. Two of the middies collapsed toward each other in a hug, then landed in a pile.

The second bomb puffed and her ladyship went down.

Claire dove through the galley doorway, tripped over a silver coffee pot lying on the floor, and fell headfirst into the dumb waiter.

A hiding place!

She yanked her feet in and slammed the door, then let out a squeak of dismay as the floor rose up under her posterior.

Good heavens. She would be deposited in the serving pantry, not ten feet away from where she had begun the day, in the dining saloon facing a roomful of pirates.

Only now they had much more reason to be angry with her.

Chapter 7

Had anyone heard?

Curled up as small as she could make herself, Claire listened so intently that her own breathing sounded loud enough to bring the pirates running if the dumb waiter's mechanism had not.

Nothing seemed to be stirring outside, though she could hear a ruckus below—one with a triumphant tone to it. Round two to Ned Mose, but they were not beaten yet. Claire now knew two things the pirates did not—the existence of the ceiling passages and the location of the weapons locker in the stern.

Slowly, she slid the door aside and wriggled out feet first. On her hands and knees, just pushing up from the floor, she froze.

A pair of boots stood in the doorway of the serving pantry. Boots she knew as well as her own.

"Hallo, Lady," Jake said.

Drawing a deep breath, she rose to her feet. She must be calm. She must use her wits and perhaps he could be persuaded to abandon this madness and help them all.

He lounged against the door jamb, what looked to be an actual bullet-shooting rifle in the crook of his arm. "I figured I'd find you here."

She had no idea where her aural detonator had gone. It had probably fallen down a shaft somewhere. "Did you? How is that?"

He shrugged. "It's just wot I'd do. You'd best come wiv me quiet-like. Captain'd like a word."

"Jake, just a moment."

"Don't 'ave a moment if you value yer life."

"Oh, stop talking like a pirate."

"I'll talk 'ow I like and there's nowt you can do to stop me. I'm the one 'oldin' the rifle now." His posture was cocksure, his tone as insolent as she'd ever heard it. But something in his eyes, in the tension around their corners, told her he wasn't completely comfortable in the role of ruffian.

He'd lost the talent for it somewhere along the way, and it was that which kept her tone gentle, and allowed the faintest shoot of hope to spring up where a rational person would find none.

"Only tell me why, Jake. Why did you throw in your lot with these men when his lordship has done so much for you?"

His face hardened, and the conflicted look in his eyes faded. "I make me own way in the world. I take handouts from Dunsmuir and I'm nowt but 'is lackey, then, ent I?"

"Certainly not. You have been earning your way. His lordship is not the kind of man to give handouts, in any case. He is fair. A gentleman. And worthy of your loyalty. As, I hoped, was I." Her throat closed and made her voice fade to a whisper.

She turned away, unable to look at him. And there, practically under her nose, was a paring knife lying next to a pile of fruit, some peeled, some not.

She gripped the edge of the counter and hoped her skirts were enough to conceal what lay on it.

Jake merely shrugged. "Takin' a gentleman prisoner is heaps easier'n regular folks. But you was harder. They needed me, and captain's gonna give me a cut of t'plunder. When we find it."

"And yet you've said nothing to him of the Mopsies. Or Willie." She reached back slowly, feeling for the knife.

He shrugged, and levered himself off the jamb. "Kids don't interest t'captain. I got nothing against t'Mopsies. No reason to hand 'em over. Once we make port, they're on their own."

"That's hard. They're only children."

He raised his eyebrows and nearly smiled. "A lot you know. Come on, enough lollygaggin'. Captain's waitin'."

As she pushed away from the counter, her fingers found the knife. Before she had taken a step, it had gone up her sleeve where once, in happier days, she had kept a spare handkerchief.

Her interview with Ned Mose went rather more poorly than the first one. The upshot was that they were all imprisoned in the crew's quarters on B deck once again, leaving the pirates to make themselves comfortable in the family's and guests' quarters above.

Claire lay on an airman's bunk, twitching and tossing and wondering how a man could possibly sleep on such a hard pallet. But she must not complain. She and Lady Dunsmuir had the only bunks, one above the other. The other pallets had all been requisitioned by the pirates for their greater numbers, forcing the men to take what rest they could on hardwood floors.

The sun rose and fell, from the limited view she could get out a tiny porthole, and still they flew steadily west, their progress slowed by the drag of the *Stalwart Lass* on the tow line. She wished she'd punctured the pirate ship's fuselages while she had the chance. But it was too late now. Below them, the landscape changed from verdant tracts of trees broken by the occasional patchwork of farmland, to more farmland, to open prairie.

"We must be nearly to the Wild West," she said to Lady Dunsmuir. "How long does it take to cross the Americas?"

"Days." Her ladyship lay on the top bunk, one wrist across her eyes. "You will know the Wild West by the color of the landscape and its aridity. Do you suppose my poor darling has starved to death by now?"

"No, I do not. He is in the Mopsies' company, and is likely in much better shape than we."

"How can you say so? He is trapped in the ceiling."

"He is not in the least trapped. *We* are trapped. If they have not been feasting on trifle and roast beef, I will eat my hat." She paused. "If I had it." Her lovely hat was gone, knocked off somewhere or whisked off her head by the wind during the escape from the gondola. Some lady in the Fifteen Colonies would come out of her farmhouse and find it perched in her garden like an exotic bird.

"I suppose we should be thankful for small mercies," her ladyship sighed. "These could be pirates from the Spanish Main, in which case we would be dead. They have no patience for ransom and a distaste for witnesses."

"The Spanish Main?"

"Yes. Everything south of the Fifteen Colonies—the Bermudas, Florida, Louisiana, all the way to the South American coast. A lawless anarchy of a place which all good society avoids."

"Dear me. I had no idea."

"It is not something spoken of in the drawing rooms of London. But in the homes of the railroad barons and shipping people, particularly those seeking trade in the southern hemisphere with the Royal Kingdom of Spain, it is a concern. One cannot fly safely through those skies at all. Hence the vigor of the Texican economy—everyone is forced to fly their way and east again."

"But our captors are ... local?"

"There is no shortage of lawlessness in the Texican Territory, my dear. The Rangers do what they can, but the country is simply too big."

"I wonder where they are taking us."

"I do not know. Usually we travel further north than this, from New York to the Canadas, so my usual landmarks and little familiarities are leagues away."

Claire gazed out of the glass, wishing she could at least open it. The room was tiny to begin with, and two women crushed into the space without even a breath of fresh air was beginning to make her a little crazy. If she could only see enough of the country to—

The floor dropped ever so gently out from under the soles of her boots.

Lady Dunsmuir sat up. "Did you feel that?"

"Are we descending?"

It happened again.

"I believe we must be. I don't know whether to be glad or terrified."

"One thing we can be glad of," Claire said. "The children have not been found."

"I hope they have the sense to remain concealed," Davina said. "When we escape, we will return to the ship. Do you suppose they will think of that?"

"I hope so."

They had dropped about a thousand feet by now. Outside, the two women heard a ruckus and in moments the key turned in the lock.

A pirate stood in the doorway. "Nearly there. Out with you."

"Where are we going?" Claire asked.

"You'll see soon enough."

They were herded, along with the officers and Lord Dunsmuir, down to the embarkation hatch where normally a set of steps would be rolled up to let the passengers on and off. But now there was nothing but the large boarding area and the open hatch, through which Claire could see the landscape sailing past several hundred feet below them.

Trees. Rolling hills. And now, water. A lake? Or the ocean? Oh, if only she knew where they were!

The captain strode up to his lordship, his neck outstretched like a rooster challenging a more powerful one. "I've had about enough of this nonsense. I've asked nicely. I've looked myself. And now I'm about done with being nice." Practically nose to nose, he demanded, "Where are those jewels?"

"I have no idea, sir," his lordship said with the conviction of one who tells the truth. He did not, after all, know where Willie had gone with them.

"You're lying!" the captain roared. He reached out one long, apelike arm and grabbed Jake by the shoulder. "Boy, tell him what you told me last night."

"They got to be in the ceiling," Jake managed, as the captain shook him.

The blood drained from John Dunsmuir's face, and Captain Hollys started forward, only to be yanked back so roughly he fell to his knees on the deck.

"He was tellin' the truth, at least. I sent him and a team of my men up to comb every inch of them passages. Found a nice cache of weapons, but no jewels. Now, once and for all, you tell me where they are, or this boy takes a long walk."

"Wot?" Jake jerked away, to no avail. The captain had a grip like a grappling hook.

"What does that mean, exactly?" Lord Dunsmuir's color had not improved.

"It means exactly this—you tell me what I want to know, or Jake here goes out that hatch. Simple."

His lordship searched his wife's face, the full horror of his dilemma in every line of his own. It was clear Jake had not told them about the children. If John Dunsmuir revealed where they were, the pirates would take the jewels and Willie's life would be in mortal danger along with their own. As long as the children remained concealed, there was hope for the desperate parents. But if he did not speak, there was no hope for Jake.

All three Dunsmuirs could be held for ransom by the threat of death. But what of the Mopsies? Their lives were worth nothing to these men. If they were discovered, would they be deemed useless and pushed out the hatch, too? And what of poor Rosie? She would last only as long as it took someone to whip out a butcher knife.

For the first time, Claire felt the sheer terror that parents feel when the children they love are threatened.

My lord, you cannot make this decision. Claire reached out a hand in entreaty. Who to, she hardly knew. Ned Mose? John? The Lord looking down from heaven?

Ned Mose roared in utter frustration. "That's it! I've had enough of you! If you weren't worth so much, I'd toss you out myself. But he's worth nothin'."

With that, Mose whipped around and before Jake could brace himself or grab something or so much as take another breath, the pirate captain had given him a mighty shove.

With a shriek that Claire would hear in her nightmares for years to come, Jake tumbled out of the hatch and fell like Icarus into the empty sky.

Chapter 8

Claire and Davina both screamed, and Claire leaped for the opening. *Oh, dear Lord in heaven, please let him have caught something ... let him be in the rigging, hanging onto a rope, something ... please ...*

But he was not.

The water gave way to land and she could not see a thing. She ran to a window, heedless of grasping hands or the laughter of the pirates.

Nothing! Not a sign that Jake had ever been there, had ever learned chemistry recipes, had ever touched a sextant or gazed at the starry sky.

Had ever lived.

Each breath practically a sob, she could not tear herself away from the glass, in case somewhere in the distance she caught a movement that might indicate he had survived. Behind her, the countess had gone into hysterics, and the ensuing hubbub formed a kind of privacy in which Claire could grapple with regret and horror and grief.

Which meant that she was the only one looking out when a most peculiar assembly floated past.

Suspended from what was clearly a makeshift balloon was her hatbox.

Her mouth dropped open. She craned to see where it was going, and in doing so, saw that they were only fifty feet in the air and coming in for a landing. The hatbox floated downward and vanished somewhere in an uninhabited landscape populated by scrubby trees.

An enormous spire of red rock filled the windows and blocked her view. One of the pirates shouted, "Port ho, sir! Prepare to secure ropes!"

She was pushed out of the way but she hardly felt it.

Her hatbox. Floating away.

The last time she'd seen it, it had contained Rosie and the Dunsmuir diamonds.

If it did still, had the Mopsies seen Jake's demise and taken precautions? Or did it mean that they had given up hope and were prepared to surrender?

Oh, she must give these wretches the slip and find the children! She had not been able to save Jake. But with every cell in her body, she meant to save the Mopsies and Willie and Tigg. Wherever he was.

And then they could mourn Jake together. Properly.

But for now, she must concentrate on staying alive and at liberty. She would do none of them any good if they locked her up, or separated her from the Dunsmuirs and the ship. She must at all costs be able to get back to the *Lady Lucy*, if only to discover whether or not the children were all right.

Especially Tigg. Why had she not seen him? He had not been locked up with the crew, and he had not been with Willie in the ceiling. What had happened to him?

Under her feet, she felt a curious sensation, one a bird might feel if it were prevented from flying. "They have moored us," the countess said.

"Quiet!" one of the pirates barked, and Claire realized that the captain and those miscreants who passed for his officers had gone while she had been pressed to the window—probably to the gondola to oversee their landing.

But what was this? They were still thirty feet in the air. How were they to get down—jump? Or be pushed, like poor Jake?

And then she saw it. A cloud of dust rose into the air ahead of it—a huge engine that might once have been a locomotive, with a tower bolted to it. Steam puffed from the stack as it made its ponderous way across the yards of crushed plants and matted bush below, until at last it heaved up next to the gangway hatch and stuck a ramp into the opening. At least, that seemed to be the goal. However, it missed the opening and crashed into the fuselage. Backed up. Fired up its engine and tried again.

This time, the ramp protruded more or less into the hatchway, and two pirates grabbed it and locked it down. Steam puffed out and up around the tower, for all the world as if it had heaved a sigh of relief.

"You lot." The pirates flanked the earl and countess and one of them gave John Dunsmuir a poke in the back with a rifle for good measure. "Out."

"Is the mooring mast not on the ground? Why are we up so high?"

"None of your questions or you'll go down the short way. It don't take so long, but the landing's harder."

With a rifle barrel in his back, the earl did not answer. Instead, with as much grace as he could muster, he handed his wife and Claire onto the ramp, then preceded them down an iron ladder in the tower, lit only by daylight at top and bottom. How the countess managed her skirts, Claire could not imagine. Even with her own tucked up, it was difficult.

This engine was nothing like the smooth, efficient wonders belonging to the Midland Railroad. This one might at one time have been pushed over a cliff, it was so banged up, and instead of normal four-and-six wheels, it had a kind of track that went round and round.

"Quit yer gawking and move."

The rifle prodded her and she resisted the urge to jump ahead. Instead, she kept her step unhurried and ladylike, for all the world as if she were crossing a gallery to see an exhibit of famous masters.

No master would ever visit here to paint the landscape. During the walk into town—apparently the engine and tower did not proceed any further than from a shack up against the wall of a cliff to the field—she had plenty of time to see it.

Dry scrub. Soil so light and dusty it was clear all the goodness had been leached out of it by weather or some chemical disaster. Canyons that dropped unexpectedly away from one's feet—some a foot across, some a hundred—and heaps of red rock like loaves of bread. And over it all stretched a pale, distant sky that neither knew nor cared that it had swallowed a boy's life.

She could not help but look over her shoulder at the *Lady Lucy*, floating serenely with her bow moored to ... ah, now she saw why they had had to disembark with the help of that tower. The *Lady Lucy* had been towed and was now snugged into a berth formed by the sheer red cliffs behind the shed, as neatly as any dock at Southampton.

Well. That would make escape problematic, but not impossible.

Her biggest concern at the moment was the increasing separation between herself and the children, to say nothing of the hatbox some two or three miles behind them, which she was now certain must contain Rosie and the Dunsmuir jewels. Otherwise, why take such a risk in launching it? The girls must have worked under some duress to rig such a contraption so quickly. Claire could only hope that they had not been discovered in the process.

കൈ

"That's it—she's away."

Clinging like monkeys to the guy ropes that crisscrossed the exterior of the fuselage of the *Lady Lucy*, the Mopsies and Tigg rested at the base of the enormous ventral fin and watched their makeshift parachute take Rosie and the jewels away out of danger. They couldn't stay long or Weepin' Willie would take it into his head to live up to his old nickname, but a minute to savor their success wouldn't hurt.

"We best not be long in finding it again," Maggie said. "Rosie won't like bein' stuck in a hatbox for much more time than she takes to land."

"Better bein' stuck than et." Lizzie was practical to a fault. "And we tied the lid down so tight ent nuffink going to get in after her."

"Lucky job the Lady's hats come in leather boxes."

"Lucky job Tigg knows 'ow to rig a balloon out of a landau cover."

Tigg looked justifiably proud. "After all them fire balloons we made, it were easy. Though between Rosie and them diamonds, it weighed more'n I expected. Come on. Willie'll be worrit."

The hatch on the dorsal fin opened inward, and the wind blew the three of them inside and down the ladder. Willie was guarding the sternsman's chamber deep in the rear of the ship, just above the loading bay—deeper even than the quarters where the captain and crew had been imprisoned.

There was no sternsman now. Every last crewman had been rounded up by the pirates. But his quarters had a bunk, and Maggie had to admit that it was right comforting to all sleep together in a tangle, like the old days in the warehouse squat on the banks of the Thames. This one had its own sink and no fleas, which in her opinion was a big step up.

Willie was under the bunk. "It's all right, old man," Tigg told him, bending to look. "With the wind and our speed, Rosie shouldn't be more'n a mile or two behind us. After the coast is clear, we'll go get 'er."

"But in the meantime, even if we're took, Ned Mose and his lot won't get what they're after," Lizzie said. "Your da wanted us to keep 'em safe."

Willie crept out from under the bunk just as the ship gave a gentle shudder. Tigg took his hand. "Come on. Feels like we've docked. Let's go 'ave a look-see and then find some grub."

The navigational gondola had no ceiling passageway, so they couldn't eavesdrop from above. But they hadn't gone far on the way to the engine pod when they heard the racket of the crew being bullied along the corridors. "They're takin' everybody off," Tigg whispered. "Quiet, now."

The port side engine pod was empty, the mighty Daimlers silent and smelling rather burned after their long journey over the

Atlantic and half the Americas. They had put down to take on kerosene, of course, but never for very long—and not at all on the forced flight into the middle of the Texican Territory.

Maggie pressed against the curved windows of the pod. "Willie, there's your mum and dad, see? Going across the gangway. They're all right."

"And there's the Lady." Tigg's shoulders relaxed just a fraction. "I reckon we get the lightning rifle back to her and start settin' things to rights."

"Rosie first," Maggie said.

"We just sent her off," Lizzie told her. "Wot we want to get her back for so soon?"

"I just don't want us to forget her. We're a flock."

"Nobody's forgetting anybody," Tigg said. "Look. I never ever thought I'd see that."

Two pirates were attempting to stuff her ladyship into the tower of an awful-looking engine. She slapped one of them, twitched up her skirts in one hand, and climbed into the mouth of it under her own steam.

"Good for you, missus," Maggie breathed. "You tell 'em." She glanced at Willie, whose eyes were shining. "Yer mum's got a spine, she 'as."

The possession of a spine, according to their Lady—Lady Claire, not Willie's mum—was a person's greatest advantage. Consequently, the children considered it a great compliment.

From the engine pod they watched their friends marched away under armed guard. They were high enough up that they could see the town, but not, sadly, exactly where the little group was being taken.

"Better get back astern before someone comes," Tigg finally murmured, when they could no longer distinguish a man from the sickly-looking pines and spiny plants that clawed a living from the soil. "They'll 'ave left a guard and we don't want to get took by surprise."

They'd no sooner got back into the ceiling when the ship moved. Maggie staggered and grabbed Lizzie's arm.

"We can't be lifting off! Not when everyone's gone!"

Maggie lost her head and pelted down the passageway to the sternsman's cabin, which had a porthole. Slowly, ponderously, the ship moved, the walls of a deep canyon closing in on it close enough that she could practically reach out an arm and touch the rock.

"They're dockin' us somehow," she reported with some relief when Lizzie caught up. "That big tower is moving us. Hear it?"

Sure enough, the sound it made growling and roaring was amplified ten times by the close walls of stone. "It's like bein' cornered in a blind alley. And I bet anyone flyin' overhead isn't goin' to look down 'ere. They'd be lookin' for a proper landing field, wiv a mooring mast an' all."

"Nothin' proper about this devilish place," Lizzie said, pushing her out of the way so she could see, too. But there wasn't anything but stone out there now.

"You wouldn't use that word if the Lady was 'ere," Maggie observed.

"Well, she ent, is she? An' it is devilish. The very devil hisself wouldn't come here on a bet, you ask me."

"Nah, 'e sent Ned Mose instead."

Lizzie grinned. "That were 'is mistake, innit?"

"We'll make sure o' that," Maggie said stoutly. Lizzie's grin could make anyone believe anything.

"We got the lightning rifle thanks to yer light fingers, so like Tigg said, all we 'ave to do is get over to that pimple of a town and break the Lady out."

"Simple. A simple pimple it is."

"It always is, Mags. You just got to have a spine."

And a lightning rifle that worked.

And a crew that outnumbered that of the pirates.

And maybe a map of the town with a big X marked where they were holding everyone.

Easy peasy, Mrs. McGreasy.

Their prison turned out to be a ramshackle house in the middle of town. The locks on the room at the top of the stairs into which she was thrust, however, were anything but ramshackle—and they were on the outside of the door. The earl came to blows with two of the sky pirates over whether or not the countess would share his prison. Apparently even he had his limits, and it was not until Ned Mose intervened that he backed away, blood dripping from his nose and onto a shirt that was no longer as pristine as it had once been.

"Fine," Mose snapped. "Let her stay with him. It's not like they're going anywhere. They can recite poetry to each other to pass the time." He pushed them into a room, but the walls were thin, and on the other side Claire could hear every word.

"Now, let's get down to brass tacks," Mose said. "We're holding you for a hundred thousand pounds' ransom."

"The family will never pay," the earl said at once.

"Maybe not, but the pigeon didn't go to your family. It went to that frumpy old bat you call a queen."

Silence. Claire's mind reeled as she tried to imagine the reception such a demand would get at Windsor. She hoped he had not addressed Her Majesty in such terms.

"I fail to see what Her Majesty has to do with this," the earl said rather stiffly.

"Simple. Your family brings in a fistful of dough for the government, what with your holdings in the Canadas and whatnot. I'm thinking a little pressure from higher up might do the trick where a pigeon from old Ned Mose might not."

"Her Majesty may be just as likely to send a zeppelin full of soldiers than a chest of money."

"And she has so many of those hanging around? I hear tell of an uprising in the Near East that's sucking soldiers like one of our dust storms."

"If that is true, she will have even less cash to spare."

"We'll see, won't we? Now, you just make yourselves comfortable. You've got a long wait ahead of you."

He was, as ever, quite serious. The day passed with tedious slowness. Claire spent most of it alternately prowling around her prison and staring out the window.

She made a number of interesting discoveries. One, the house in which they were locked—all the houses and buildings, really— sat on sturdy stone footings, all of which were at least ten feet high. Hence the steep climb to get her into this room. Again, escape would be difficult, but not impossible.

Two, the town protruded out of an expanse of scrub that had been scored by some kind of force—as if it had been in the path of something with the power to score deep trails in the soil. It almost looked like the paths the creeks made in the sand at Gwyn Place as they ran to the sea—sinuous and braided, but relentless in their drive to join the larger body of water.

But there was no water here. Not for miles and miles. She felt rather lucky that there was a sprigged china pitcher full of it on the nightstand—and it was evidently meant to do double duty for washing and drinking.

Three, and most interesting of all, someone had forgotten to lock the single sash window. They must be laboring under the delusion that a drop of nearly twenty feet would dissuade anyone from trying.

At sunset, a woman brought her a bowl of soup and some bread, but Claire's attempts at conversation only resulted in a terrified look and a crablike scuttle for the door. The sound of locks turning put paid to that.

She polished off the soup, which contained not much more than beans and some kind of ground-up meat whose provenance she was in no position to question.

Then she tapped on the wall. "John? Davina?"

"Claire, are you all right?" The earl's tone was low, but she could hear him clearly.

"Perfectly. Is your nose broken?"

"I don't believe so. But Davina is not well. Fear for Will is wearing down her ability to cope."

"Have you a window in your room?"

"No, I'm sorry to say. I suspect that's the only reason they allowed us to stay together. There is no way out, no matter how much plotting we do to escape."

"I have one. I simply need to engineer a way to use it."

"Have you sheets with which to form a rope?"

"Sadly, no. That was the first thing I thought of. I wish now I'd brought my evening gown. It has a train that would have done the job admirably."

"Alas. Hindsight. If I had not lost my head and hidden the jewels, we might have been—"

"Dead, John."

"There is still the ransom."

"They are only ransoming us as a fallback plan. If they had had the jewels, their hundred thousand pounds would have been in hand and there would be no reason to keep any of us alive."

He was silent a moment. "And what of your family? Will they be willing to negotiate?"

Claire choked back a laugh. "My family—my mother and brother—have the land they sit on and not much else. She has leased our acres to a neighboring squire, but that income is only enough to keep them in pastry. There is nothing left to ransom me with."

"Then escape is your only option."

"Not without you. And the children. And Captain Hollys and the crew."

"Don't be foolish, Claire. How can one girl elude a shipful of pirates and set nearly thirty people free?"

Put like that, it was a little daunting.

But Ned Mose and his motley crew had never dealt with the Lady of Devices.

Chapter 9

The locks ground and Ned Mose kicked the door open. By the time it had banged against the wall and rebounded on him, Claire was sitting demurely on the bare pallet, ankles crossed, hands in her lap, just as Miss Follet at St. Cecilia's Academy for Young Ladies had taught them a lifetime ago.

He narrowed his gaze at her. "What are you up to, you minx?"

A lifting of the brow in inquiry was his only answer.

"Stand up. Turn around and show me that holster of yours."

She did so, and was subject to a number of jerks and tugs. "Are you interested in designing one?" In the process, he investigated the contents of her pouch.

"Shut up. What are these?" He sifted the gears and bits of machinery through his fingers.

They were the parts that went into a fire balloon. "Mr. Yau gave them to me. I thought I might crochet a purse and weave them into the design. That spiral gear is particularly pretty if you don't think about its original use."

"You ain't gonna be crocheting purses anytime soon." He pocketed them, and her heart sank. "Where's my rifle?"

She tried to keep her expression calm as she gazed at him. "In your hand?"

"Not this one, you aggravating chit. The one I took off you. The one that don't work."

The lightning rifle had gone missing? "I have no idea, captain." She adjusted the pins in her chignon. "You are welcome to search, however."

"Don't give me that. That rifle was in my cabin on *Lady Lucy* and now it's not. The only other person with an interest in it is you."

"I have been here all day, not gallivanting about the landscape stealing arms. I suggest you look to your crew, sir."

An irate glance about the cabin told him that even if she had managed to get her hands on the rifle, there was nowhere to hide it. The room held only Claire, the bed and pallet, a brass chamber pot, and the sprigged-china water pitcher.

"My crew is true. If I find out you had something to do with this, and lied to me, you're not going to like what happens." He glared at her. "I've been making inquiries about your ransom. Seems you're not a very good investment."

"I am sorry," Claire said quite sincerely.

"Yer queen knew who the Dunsmuirs were smart enough, but she didn't have no idea about you."

"Are you in communication with the queen?" How on earth had he pulled that off? A simple tea with her took weeks of management and involved several layers of the military, not to mention household staff.

"Don't take that tone with me. Course not. But I made headlines in the London papers two inches tall," he said with rather more pride than this should normally warrant. "In New York, too. I seen 'em. Pigeon brought 'em this morning. My demands were plainly laid out. I expect to hear something tomorrow on the Dunsmuirs."

She was silent. He was not expecting to hear about her. "Was I ... mentioned at all?"

"Pricked your pride, has it, that no one cares about you enough to want to ransom you?"

"I don't think it's a question of caring. It is a question of resources. My family have none."

"You got a fancy title and no money?"

"I'm afraid so."

He snorted. "Might have to make your own way in the world, huh, girlie? Ain't that a shame."

"I have been, sir, and quite successfully. I ran a home for indigent children up until very recently."

"Indi—ing—"

"Orphans."

At this, he stopped playing with the fire balloon parts in his pocket, pulled them out, and absently dropped them out the window. Claire bit back a cry of distress.

"You some kind of bluestocking do-gooder?"

"No, merely an impoverished woman making the best of a bad situation."

"So what are you doing with the Dunsmuirs, then, with satin dresses in your cabin and them fancy boots on?"

"I have precisely one satin dress to my name. And these boots were bought in Leadenhall market off a rag picker who'd had a good day."

Now he was looking at her as though she'd inconvenienced him—worse, that she'd somehow lied to him and he'd made a bad bargain because of it.

"I'm sorry to have misled you. Had I known we were to be skyjacked I would have been more clear about the situation."

Sucking in his lower lip, he thought for a moment. "Oh well. Buck up. Maybe someone will come forward yet."

"One can always hope," she said pleasantly. "However, if that turns out not to be the case, what might you do with me?"

"I dunno. I ain't never skyjacked a working woman before. I'll have to think on it."

And with that, he turned and left with a slam of the door. The lock ground into its housing once again, and as soon as the sound of his boots on the stairs faded, Claire darted to the window and leaned out.

Twenty feet below lay the scattered parts of her device. First thing on the agenda was to get down there and collect them.

Second thing was to find out what had become of the lightning rifle.

It would have been far too easy for Ned Mose to shake it out of any of his crew members foolish enough to steal from him. Who would risk being shot for theft, or whatever the punishment was out here for such things? If it had gone missing on the *Lady Lucy*, there was only one explanation.

The Mopsies.

They must have lowered themselves from the ceiling and taken possession of it, and by now they would have discovered it did not fire. All she had to do was reunite with them, pull out the trigger coupling concealed in her hair and replace it, and their odds of success would increase immeasurably.

Off in the distance, thunder growled in the twilight sky. The prospect of rain in this dry landscape seemed impossible—the state of the plant life proved it. But rain and night notwithstanding, a sense of urgency was growing under her breastbone. If Rosie was indeed in that hatbox somewhere out there, she would make a meal for some creature unless someone did something quickly.

She had to get out of this room!

Sitting on the windowsill, she leaned out and surveyed, not the wall below, but the wall above.

Urgh. Nothing but sheer wood planks. Five or six feet away was a rusty drainpipe, but it looked so unstable it would barely support a spider, never mind a young woman. Claire could just see herself leaping for it, and it promptly tearing away from the wall. Frustrated beyond measure, she slid back into the room.

Just in time to hear someone release the lock.

Ned Mose came in bearing a lamp, and Claire blinked, her eyes adjusting to the light.

"What are you doing?" he demanded.

"Gazing at the stars and feeling homesick."

He snorted. "You won't have much longer to do that. Buck up, girl. Seems you're to be ransomed after all."

Claire stared at him. Impossible. Lady St. Ives would not sacrifice Claire's baby brother Nicholas's inheritance, even for her own daughter. Would she? "You've heard from England already? How is it possible for the pigeons to travel so fast?"

"If they don't have so far to go, it ain't difficult."

"I don't understand."

"They read the New York papers up in Santa Fe. And telegraph works as well there as it does in New York." He sounded indignant, as if she'd impugned the literary abilities of the outposts in this godforsaken land. "Turns out you got a friend up there with a bit of ready cash."

Andrew!

Hope leaped in her heart and she put a hand to the wall to steady herself. His letter had said he was in pursuit of Lord James Selwyn. Had he located him so soon? Had he sold their Kinetick Carbonator to lawful buyers instead of the thieves who had spirited it out of England?

Ned Mose was watching her closely. "I sent a message back saying I was willing to negotiate, since if I was looking to recoup my costs I wouldn't get much out of you otherwise."

"That's ... comforting."

"So this Selwyn fellow should be here by tomorrow night at the earliest, if he takes ship. Train'll take longer."

Something was wrong with her head. Claire felt as if her ears had stopped up. He couldn't possibly have said what she thought he'd said. "What was that? Whose name did you say?"

He pulled a piece of yellow paper out of his pocket and squinted at it. "James Selwyn. What's the matter? Is he a friend of yours or not? Don't matter anyway—long as he's got the cash I don't care who he is."

And with that, he walked out and closed the door.

Claire heard the sliding of the lock as if for the first time. Locking her into a room—a house—a life she could not seem to escape, no matter how she tried.

৯৵

Lizzie nearly came to blows with Tigg over the question of who would stay with the airship and who would go and find the Lady.

"Our Willie can't leg it all that way and back," Tigg said as firmly as a person could with a six-year-old clinging to him like a burr. "Besides, 'e won't leave the ship." Willie shook his head vigorously. "His dad told him to stay put, and nothin' short of a bomb's gonna make 'im go."

"Fine," Lizzie snapped. "He stays. But we can't leave 'im alone. What if t'watch finds 'im? He can't defend 'imself."

"That's why you're going to stay wiv 'im," Tigg said patiently. "Girls stay with the kids and look after 'em."

"Wot?" Maggie goggled at him. "Tom Terwilliger, I ent never heard you spout such nonsense in all me life."

"That's wot Mr. Yau says."

"Mr. Yau don't know us very well," Lizzie said grimly. "Who's been scouting for Snouts since we was little tykes, eh? It weren't Mr. Yau, now, were it?"

"Besides, all *his* opinion got 'im was locked up," Maggie put in. She had nothing against Mr. Yau—had quite admired him and his red sash, in fact. But being left to mind the children just because she was a girl was plain silly.

"Me and Maggie will take the rifle to the Lady. We know wot we're doin'. And seems to me knockin' out the watch is more your job, now that Jake went over to the other side."

Tigg's eyebrows drew down in a way Maggie had never seen before. "Don't say 'is name in front of me again. I catch 'im, I'll give 'im what for, see if I don't."

"Cheer up," Lizzie told him. "Maybe they made him stand watch. You c'n fill yer boots then."

"T'engines need checked," Tigg said, clearly torn. "When Mr. Yau comes back, likely he's going to want a fast liftoff."

Lizzie could sense her victory close at hand. "They did smell a bit on the burnt side, didn't they?"

Tigg nodded, as if he'd made his final decision. "All right, then. Willie and me will get the *Lady Lucy* ready to cast off when you come back with everyone. We'll do for the watch quiet-like. And don't forget Rosie."

"As if it were all 'is idea," Maggie muttered indignantly to Lizzie as they hurried through the ceiling to the cabin they had shared.

"Never mind. Let 'im think wot 'e wants, long as we get to do wot we want. Tigg belongs wi' them engines and we belongs out there, sussin' out the situation, an' that's that."

They changed quickly into raiding rig—black skirts and stockings, their hair braided tightly so as to stay out of the way. "Will we want a rope?" Lizzie asked, tipping up the false bottom of her travel bag. "And a fire balloon?"

"Best take both. You never know. Here, use my sash an' tie the rifle on my back. You got the Lady's ring still?"

"Round my neck. The pearls?"

"Under my cammy." Maggie grinned over her shoulder as Lizzie cinched the last knot. "We're as rich as Rosie, an' that's a fact."

The humor of the situation lightened their feet as they crept down the gangway. Silence and darkness greeted them. "Wonder where t'watch is?" Maggie whispered.

"Long as 'e's not 'ere, I don't care. Come on. Hope you remember 'ow to shimmy down a rope."

"No need. Look, 'ere's the airmen's ladder."

Working quickly, they opened the hatch and tossed the bundled ladder out, where it unfurled and hung within jumping distance of the ground. Maggie had been in plenty of high places, but she still forbore to look down, concentrating instead on the immediate sight of the rungs in front of her eyes and under her boots.

There was no watch on the ground, either. She'd only been on an airship twice—once down to Cornwall and this time—but even she knew that an airman stood watch on the mooring ropes at every field.

"Lot of confidence, this Mose bloke," Lizzie muttered. "Only four guy ropes and no watch to be seen."

"Lucky for us. Come on."

Snouts had always told them to avoid roads and open land if they could, so they crossed the curious shallow course cut into the ground in order to approach the town from the opposite side. There was more cover over here—the thorny bushes stood a mite taller, and Maggie could smell the scent of pitch from the stunted little pines, breathing in the night air.

You would think a deserted wasteland would be quieter, though. Above the steady wind, she could hear something else.

"Liz? 'ave a listen. Wot's that?"

Lizzie cocked an ear. "Wind."

"No, under that. Deeper."

"Sounds like a train comin'."

There had been train tracks—she'd seen them from above as they'd come in. "Ent no train runnin' in the middle o' the night. Besides, them tracks are on t'other side."

"I don't like it." Lizzie picked up her pace. "Might be a ship o' some kind. Let's move."

By the time they got within sight of the town Maggie could hear more than just a roar—it sound like a band of trolls in full cry. "Lizzie! Get up on that rock! It ent no ship!"

They flung themselves at a pile of rocks, each the size of a house, all tipped and tilted as though a giant child had knocked them over one day and had never picked them up. Kicking and scrambling, Maggie pulled herself up onto the last one and looked over the top just in time to see a huge wave of water engulf the town.

The sound of it! The worst thunderstorm she'd ever been out in was like a baby's temper tantrum compared to this. The water roared, while big rocks and pieces of trees chunked against the stone bases of the houses, whirling off whatever it could grab.

"We could've been out in that!" Lizzie shrieked, and they clung to each other as the mad flood scoured through the buildings and out the far side, washing away their footprints in ten feet of water.

The edges of it came within a few yards of their perch, but it was like a flood tide in the Thames basin. It made its mark and then began to recede. The stars had barely moved in their wheeling arc across the sky when the roar became a rush, and then a chuckle, and finally a whisper, as if the whole town let out a breath.

Nothing moved but the watercourse, running and trickling and sighing after the bulk of it had stampeded off and what was left leached into the ground.

"D'you think they survived?" Lizzie's voice cracked.

"Dunno. Wot kind of idjits plant a town in t'middle of a riverbed?"

"Idjits who don't want company?"

Silence while a few more minutes passed.

"Mags?"

"Yes?"

"I'm afraid to go down there. Wot if it comes again?"

"It comes regular like, if that watercourse is any indication."

"Tonight, I mean."

"That's a chance we got to take. The Lady's down there, and Willie's mum and the captain and all. We gotta spring 'em before dawn. Seems now would be the best chance, while everyone's—"

Recovering? In shock? Dead? It was hard to find a word that would do justice to this stunned silence that lay across the land.

"I don't think I can move."

"Buck up, Liz." Maggie pushed herself to her feet. Truth be told, she'd far rather put her arms over her head and have a good cry, but that wouldn't do the Lady any good, nor any of the others, either. "Now's our chance."

"I can't. The noise, Mags! Ent no surviving that, you get caught in it."

"It's down to a trickle now, see? Come on. The Lady's countin' on us."

Cajoling, urging, and finally pulling on her arm, she got Lizzie down the rock. Their two figures cast long, vague shadows ahead of them as they ran toward the first of the buildings.

Starlight made a shadow. Who'd have thought?

❦

Any hope of sleep fled. Claire lay on her pallet as though she had been paralyzed—and perhaps she had.

She had no plan, no action she could take. All she had was the slim hope that, after the ransom had been paid and she was under James's protection, she could somehow give him the slip and find Rosie and the children.

I cannot let him pay the ransom.

Of course you can. It's your money. He stole it. You would practically be ransoming yourself.

It is Andrew's and mine and Dr. Craig's and the children's.

Regardless. Let him pay it and gain your freedom.

Yes, but at what cost? Would James be willing to assist her in freeing the Dunsmuirs and the children? Would he stand up to Ned Mose and the pirates for their sake? Would he be willing to comb the countryside in search of Rosie? Or would he take the Dunsmuir diamonds the same way he had taken the Kinetick Carbonator and return to Santa Fe, his investment tripled?

Her throat thickened with tears.

No. She must not give way to despair. There must be something she could do.

Perhaps the drop was not as far as she thought. If she hung from the sill and dropped to the ground, why, that would subtract six feet from the twenty-foot total.

She pushed up the sash and leaned out.

Fourteen feet was still a very long way. Long enough to break an ankle. And then where would she be—unable to run or save or do anything for anybody. Who knew if there was even a doctor in this place to set the bones?

The stars she had lied about gazing at before twinkled down on her.

At least, some of them did. The rest had been obscured by thick cloud. And in the distance, she heard a rushing, roaring sound, almost like the wind. No, not wind. Water.

Water. Oh, dear heaven.

The torrent bore down upon the town like a train, rushing in the path it had clearly cut many times before. There was nothing she could do but stare in motionless horror as it raced toward them, slurping up a half mile, then three hundred yards, then the last hundred feet.

With a bone-shaking sussuration, it leaped forward, rushing between the buildings, slapping against the stone foundations—stone, that was why the first floor of even the most wretched house was stone—heaving great whitecaps up into the air as force met resistance.

The sound was deafening, the shuddering of the house as the water engulfed it terrifying. Why, one loose board or stone and the water would tear in and the entire house would go whirling off into the maelstrom.

Off into the maelstrom.

Claire yanked the window up. The water shot past a mere ten feet below her. The house shook once again as something—a tree trunk that must have been uprooted miles away—struck the side of it like a battering ram and spun out into the current.

Floating.

Claire's horror snapped into intelligent thought. In less than a second she had swung her legs outside. She sucked in a deep breath, clutched her chignon where the precious coupling hid, and leaped feet first out of the window into the roaring night.

Chapter 10

Cold.

Claire had swum in the sea below Gwynn Place, but even that had not prepared her for the chilling cold of water that must have come from mountains far away. One hand clutching the back of her head, she struggled for the surface with the other, hoping her boots would stay laced to her legs and thankful that at some point earlier, she had rucked up and fastened her skirts.

Her head broke the surface just in time for her to see a solid wall looming up. Kicking furiously, she allowed the current to take her around it rather than mashing her into it, where she would be pinned like a struggling butterfly until it receded.

The current pushed her into the street and widened out into a rushing river, carrying her like a piece of gasping flotsam all the way through town in a matter of seconds. She had no choice but to let go of her hair and use both arms to half-swim, half-steer herself, mostly feet first to fend off posts and structures.

Once free of the unnatural canyon made by the houses and store fronts, the water spread, scouring yet deeper the channel she had seen on the way in. Before long, her weight and her sodden skirts made her drag along the bottom until at last she could gain her footing.

She staggered up a sandy bank and collapsed upon it, gasping and crying at the same time. *Thank you, blessed Lord, for saving my life.* Oh, how foolish she had been—but bruises and filth notwithstanding, she was free!

The coupling! She clutched at her chignon. Thanks to the wire pins and the thickness of her hair, not to mention the ivory pick, she had a fine sopping mat decorated with leaves and bits of flotsam. And here it was. Nothing had ever been so welcome as the feel of that U-shaped bit of brass. She may as well leave it, because nothing would dislodge it from this mare's nest.

And now she must rest. Just for a moment. Her limbs felt so heavy ...

The cold woke her.

Shivering, she rolled to a sitting position, her wet clothes clinging like the hands of the dead. How could such a hot, dry place get so cold at night?

She drained the water from her boots, wrung out what she could from her skirts, and pushed herself to her feet to get her bearings. Below her, the river chuckled and bubbled, but even as she watched, it seemed to be receding, soaking into the thirsty earth and losing itself in the flat spread of the plain. How strange and wonderful and deadly—coming and going in what seemed like a mere flash of time.

She, meanwhile, felt as though she'd aged a year. And how long had she been unconscious?

In the distance somewhere lay the town. And ahead loomed a thicker darkness that blacked out the stars.

The cliff?

There had only been the one, that she could remember—a red sandstone monolith cut by centuries of wind and storm, with caves scoured out of its faces and pinnacles left where rock had fallen away. There had been a shack snugged up against it, directly to the west of the canyon where they had moored the *Lady Lucy*. She would simply have to circle around to avoid being detected by whoever lived in the shack. And as far as boarding, there must be a way other than by the locomotive tower. If she had to shinny up a mooring rope, she would do it.

But now she needed to decide between two urgent questions—and quickly, before her shivering and chattering teeth became uncontrollable. Should she strike out to the east and try to locate Rosie and the hatbox before one was discovered and the other eaten? Or should she secure the girls and Willie and the lightning rifle?

On a moment's reflection, the airship won out. The children's safety was most important. And with the lightning rifle, at the very least, she could shoot any threat to Rosie.

With a sense of relief at having real work to do once again and a clear path to it, she turned toward the cliff.

A dark shape rose out of the river course behind her. "Hey!" it shouted. "This stretch is mine!"

Claire gasped and whirled, in the same movement snatching the ivory pick from her hair. "Who's there?"

"What do you mean, who's there?" The voice sounded indignant. "This is my stretch. You go find your own."

Now there were two figures, moving toward her cautiously, as though she presented some danger.

That was comforting. In a way.

"I have no idea what you mean. I was carried here by that— that—" What did one call it? "That act of God." Briskly, she rubbed her arms.

"What, the flash flood?" The voice rose to such a pitch that Claire realized with a jolt that the speaker was a woman. "How did you survive that? Who are you?"

She carried the lamp close enough now that Claire could see the outline of a body. Rolling the pick in her fingers, she glanced from the woman to the dark figure moving next to her.

"I'm Claire. Who is that with you?"

"Oh, that's Nine. I'm giving him a trial run. He's an automaton. See?"

She lifted the lamp just enough for Claire to see a metal contraption vaguely human in shape, with buglike eyes and enormous feet. She stumbled back. An ivory hair pick would do nothing against a brass casing. And who knew what malevolence was contained behind that blank stare?

"Oh, don't worry, he's harmless. He's a metal picker. Like I said, we were just doing a trial run when I saw you climb up the bank. Say, you're all right, ain't you? Nothing broke? Or worse?"

The woman lifted the lamp to examine Claire's face, and in the light, Claire took in what appeared to be a mechanic's overall and a leather cap on which were perched a pair of goggles. They bore no resemblance to the driving goggles she owned herself; in fact, they seemed to be made of sterner stuff. Poking out from under the cap were a few strands of frizzly blond hair.

"Are you a w-welder?" she asked.

The woman—no, girl, really, she couldn't be more than a year or two older than Claire herself—wagged her head back and forth. "Welder, tinkerer, picker. You name it, I probably done it. Alice Chalmers, at your service." She stuck out a gloved hand.

Claire moved the pick into her left and shook it.

Alice gazed at her as if she couldn't believe she was real. "You look like a drowned rat, so your tale must be true." Shaking her head, she said, "Come on. You could probably use a hot toddy before you get hypothermia, and you can tell me all about it. I'm that keen on a good story."

A hot toddy sounded divine, but her story was hers to keep. Too many lives depended upon it. "I'm so sorry, I can't. I have urgent b-business. Where do you live?"

"Over there." She jerked her head in the direction of the cliff. "Got a place to myself. I make my living picking and wrecking, sometimes mooring. Whatever it takes, you know?"

"You mean the sh-shack by the cliff?"

"Sure, where else?"

"Are you the operator of that locomotive tower?"

"Sure am. Built it, run it, fix it every time it breaks, which is daily. Say, how'd you know about that?"

Claire felt the irrational urge to weep.

Out of the frying pan, into the fire, as Mrs. Morven used to say.

❧

It wasn't so hard to find where the Dunsmuirs and the crew were … all you had to do was follow the sounds of fighting.

Somehow the crew had seized their chance in the calm after the deluge, and the pirates were giving back as good as they got. The street was filled with debris—tree branches, rocks as big as one's head, pieces of buildings—so when Lizzie tossed her a jolly great branch to use as a club, and picked up a rock in each hand, Maggie prepared herself.

She wasn't so keen on fighting. She was a fine scout and even better on watch, but she had to admit that being ten and not very tall had its disadvantages in a scrum.

But there were ways to turn disadvantages upside down.

Darting in and out of the fray like birds, Maggie swung her club at the head of a pirate who held the first officer down in the mud. When he collapsed with a grunt, Mr. Andersen finished him off with his own air rifle. Lizzie had a good eye and deadly aim, so she chose her targets and launched rocks one after the other. Maybe they landed hard enough to do damage and maybe they didn't, but they distracted their opponents just long enough for a crewman to get the upper hand.

Even his lordship fought like a madman. He'd stuffed her ladyship behind a cart loaded with what looked like engine parts, snatched up a healthy length of pipe in each hand, and was wielding them like a proper dockside drayman.

Someone caught Maggie from behind and smashed the breath right out of her. She dropped her branch and clawed at the iron fingers around neck and waist, a scream choked off before it fairly got out of her throat, her feet kicking and trying to find purchase on flesh.

"Aiyeeyah!" The most unnatural cry she had ever heard came from somewhere behind her captor, and in the next second his head jerked forward, clocked her on the back of the noggin, and something made an awful snap. She fell, rolling clear and scrambling to her feet so quick Snouts would've been proud.

The pirate lay dead in the mud, and Mr. Yau nodded at her as calmly as if she'd come into the engine room for a lesson in mechanics. "Thank you, sir," she managed to gasp, remembering at last to drag in some air.

"Duck, missy."

She dropped to the ground and his leg lashed out, catching a pirate under the chin and snapping his head back with lethal force. There was that sound again—the sound of neck bones being permanently snapped. The pirate's weapon fell on her and she caught it.

"Take this, sir."

"No need." He waded into the fray with pleasant determination while his appendages moved so quick the eye could hardly follow. Every man he touched fell.

What wouldn't she give to know how to do that.

However, as the Lady might say, one made the best of one's circumstances. Maggie hefted the rifle. All right, then. If a pirate could shoot it, so could she.

It had a big fat barrel and weighed a ton. Must be a royal sized bullet in there.

Someone roared with rage and she sucked in a breath. The earl. Two pirates advanced on him, screaming for him to put his weapons down and surrender. Both of them had air rifles trained on him and while Mr. Yau and two of the crew were fighting their way to him, he was so mad and so determined to protect her ladyship that they'd have to shoot him.

But Maggie couldn't raise the gun. The blasted thing was so heavy it wobbled all over the place. Aiming at anything but a warehouse was out of the question.

Her ladyship's cart!

Maggie dashed behind the earl and took up her position. If anyone but the countess saw her, she'd be surprised, but in a trice her ladyship took in what she was up to.

"John!" she shrieked. "Duck!"

It was a rare man who would do what his wife screeched at him in such a tone, but the earl seemed to be that kind of man. He dropped like a stone, leaving the pirates gawking at him for just a second.

A second was all Maggie needed. She pulled the trigger, wondering what on earth she'd got them all into—

A pair of cannonballs, each as big as her fist and tied together with a length of chain, exploded out of the big bore of the rifle. Whirling like a very dervish of destruction, they struck the pirates and then whipped around the two of them, cracking their skulls and tying them up tight all in the same graceful swirl.

The countess shot her the kind of triumphant look that Maggie had only seen on the Lady's face when she'd got her times table right or fixed the mother's helper that cleaned the cottage. Except the Lady didn't look quite so bloodthirsty when she did it. "Well done, Maggie. Well done indeed."

The earl scrambled up and joined them. "If I'd had any idea you were such a good shot, I'd have come and found you first."

"Where's Will?" the countess demanded. "Is he with you?"

"Not likely. 'E's on the ship, 'elping Tigg get 'er ready for lift-off."

"He's safe." Her ladyship's eyes could burn a hole in a hanky. "You're sure he's safe."

"Safe as houses, ma'am."

The intensity in her gaze was dissolved by relief. "Good heavens, Maggie. You just saved my husband's life. I think we can dispense with the ladyships and ma'ams. My Christian name is Davina, and I would be honored if you would use it."

Goodness. Wait till Lizzie heard!

"I—well, all right, then, yer la—er, Davina."

"If you ladies are finished with the proprieties, perhaps we might consider getting back to the ship," his lordship said. "Maggie, is that rifle on your back operable?"

"No, sir."

"Has that thing in your hand got another shot?"

"No, sir."

"Can you use it as a club if you must?"

"Oh yes, sir."

"Right, then. It appears our side is carrying the day. Let us locate Ian and Jack as fast as possible. If I do not see my son within half an hour, I won't be held accountable for the consequences."

As it turned out, Maggie could have stood to find Captain Hollys about two seconds later than she did. Then she would have missed the sight of some dilapidated old sword going right through a raggedy pirate's chest. Why that bothered her more than having a man's neck broken right next to her ear she couldn't say, but there you were.

Compared to the Texican Territory, life in Blighty was tame. In fact, she'd almost be willing to shake the Cudgel's hand after this.

Almost.

They found Lizzie with Mr. Yau, and after that, the officers rounded up the crew right quick. They dragged the wounded and dead into one of the houses the captain said had been used as a prison, made the former as comfortable as possible under the circumstances, and left the latter for Mose to deal with.

"Where is Ned Mose?" Maggie ventured to ask Mr. Yau. The man had saved her life—she felt a connection to him now that went deeper than admiration for his sash and his skill with the engines.

"I don't know, little missy." She and Lizzie had to jog to keep up with the pace they set across the wash and along the bank on the other side. "This is merely a skeleton crew. If the entire band had been here, the outcome would have been much different. Apparently they have urgent business elsewhere."

"Pirating other people, maybe," she grumbled.

"I think not. The *Stalwart Lass* is disabled, and unless they have taken the *Lady Lucy* to do so—ah."

Maggie looked up to see the smooth fuselage of the Dunsmuir vessel protruding from the canyon, exactly as she and Lizzie had left it.

Her ladyship picked up her skirts and broke into a run.

৵৽

Alice Chalmers grasped her arm, but Claire was shivering too hard to shake it away. "Come on. We've got to get you warmed up. I'm surprised you ain't dead. Not many people get washed up out of the flash floods alive."

She was of no use like this—better to be restored to herself than to let the night air finish what the water had not. The shack was several hundred yards away, and by the end of it, sheer stubbornness was all that kept her on her feet.

Alice ushered her inside, poked up what appeared to be a boiler combined with a stove, and stuck a hand into the hot water reservoir. "Won't be a shake. Meanwhile, better knock back some grog. That'll help."

She handed Claire a brown bottle. *Another thing mama need never know.* One swallow was enough to make her splutter and cough, but oh my, it burned all the way to the pit of her stomach.

A thick, uneven slice of bread and honey, and a chunk of surprisingly creamy cheese went down next. Claire began to feel as if walking out the door might not be such an insurmountable task after all.

"D-Does this happen often? This flash flood?"

"All the time. The minute you hear the thunder up in them hills, you batten down the hatches. Me, I'm out of the way, so I just wait till it all goes down, and then I see what there is to see."

"But why build a town in the middle of a riverbed?"

"They didn't, originally. But the water goes where it wants, so there's not much to do but live with it. They could move the town, I suppose, but there's no guarantee it won't be just as bad in the new place. Here, have a wash. I make the soap myself. We'll do your clothes after."

"No, really, I must be on my way."

"Best listen. I been living out here close on five years now. If you don't want to be scratching red sand out of places you never knew existed, you'll want to wash it away. Here, behind the curtain. I'll bring you a tub. Take your time."

Other than bolting for the door and raising the alarm, she couldn't see any course but to obey. If Rosie had not been eaten by an animal yet, then perhaps chances were good she would make it to the morning. It would be better to search by daylight anyway.

The hot water felt better than any satin gown ever had.

Claire washed her hair with the lavender-scented soap—where did Alice Chalmers get lavender way out here?—and scrubbed the sand out of her skirts and blouse as well. The holster and her leather corselet had fared quite well, so she hung them on the back of a chair to dry out. When Alice brought more water to rinse everything in, she felt nearly human again.

"Thank you for rescuing me." She sat by the stove, which had been roused to a fine heat to dry her clothes, and drank the tea that magically appeared. "And feeding and washing me. I owe you much more than I can repay."

Alice shrugged modestly. "It ain't often I get to talk with another girl. Mostly it's that rabble off the *Stalwart Lass* and the ya-hoos in town. There's a few ladies, and I'm pretty good friends with some of the desert flowers over at the honkytonk, but mostly I keep to myself."

Claire had no idea what a desert flower or a honkytonk might be, but at the mention of the *Stalwart Lass*, her guard came back up. It was far too susceptible to the blandishments of hot water and food. "Are you part of the crew? Of the *Lass*, I mean."

"Not me. They need a place to land, and I got one. That's about the extent of it. Not that I own this." She waved a grimy hand to encompass the cliffs and the desert outside. "Nobody does, really. All I got is in this one room and my locomotive tower. Oh, and the automatons."

Plural? There were more? A prickle of unease ran up Claire's spine.

Alice's face took on a dreamy expression as she gazed into the distance over the stove. "Someday I'm going to get to Santa Fe and have a real manufactory. I bet they could use some good automatons up there. And mine are good. They don't look like much, but they work real well. See?"

She pulled over what looked like a leather mail pouch, and sifted through its contents. Gears, pulleys, tools—even jewelry and kitchen implements. At the bottom was something that might have been a mechanical arm such as the one employed by Ned Mose. "Nine found all this. He's got a magnetic charge in his feet, see? Saved me weeks of combing the sand with a big rake, like some of 'em do."

She smiled, and Claire realized she wasn't gazing into the distance at all. Nine stood behind the stove as if that were its resting place. She resisted the urge to push her chair back and put it between them. She must control this irrational aversion. There were a few automata in England, used mostly by the *nouveau riche* as butlers at parties, but people of good society employed actual humans. Were they so common in the Americas that this apparently uneducated girl in the middle of nowhere could build them?

"Have you training in mechanics?"

"I had a year at the engineering school down in Texico City, but mostly I just tinker until something works. Nine, come here."

Claire sucked in a breath as the machine whirred and took several steps closer. In the light, she could see that its arms and legs were jointed roughly where human joints would be. In fact, the arm assemblies looked familiar.

Distressingly so.

"How very clever. Have you ever considered building these limb assemblies for people who have lost theirs in some accident?"

"Oh, sure. I made the one Ned Mose wears. Pretty proud of it, too, with the telescoping forearm and all. Ever seen it?"

Claire evaded the question with another one. "You made it for him, but he's not your employer?"

If all she did was look after air traffic, and she didn't associate with the sky pirates except to take money from them, then maybe this girl would help her.

Alice laughed. "Not him. I'm not what you'd call an employer kind of girl. No, didn't I say? Ned Mose is my pa."

Chapter 11

"But we can't leave Rosie!"

Maggie could count on the fingers of one hand the times she'd put her foot down and acted the way Lizzie did every day of her life. If a point needed to be carried, Lizzie usually did it. But in the crunch, Maggie could stiffen her spine and make a fuss with the best of them.

This was a crunch, and she was prepared to fuss as much as it took.

"Maggie, dearest, we have only moments in which to escape." The countess knelt next to her so that Maggie, who had grown quite a lot in the past couple of months, thank you, could actually look down into her face.

"The Lady will never leave wivout Rosie. And what about yer jewels 'is lordship was so keen to keep safe?"

"We have learned a lesson or two about the relative value of jewels," the earl said grimly. "Davina, you must tell her. There is no getting round it."

"Tell us wot?" Lizzie's face took on that mulish look she got when she suspected a gull. It took a lot of skill to put one over on her—and hardly anyone succeeded. "Why're you lookin' at us that way?"

"My dears," Davina said softly, "I'm very sorry to tell you that Claire is ... gone."

"Gone?" Like a blow to the stomach, Maggie suddenly realized what she'd done. They'd gone to free the Lady, and in the shock of the flood, the fighting, and the mad dash back to the ship, she'd completely forgotten about her! "Where is she? Why didn't she come wiv us?"

"She was gone before the fighting started. We—we are very much afraid that there has been foul play."

Maggie snuck a glance at her sister, whose face was as blank as her own must be.

"Immediately after the flood receded, Mr. Yau employed his skill at the ancient Eastern practice of *juh-doh*. The door was no match for him, and he and Captain Hollys came to free us. Mose was holding Claire next door, but when we got in, we found no one."

"She 'scaped, then." Why were they leaving it to her to point out the obvious?

"We are very much afraid she was pushed. Due to—to economic circumstances that are too complicated to go into now, the pirates discovered there would be no ransom for her. We— oh girls, how it pains me to say this! We believe she was pushed out the window during the worst of the flood, and drowned."

Maggie stared at her ladyship, her stomach pinching and a horrible cold creeping over her skin. They must be talking about someone else. Not the Lady.

"The day the Lady lets someone push her out a window is the day the queen leaves Windsor and turns 'erself into a Billingsgate doxy." Lizzie's tone brooked no argument. Maggie couldn't have said it better herself.

"An admirable sentiment, but misplaced, I fear."

"I don't believe you fer a second, but no matter. We still 'ave to collect Rosie." Maggie braced herself for some truly epic fussing.

"Your lordship!" A middy, covered in mud and with the sleeve of his uniform hanging off his wrist, appeared in the hatch from the navigation gondola. "Captain says to tell you up ship in five minutes, sir."

"No!" Maggie shouted. "We have to go find Rosie!"

"I'm sorry, darling." Her ladyship looked close to tears. "You were brilliant and brave to send Rosie and the diamonds off the ship to safety, but I'm very much afraid we must leave them behind in order to save ourselves."

"Please, yer ladyship." Lizzie, reduced to begging? Maggie could hardly credit it. "It won't take but a moment. We saw where the hatbox went down, not a mile away, past that big pointy rock. It's near dawn—she'll be callin' for us. We c'n find her in two shakes of a lamb's tail."

"Captain says you ent got one shake," the middy observed from the hatchway, not without sympathy.

"Thank you, Mr. Colley, that will do," the earl told him. "Tell the captain we are ready to lift."

"We aren't!" Maggie shrieked.

"Maggie, the diamonds are not worth the lives at stake here," the countess said desperately, trying to put her arms around her.

"I don't care about the bloody diamonds," she screamed, yanking herself out of reach and practically standing on her toes like a rooster about to attack. "I care about Rosie! We're a *flock!*"

"You don't even know if the Lady is dead and you're going to leave her? What kind of people *are* you?" Lizzie demanded.

"Dear heaven, Davina. This is no time for argument. Mr. Andersen, take the young ladies to their cabin and lock them in. We have no time to waste."

"No!" Maggie cried, and dodged, but no matter how she struggled, the chief steward had a grip like a manacle.

"You can't do this!" Lizzie screamed all the way down the corridor, until Mr. Andersen thrust them into their cabin and closed the door on them with inexorable politeness. The lock clicked over.

Lizzie launched herself at the door, kicking and pounding on it, to no avail. She collapsed in a heap at its foot, tears and snot streaming down her face.

If ye can't get out the door, ye numpty, look for a window.

Snouts's voice, irritating as it was, came to her out of the depths of memory. Maggie leaped for the porthole.

What luck! "Lizzie!"

A storm of tears was her only answer.

"Lizzie, a guy line!" She shook her sister with rather more violence than usual. "There's a guy line right outside this porthole. Think we can get out?"

Lizzie lifted her head and wiped her nose with her muddy sleeve. "If we can't, I'll die tryin' before I stay aboard this tub one more minute."

❧

Claire's stomach clenched so hard the bread and the cheese threatened to come back up.

Ned Mose was this kind girl's *father?*

She pretended interest in Nine's arm while she controlled herself and tried to think what to do. She had been a fool to let Alice's ingenuous gaze and disarming way of speaking get past her guard. Her admiration for Alice's talent with mechanics was likely to get her sent straight back to that locked room. Alice was no society belle, trained not to use her mind except to dabble in conversation with possible suitors. Behind that open gaze lay a quick brain that seemed to be always working.

"So I'm thinking, from that white look on your face, that you were one of those rich folks Ned took off the *Lady Lucy.*"

She could deny it, but the prospect of having to come up with a Banbury tale to explain her presence here was just too exhausting. "Yes, I am. I've been locked in a room for two days, being driven nearly mad with anxiety. I have urgent business to attend to."

"So you said."

"You may tell him I was here if you like, but by the time you do, I will be long gone. And if you try to restrain me, be assured I am no stranger to violence."

Alice raised blond brows, scratched her scalp, and pulled off her leather cap. She shook out hair that was a frizzled, curly mess. With a little care it could be beautiful—there was certainly plenty of it. "I don't see how you're going to leave, unless you plan to pilot that airship out of here, or take my locomotive tower. In that case, you'd be better walking. A good horse can beat that thing any day. What makes you think I'm going to tell him?"

"Why wouldn't you? You're his daughter—you said so yourself."

"That's got nothing to do with nothing. I'm my mother's daughter, too, and you don't see me working at the honkytonk, do you?"

Ah. So that was what a desert flower was. A street sparrow. A dollymop. A woman forced to make her way using any method she could.

She gazed at Alice, who got up and refilled her teacup. "Just because they have the use of the field don't mean I agree with what they do. I gotta eat, same as anyone else. And if I say that no killing is to happen during any mooring or lift, then I suppose being his daughter is some advantage. At least he gives me enough credit to indulge me."

"So …" Claire hardly dared say it. "You do not intend to hand me over to him?"

Alice shrugged. "Not my affair. Pulling a half-drowned girl out of a flood path is my affair, since this is my patch. All this flat, from the nose of the mesa down to Spider Woman, that's mine. I got no call to interfere with you once you're on your feet again."

Hope was an amazing thing. It grew and bloomed even in the most trying and inhospitable environment.

"Thank you for that."

Alice twinkled at her. "Us girls gotta stick together, or the men will run us over."

"What is a *may-so*? And Spider Woman?"

"*Mesa*. That's Spaniard for *table*, because of their flat tops. And Spider Woman, that's a big old rock spire down at the end, where the wash flattens out. There's a legend among the Navapai hereabouts that she sits up there on top and spins out the lives of men."

"I see. And the Navapai?"

"Indians. We rub along all right so long as you don't try to cheat 'em. They're like you about automatons—no, I saw you. The Navapai, they think they're the walking dead."

Claire began to feel some affinity for these mysterious people. Perhaps they were the desert equivalent of the Esquimaux in the Canadas.

"So, you got an interest in mechanics?" When Claire nodded, she went on eagerly, "Sometimes the pigeon brings papers from the big cities, and I can see what people are inventing. That's where I got the idea for One way back. This man in New Jersey took a basic household automaton and outfitted it for his cotton mill. Doubled production in a year."

"One? So Nine means you've built nine automatons? Where on earth do you get the parts?"

Alice flushed and looked away. "Here and there. Resolution ain't much of a town, but traffic does come through."

"Is that what this place is called? Resolution?"

"Yep. Been here ten years or so. Might not be here ten years from now, though. The floods are starting to get on people's nerves. Say, maybe you've seen this one?"

Claire thought she meant a flood until a scientific magazine was thrust into her hands.

"Andrew Malvern has an article in this issue." Claire looked up in surprise. How strange to hear that name out here in the middle of nowhere, in those flat Texican accents. "They don't come often enough, you ask me. He could fill a whole subscription just by himself." Alice bent to show her the page, and sure enough, there was Andrew's daguerreotype next to the byline. The article outlined his theories on coal production and how technology could help the railroad industry.

"Are you an admirer of Mr. Malvern?"

Absently, Alice took the magazine from Claire before she could read much more than the first paragraph, held it at arms' length, and gazed at the picture. "He's so brilliant. And his writing is so entertaining. I wonder if he really looks like this. Before I die I've determined to meet him. Haven't figured out how yet, but I will."

"How very strange life can be. Alice, I have been Mr. Malvern's laboratory assistant these past two months. We worked on that very project, with the coal."

Alice lifted her head and goggled at her as if she'd just announced she was the queen herself in disguise, come for a visit. "You?"

"The very same. Along with a young man named Tigg, who is part and parcel of my urgent business."

Alice shook herself, much in the manner of a dog climbing out of a lake soaking wet. "Well, I never. His assistant, you say. Boy, what wouldn't I give ..." She glanced through the cabin's two windows. "Dawn's a few hours away. What business is it that's so urgent you can't catch a few hours' shut-eye?"

"I must rescue a friend who is marooned some distance to the east of here."

"Marooned? Is it this boy? Is he injured and can't walk into town?"

"It's possible. Thank you for rescuing me. But I really must set out."

"I'll come with you. I know the terrain and you don't."

"Thank you, but—"

Alice held up a hand, as if to stop her refusal. "Shh. Someone's coming."

They'd discovered she was gone. And what more logical place to look than downriver for a dead body, or at the shack for a live one?

"Alice—I must hide."

Frantically, she cast around the one-room cabin for somewhere to conceal herself. The stove, the chairs, the cupboards, the automaton—those were the sole contents of the shabby room.

"Here." Alice snatched up her corselet, holster, and damp skirt, pushed them into her hands, and tilted a ladder against the wall. "Loft."

As someone pounded on the door, Claire practically leaped upward and found herself in a crawl space barely high enough to fit a couple of crates and a strongbox. She rolled over them and lay face down on boards that were placed carelessly enough to give her a limited view of the room below. Unfortunately, anyone looking up could also see her white corset cover in the spaces between the boards.

Perhaps they would not look up.

Alice tossed the tea things in a metal washbasin and answered the door. "Pa. What brings you out here at this time of night?"

He pushed two or three of his crew into the room and slammed the door.

"I been out picking and Nine found—"

"Quiet, girl. I need to think."

"Fine. You do that. Tea?"

One of the pirates looked hopeful, but was crushed by a glare from Mose. Alice filled the basin from a metal spigot poking out of the rear wall, and washed up the tea things as if her father and his temper were a common sight in her little home in the middle of the night.

Perhaps they were.

"So here's where we are," Mose said abruptly, apparently having had enough time to think. "I got the Dunsmuirs up for ransom, and a cache of missing jewels. The *Stalwart Lass* is crippled, maybe for good, but I got another ship we can strip for parts."

Lying prone some three feet above his head, Claire pressed her lips together. *We'll see about that.*

"I got someone coming to ransom a prisoner, but the rascalous girl escaped." His ocular assembly whined as it focused on his daughter, in and out. "You seen her?"

"Who? Your prisoner? It's been a while since anyone gave you the slip, Pa."

"Girl vanished out of a locked room."

"You don't say."

"Only explanation is she fell in the flood, but that don't seem likely. People don't just fall out of windows."

"Maybe someone pushed her, Pa. And locked the door behind him when he was done."

He was silent for a moment while Claire silently applauded her. How clever to plant yet another doubt in his mind about his own men! Who knew when that might bear fruit?

"Ain't none of us would do such a thing, Ned," one of the pirates ventured. "Not if there was money to be made off her. Say, Miss Alice, you got anything to eat around here?"

"I could whip up a mess of biscuits if you wanted, Perry."

Claire couldn't see Perry, but from the sound of his voice, he was young. A hungry age, maybe somewhere between her own age and Jake's.

Jake … Jake. Oh, if only I'd—

"Shut up, Perry. We got work to do." Mose began to pace, though the cabin was so small he couldn't take more than a few steps either way. The ocular assembly adjusted to his course every time he made the turn. "So I'm thinkin', since I got no girl to hand over for the ransom, I gotta do something else. I don't see any choice."

"Pa, no." Alice's tone was hushed with pain and pleading.

"Don't take that tone with me. You think I like wrecking? But what's this fancy man gonna do once he finds we got no girl? He'll have the Rangers down on us quick as that flash flood and twice as mean."

"Rangers been here before and we gave 'em the slip, Ned," one of the pirates offered.

"Got too much to lose this time. Got a house, and a woman. And I'm getting too old to pick up and run every time someone takes exception to the way I manage my business."

"So you're set on this course, then?" Carefully, as if it were fine Limoges that would shatter at a breath, Alice put a dry saucer into a crate tacked to the wall as a cupboard. "You want to wreck this ship that's coming?"

Claire suddenly realized what they were talking about. *Wrecking.*

Wreckers operated in Cornwall, too—setting out lights on the cliffs on stormy nights. A ship would steer toward the light thinking it indicated a safe harbor, only to be wrecked on the rocks. The loss of life was terrible—some wreckers even made sure it was total. Meanwhile, the cargo washed ashore for the wreckers to pick over, use, or sell. Claire had heard them use the word and it hadn't sunk in that the despicable practice could mean the same thing out here in the desert as it did at home in Cornwall.

"I do. Pigeon came saying they're a hundred miles off. The boys will help you set out the lanterns."

"Pa—"

"No arguments, girl. Do it or you'll be sorry you didn't."

It took an act of will for Claire to remain motionless. The ship was coming—James's ship. No matter what he had done to her, he was still part of her past. They had broken bread together, conversed together. He had asked her to be his wife.

If she did not do something, he would be lured to his death.

And it would be all her fault.

Chapter 12

Alice did not give up, despite the fierce brows and downturned mustache of her father. "There must be a different way. Why not just take 'em prisoner when they get off?"

"Because then we'll have more witnesses than we do already. My mind is made up, girl, so quit your whining. We'll run 'em into Spider Woman same as always."

"Pa, they're innocent people trusting you to do a proper deal."

This appeal to his better nature seemed to have no effect on Ned Mose. "Cheer up. You can make yourself another automaton from the plunder. Ten's a nice round number."

They had wrecked *nine ships?*

But how did they coax a ship out of the sky and run it into a rock?

The pirates swept Alice out with them, and in a moment Claire heard the locomotive tower fire up. But, in the grip of cold horror, she could not move.

Spider Woman. That spire of rock with the woman spinning on top of it. Spinning out the threads that would end the lives of innocent men.

She rolled over the crates and fell to her hands and knees, fighting the nausea down. Alice had not been able to put the ladder back up. Never mind. She'd dropped from the tops of walls higher than this.

As she landed lightly, she heard scraping and cursing somewhere behind and above the shack. Then the sound of metal on rock and a shout of "All the lamps. No, all of them! Hurry up, you fleabitten coyotes, or they'll be on us!"

There must be some kind of equipment storage up in the cliff, reachable only by the tower. Evidently they valued their equipment more than the life of their tower operator— considering the unpredictable flash floods and goodness knows what other natural disasters this place was subject to.

Her fingers felt almost numb as Claire pulled her damp clothes on. She snapped the corselet together and snatched a knife with a thick bone handle from beside the washbasin, wrapping the blade in her scarf and slipping it diagonally into the leather. She'd never laced her boots so fast in all her life.

She slipped out of the shack and into the inky shadows where it met stone. And it was there, as she watched the tower chug across the ground toward Spider Woman, that the full scale of the enterprise hit her.

They were not carrying lamps to light their way across the flat. They were going to set them out on either side of Spider Woman to indicate a landing field, and when the zeppelin glided in, it would smash right into the vast spire of rock.

What could one almost eighteen-year-old girl do against two dozen pirates, a locomotive tower, and this hostile landscape?

Claire examined the impossibilities as they raced before her mind's eye.

Could she release the *Lady Lucy* and take it up, turning it somehow so that it would obscure the lamps from the view of the incoming ship? Assuming she could release the mooring ropes and get aboard before it floated away, how would she manage both steering and engines? They were hundreds of feet apart, and by the time she got one going, the other would have become uncontrollable.

Keep it simple.

Could she run out and kick over the lamps? Yes, and then they'd catch her and this time, they'd save themselves the bother of locking her up. They'd simply shoot her on the spot.

Could she run to town, then, and release the Dunsmuirs and the crew? That would be an excellent plan if she had more than a few minutes. By the time they got back, James would have fallen out of the sky and landed among the wreckage, twisted and broken.

She couldn't even send a pigeon up to tell them something was wrong. Or wave a flag or those lamps that the railway men had to signal a train to—

Wait. Lamps.

One lamp.

All she needed was one lamp with which to signify danger, up high enough to catch the eye of the navigator and make him wonder why there was a danger signal where logic said no signal should be.

Her scarf was red. She could wrap the lamp in it. It would probably catch fire, but she had to take the chance.

With only the vaguest idea of where exactly Spider Woman was in the dark, Claire followed the sound of the locomotive tower, keeping fifty yards to the side and praying the night would conceal her. No point trying to keep quiet—the locomotive, grumbling along on its rotating treads, made enough noise to cover the sound of an approaching army, never mind one person.

She must steal a lamp. Now, while everyone was facing the monolith that rose out of the desert floor, blocking out the stars.

Crouching low, she ran in and snatched up the first one on the makeshift landing field, then darted back out to the perimeter.

Blast, it wasn't a flame at all! It was the same substance as in the moonglobes, and the more she agitated it by moving, the brighter it glowed.

She tore off her skirt and wrapped the lamp in it, then took off at a dead run for the foot of Spider Woman.

This was no time for modesty. Besides, it was dark.

She didn't know what she expected, but it was not the scree of fallen rock and shelves of rough, sandpaper-like stone that made up the base of the huge formation. It was unstable and broken and was probably going to kill her—but better that than to live with the knowledge that she had watched a ship full of people die and had done nothing to stop it.

Perhaps this would balance her accounts with the Almighty over the matter of Lightning Luke.

Her foot slipped and she banged a knee on an outcropping. A word escaped her she had heard Snouts use and never imagined using herself—but when she lifted her head to grit her teeth in pain, she saw that the locomotive tower had passed the rocks and was laboring away into the dark on the other side. Alice was placing lamps. The pirates would conceal themselves in the monolith's shadow. She had a few moments to gain some ground.

If only she could stuff her bundle in the holster and use both hands! If only her underthings weren't white! It was of no use at all to have a black skirt and stockings in one's raiding rig and have a white batiste corset cover and pantalettes. If she survived this, by George, she was going to have black underthings made just as soon as she found civilization.

Another ledge. Another outcrop of rough stone.

Pull, scrape, heave. Again. And again.

Scrape. Claire halted. She could hear her own boots on the rock.

The locomotive had shut down.

And in the distant night sky, she heard the now-familiar clattering purr of steam engines. They were not Daimler engines, that was certain—the Germans were dab hands at a smooth operation that didn't make so much noise. These must be made here in the Americas.

What was she thinking? *Climb!*

Ten yards further, the scree smoothed out and the stone leaped straight up in a face so smooth it could have been cut with a spinner's knife. She could go no further.

How far up was she? And how long would it take them to scale the tumble of rocks and earth to catch her?

No matter.

Claire unwrapped the lamp, which was glowing like a small sun from all her exertions. She yanked her skirt back on and slid the knife out of her red scarf, jamming it into the back of her corselet. Then she wrapped her scarf around the lamp, grasped the handle, and swung it in wide, swooping arcs, the way she had seen the switchmen do on the tracks. Only this time her movements were exaggerated, almost balletic, the red glow of the lamp curving up, down, and up again.

The hum of the approaching airship did not change pitch. Or course.

She must get their attention. She must.

Please, Lord. Let them see. Let me be in time.

Down, out, up again. Down, out, and up. Again. And again.

Her arms were getting tired, both from the climb and from the weight of the lamp.

Down, out, up.

Two hundred yards.

Down, out, up. Down, out, up.

One hundred.

Oh, God—oh, God—

Down, out—

Fifty.

—up.

The engines coughed, hitched, and growled in a change of pitch that told her they'd been thrown, protesting, into full reverse.

Down, out, up. Down, out—

The fuselage floated over her head and scraped along the face of Spider Woman as if kissing it hello.

Claire cried out and, far above in the gondola, got a glimpse of a man's face, his mouth stretched in a rictus of terror, his hands flashing as he ratcheted the wheel over, its spokes blurred in the light of the running lamps.

He had not given up his post.

Neither would she.

Whoever he was, they were bound in this moment of horror as the sheer rock released its burden. Canvas tore, but the great gas bags housed within did not, and the ship turned as ponderously as a whale in the open sea.

Something landed ten feet down the slope, as heavy as a body. Claire screamed and dropped the lamp, and darkness plunged down on her.

Another body. And another and another—had so many died?

Straining, she tried to see movement. And then she realized what had happened. They were releasing the sandbags, lightening the ship enough to take them aloft again. Sure enough, as she sat there amid the wreckage of the lamp and the splattered sandbags, the breathing, living presence of the ship rose to block out the fading stars, its engines once again set full ahead.

Before her heart had slowed to its normal rate, the airship bearing her former fiancé had climbed to cruising altitude. As it moved off into the glimmer of gray that presaged the dawn, a silence that was almost holy fell upon the spire of rock lifting into the night.

Chapter 13

A howl of pure rage echoed among the rocks, somewhere on the ground behind Spider Woman, as the sound of the airship's laboring engines faded into the distance.

Claire picked herself up and retrieved her scarf from the wreckage of the lamp, but it was soaked in the chemical compound from which the light had emanated. Nothing emanated from it now but a harsh, sour scent that burned her nostrils.

It had served its purpose well. She could see the outlines of objects now—well enough to scoop up the crumbly clay earth and cover the scarf and the wreck of the lamp. Then she picked up one of the lengths of rope that had secured the sandbags to the ballast irons, and wound it around her waist, over the corselet.

One never knew when one might be glad of a length of rope. Earlier tonight, for instance.

For the moment, though, the most urgent course of action was to stay out of sight until Ned Mose and his gang of wreckers had gone back to town. She shuddered to think what might happen to the Dunsmuirs and the crew in that event, but the truth was, she was powerless in the matter.

However, she could do one thing. She could find Rosie and the hatbox and put a little distance between herself and Mose's rage at the same time.

The sun had not risen, but the rocks had taken on shape and substance now. She climbed down somewhat more carefully than she had scrambled up, keeping a sharp eye on the ground below in case someone rounded the base of the monolith. In her black raiding rig she could give a fair impression of a shadow if she had to, despite the red and ochre colors of the rock.

The sound of the locomotive tower's engine firing up halted her so suddenly that she skidded on gravel. Taking refuge in the inky shadow of a huge tumbled boulder, she stretched up just enough to see the tower rumble off toward the wash and Alice's shack. When no one followed on foot, Claire assumed the pirates were crammed inside.

That did not mean Ned Mose wouldn't send someone to see what had alerted the Texican airship and caused it to evade their trap.

Darting from rock to rock, holding her breath and feeling exposed every time she was forced to step out on a ledge and drop the next level down, she made her way back to the desert floor. Her hands were scraped raw from the sandpaper consistency of the rocks, and all the knuckles on her left hand had been bruised when a handhold had crumbled.

But she was free. And alive. And so were James and the crew of that ship.

Knuckles would heal, and torn stockings could be mended. But if that ship had gone down ... Claire shuddered.

She began an easy run in the direction the hatbox had taken, angling away from Spider Woman and toward the lake over which they had passed. Somewhere between the water and the spire of rock, there had been a stand of scrubby trees, bigger than the round bushes that seemed to uproot themselves and go rolling across the landscape, but smaller and less densely leafed than any tree back in England.

She had just passed an outcropping of rock that jutted out of the side of a much smaller wash when the sun broke over the horizon and painted it with gentle shades of yellow and cream. This country, harsh as it was, had its beauties, then. Who could have imagined that ordinary rocks could possess colors from scarlet and carmine to lemon yellow and deepest ocean blue? Someone who made a study of geology could make his fortune writing papers about—

In the distance, she heard the sound she had been waiting for—and dreading.

An engine.

She whirled and flung herself at the base of the outcrop. There was no shelter—it was merely a heap of rock piled in the middle of a hump of land—but the eye saw what it expected, did it not? Not what was there.

She stretched out at the base of it and did her best impression of a shadow.

The sound grew louder, and then she saw it.

The great golden fuselage of the *Lady Lucy* fell up into the sky above the red mesa, made a quarter turn to the north, and moved gently off into the clear bright morning.

ॐ

Claire lay in the dirt, leaning on her elbows, her mouth hanging open. Under the twin blows of shock and dismay, it didn't even occur to her to leap to her feet and signal, and by the time it did, the *Lady Lucy* had already reached a thousand feet, where no one save a hawk or an eagle could see a small, disbelieving figure jumping up and down, waving frantically.

She sat abruptly in grass that had once been green, but was now burned and dry from the sun.

They had left her!

Marooned her in the middle of a desert, without a single ally or even so much as a drink of water!

How was this possible? Granted, she had been somewhat distracted in trying to save the lives of an entire ship and crew, but for goodness sake, couldn't they at least have sent out a search party when they found she was missing?

They must have freed themselves and returned to the ship immediately after the floodwaters had receded. Clearly she had been a little hasty in jumping out of the window when if she had merely waited half an hour, she could have walked out the door with the rest of them, and at this moment be floating off into the air, blissfully unconcerned about what was happening on the ground.

No, that was not true. For who else had they left?

Rosie, that was who.

Ooh, if she ever saw the Mopsies again in this life—and even in the next—they were going to get such a spanking as they would never forget for the rest of eternity. They were a flock! They might consider Claire able to take care of herself, but she would never have imagined Maggie and Lizzie would leave Rosie behind to starve to death tied up in a hatbox.

Well. She had set off to find Rosie, and find her she would. Even if there were only two remaining members, they were still a flock.

She got to her feet, dusted off the front of her sadly abused shirtwaist and the swag formed by her rucked-up skirts, and resolutely did not look toward the north as she set off once again.

A cry sounded behind her. A bird of some kind. An eagle, perhaps, circling and wondering if she would make a tasty morsel.

Another cry, urgent, breathless.

Then— "Lady! Lady! You're not dead!"

Eagles did not speak English—especially the kind born within hearing of Bow's bells.

She turned, hardly able to believe the evidence of her own eyes. "Mopsies?"

"Lady!" Lizzie burst into tears and flung herself at Claire so hard that she staggered.

"She told us you was *dead*," Maggie exclaimed in tones clogged with betrayal.

Claire had never been at once so happy to see anyone, and so dismayed. The Mopsies. Left behind as well. Innocent children! What was the world coming to?

She fell to her knees and hugged both of them so hard Lizzie squeaked.

"Who told you?" she finally found voice enough to say, releasing them.

"Her ladyship. She said someone pushed you out a window into that flood."

"She was correct in general, though not in the particulars. I jumped. It seemed a good idea at the time. But why are you here and not on the *Lady Lucy*? Did you see her lift just now?"

"Aye." Maggie grinned. "Such a to-do there'll be when they open our room and don't find us. Oh, and 'ere—" She turned and presented her back.

"Good heavens." With quick fingers, Claire undid the knots in the silk sash and freed the lightning rifle. "I am utterly lost. You had better tell me the whole story while I put this back together."

By the time the Mopsies had finished catching her up, their words tripping and tumbling over one another as each jostled for her part of the night's work, Claire had put the coupling back in its place and blasted a nearby stump to kingdom come.

It felt extremely satisfying.

"I cannot believe you shimmied down a guy rope," she said. "You could have been killed!"

"Well, we wasn't," Lizzie said, ever logical. "But Rosie might be. We came to find 'er and we found you instead!"

"As well, you mean. Come, we must locate a stand of trees about halfway between here and the lake. I believe she may have touched down there. And as we go, I'll tell you my side of these events."

They were as impressed with her diverting the Texican ship as she was with their sliding fifty feet down a guy rope.

"Each of us is a lady of considerable resources," Claire said at last. "Which we will have to employ shortly now that we are left behind."

"Wot about that Alice?" Maggie wanted to know. "She might help us."

"I hope so, but other than a bite of tea, I cannot see her being able to give much assistance. Her father will see to that."

"Lady." Lizzie tugged on her sleeve. "Ent that them trees you was talkin' of?"

A swale sloped gently into what might have been a creek bed in a moister climate. But the trees must have found something there with which to nourish deep roots, because a line of green followed the turns of its dry banks.

"I shall take the far side, if you two will cover this side," Claire said. "Walk a hundred yards in each direction and meet back here if you don't find her. We will move outward after that."

"And don't forget to look up," Maggie reminded them. "You know 'ow Rosie is."

The copse had hardly a hundred yards to its name, but Claire searched every foot of it, including peering through the branches of the trees for a flash of reddish-brown feathers—even one lying on the ground might have been a clue. That is, if one assumed Rosie had escaped the hatbox. If she had not, then they could be guided by the mottled colors of the balloon.

But after an hour, both searches had borne no fruit.

"Move away from the wash twenty paces, and search again," Claire said. "And you might call. Rosie will answer if she is able."

"Because that's 'ow birds tell who's in their flock," Maggie said.

"Polgarth the poultryman taught you well in our brief visit." Claire smiled. "We are a flock, and Rosie knows all our voices."

Maggie put a hand on Claire's skirt to stay her. "I *knew* you wouldn't leave us. I *told* 'er ladyship so, I did. Cos we're a flock."

A lump rose in Claire's throat, and she knelt in the dust, taking both their grubby hands. "We are more than a flock. I consider the two of you my family. When his lordship filed our traveling papers for this voyage, he registered you officially with the Foreign Office as my wards. That means that nothing can separate us except our own free will."

"Wot about Tigg?"

"Him, too. But not Jake, because he was above the age of fourteen."

"That rascal Jake," Lizzie exploded, dropping Claire's hand. "I'd like to know how 'e feels now, left alone wi' them pirates. I bet he's missing us bad and wishin' 'e'd done things different."

Claire's heart drubbed in her chest, making her a little light-headed. "My dears—" Did they not know?

But then, how could they? The girls and Willie had been concealed in the ceiling during those dreadful moments, and then they had all been separated. Oh, if only there had been anyone else to say these words!

But there was not. There was only herself to say what must be said, to look after these two little lives when she had no idea what the next hour might bring.

"Lady, don't look like that." Maggie's gaze searched her face. "Did summat happen to Jake?"

There was nothing for it. She had never lied to these children, and she was not about to start now. "Ned Mose lost his temper and pushed Jake out of the hatch," she said in as soft a tone as she could manage.

What little color was left in Maggie's face drained out of it. "Wot hatch? There's any number of—"

"An outside one. The one in the main gangway, where we embark and disembark." Claire swallowed. "He would not tell where you and Willie were, so Mose threw him out. We were three hundred feet up." Her throat closed and she whispered, "There is no way he could have survived."

The tears overflowed Maggie's eyes and she threw herself into Claire's arms. "I wish we'd never come on this awful voyage," she sobbed. "I want to go home."

"I'm glad," Lizzie choked out. "'E 'anded us over to them pirates and it's no more'n he deserves." But her eyes were piteous.

"Do not blame him, darling," Claire told her over the top of Maggie's head, and held out a hand to gather her close once more. "I have no doubt he was forced to do what he did. But whether he was or was not, no one deserves an end like that. We cannot even give him a Christian burial—we don't know where he—where he is."

It took several long moments before Maggie's sobs turned to hiccups and at last to sniffles. Lizzie kicked viciously at a clump of dry grass. "We might not know where 'e is, but we'll find Rosie. I know we will."

And not half an hour of dusty searching later, a cry went up. "Lady! Over 'ere!"

Claire took off at a dead run, leaping into the wash and out again like a species of antelope. Maggie waved her over to a clump of rocks, and there was the balloon, snagged on it.

"Is she here? Is Rosie here?" *Please don't let her have been eaten. Please don't make them endure one more loss on this morning of terrible losses.*

Both girls knelt on the ground with the hatbox between them. In a trice they had yanked off the cords securing the lid, and Rosie exploded out of it like a pheasant flushed from the grass. With a squawk of indignation, she stalked in a circle, ruffled her feathers, and glared at the girls as though she had not forgotten who had put her in there.

Lizzie sat back on her heels, grinning. "Aye, Miss Rosie, it were our fault, but yer not some nasty pirate's breakfast, now, are ye?"

Rosie turned her back on her, and both girls giggled in sheer delight at the perfectly ordinary sight of the hen scratching and pecking up the grass seeds.

Claire drank it in, feeling as though she had come up for air after a long time underwater. One small red hen, safe as houses.

Compared to the dreadful events of the last twelve hours, it seemed like a wonderful blessing, indeed.

Chapter 14

The Mopsies gave the all clear, and Claire knocked softly on Alice's door. It opened immediately.

"I wondered where you'd got to. Get inside, quick, before someone sees."

"I have company." She turned and whistled, a skill that would have sent Lady St. Ives into a paroxysm of embarrassment. The Mopsies materialized and slipped inside with her before Alice could do more than gawk.

She did have the presence of mind to close the door, however. "And who are you?"

They both buttoned their lips and glanced at Claire. Snouts's training on one's behavior during questioning had sunk deep.

"It's all right, girls. This is Miss Alice Chalmers, who is Ned Mose's daughter—" Both Lizzie and Maggie stiffened with alarm. "But she is a friend to us. Remember? I told you she makes a fine cup of tea."

Lizzie did not take anyone at face value. "'Ow can she be a friend when she's—after wot 'e done to Jake—"

Alice worried her bottom lip with her teeth. "What pa does got nothing to do with what I do. You're safe with me, and I promise on my honor I'll do nothing to harm you or Claire here." She peered at Claire, having just noticed the hatbox. "Is that a chicken?"

"This is Rosie," Claire said. "She has come all the way from England as one of our party, and met with a mishap on the way. All is well now."

"Our Rosie's not to be et," Maggie told her with as close to a threat in her brown eyes as Claire had ever seen.

Alice nodded, eyebrows raised at the sight of Rosie reposing in the hatbox. "Understood." She focused on Claire. "You got an explanation for last night?"

If Alice was to be trusted, now was the moment to test it. "I climbed up and signaled the ship. The navigator diverted it at the last minute and, as you probably saw, it went on its way."

"I figured you must've had something to do with it. You've got to get out of here afore pa finds out you didn't die."

"I agree with you. Is there a train?"

Alice snickered through her nose. "There's a track. Ain't never been a train since I come here."

"It's only a matter of time before your policemen—what did you call them?"

"Texican Territory Rangers. You're right there. Once that ship gets back to Santa Fe they'll be on their way pronto. So pa will be after you and they'll be after pa. You ask me, Resolution's gonna be too hot to handle by this time tomorrow."

"What do you suggest, then?"

Alice gazed at Nine in his corner. Claire found a moment to be thankful that an automaton named Ten was not, after all, under construction. "Way I figure it, between rage and disappointment, Pa'll get tanked up and go on a tear the rest of today. Probably kill somebody by sunset, then sleep it off. By dawn the Rangers will be here and there'll likely be a gunfight."

The Mopsies' eyes grew huge.

"So if I was you, I'd give him and his crew enough time to get properly sauced, then make your escape."

"In what?" Lizzie wanted to know. "The Lady shot the engine out of t'*Stalwart Lass*."

"Is that what happened?" Alice's eyes shadowed and she couldn't quite meet Claire's gaze. "That engine was a fine piece of work. I used an old schematic from a Royal Society journal. I was kinda proud of it."

Claire put a hand on her arm. "I'm sorry, Alice. But we had just been boarded. With the children's safety at stake, I could not risk being separated into two ships, so I disabled the *Lass*."

"She were a good piece of work," Maggie said. "Caught us fair and square."

"She had speed, she did." Alice's face brightened a little with the praise. "There ain't much left, but I guess I can rebuild her." Then her expression became downcast again. "Guess I'll have to. Pa's not gonna like bein' groundbound for long. On the good side, the Rangers won't confiscate her if she can't fly, will they?"

"You would know better than I."

Alice shook herself and pasted on a smile. "So we have a little time yet. Who's for some breakfast?"

Both Mopsies came to attention. Lizzie said, "We would've 'ad eggs 'cept Rosie 'ad a rough landing, so she ate what were in the hatbox."

"You can put her out back if you like. I got a little garden there, with a spring."

"Why don't you take her, girls?" Claire suggested. "And perhaps clean out the hatbox if there's water." The Dunsmuir jewels were encrusted with yolk and dirt and excrement, having lain in the bottom of the box without a covering. But no one but themselves need know.

"Give me a hand with breakfast, Claire, and we'll have it outside. That way, if we get company, at least I can fob 'em off long enough for you to scamper up the ladder into the supply cave."

When they carried out the bread, honey, cheese, and a stack of bulbous green vegetables Alice called *poblanos* that she had grilled on the top of the steam boiler, Claire saw what she meant. Tucked between the back of the shack and the wall of the mesa was a small plot of tomatoes, poblano plants, and corn, between the rows of which Rosie had made a dust bath. An iron ladder led up the rock to a cave, and from further up, a streak of glistening moisture indicated the spring that watered the garden.

The girls eyed the poblanos with suspicion. "Eat up," Alice said. "They're not the capsaicious kind, so they won't burn your innards."

"Capsaicious?" Claire examined a poblano with interest. "Gaseous capsaicin comes from a plant like this?"

"Indeed it does. Horrid stuff. Only the most vicious rabble— criminal gangs and the like—would use it on a living creature."

The Mopsies exchanged peculiar looks while Claire bit into her bread and cheese to prevent herself from saying anything rash.

"So here's what I think," Alice said, using her bread to mop up a puddle of golden honey. "You don't have much choice but to use a velogig. People think they're stupid toys for rich folk to play with, but I'm thinking beggars can't be choosers."

Three pairs of eyes—four, if you counted Rosie's—waited for an explanation.

"What, you've never seen a velogig?"

"Wot, you've never seen a steam landau?" Lizzie muttered.

There was nothing wrong with Alice's hearing. "Nope, I haven't, but not because I haven't wanted to." Her eyes turned dreamy. "Some day, when I'm rich and living in someplace classy, like San Franciso or Edmonton, I'm gonna have my very own landau. The latest model, too, like a six-piston Henley."

"You should see the Lady's," Maggie put in. "You could've, if it hadn't flown off."

Slowly, Alice turned to gawk at Claire. "You own a landau? And it was on your airship?"

Her mouth full of bread and cheese and poblano, Claire could only nod.

"And I missed it?" The girl's eyes filled with tears. "Why didn't you tell me?"

With a mighty swallow, Claire downed the mouthful and gulped some tea. "It's a four-piston Dart, and I've been rather occupied. I had no idea you were interested."

"I've never seen a landau. Nowhere to run 'em in these parts—just a lot of open country full of gopher holes and slot canyons. But oh—" She gazed into the garden as though it were Paradise. "—just wait till someday comes."

"I'd like to see mine someday, too, and sooner rather than later," Claire said. "Do you suppose the *Lady Lucy* is headed for Santa Fe?"

"Must be. It's the only place to put down for two hundred miles if you don't want to get your pants full of pinon needles and rattlers. That man who was coming to pay your ransom—he came from there, too. Nearest detachment of Rangers is stationed there."

"So we must make for Santa Fe on this—this velogig."

"It's crazy, but if you're going to try crazy, this is the country to do it in. Wind never stops, see."

"These vehicles are wind powered?"

"Vehicle. Only got one, off a big old double-fuselage Hemmings—" She stopped and seemed to find Rosie's lolling in her dust bath fascinating.

Claire glanced at the Mopsies, but they were both fully occupied with food. "You acquired it in the same manner as the parts for One through Nine."

"Yep," Alice mumbled. Then she looked up, her eyes so distressed and yet so clear that Claire wondered how she could be so openhearted when her father was so ... so heartless. "You ain't holding that against me, are you? I—I don't think I could stand it if you did."

Claire put gentle fingers on her hand and squeezed it. "If you knew the things I've done in the name of survival, you would not ask me that."

Alice's gaze held hers. "Maybe someday, when we both have our landaus and one of us isn't running for her life, we can sit down and have a cup of tea and talk it over."

"Maybe. I look forward to that day."

Alice sat back. "Well. Let's do our best to make it happen, then. You girls done?" Even the suspect poblanos had disappeared. "You want to catch that hen and box her up again, Claire and me will get the velo ready. And then I'll pack you some food and water. You can't carry much, since weight matters, but the three of you plus a couple days of food can't weigh as much as the sporting man we ran—uh, who used to own it." Rosie was returned, protesting, to the hatbox while Alice climbed the iron ladder and began tossing bundles down.

Claire could not imagine what a velogig could be. A boat that ran on land? Some kind of flying machine?

Whatever picture she had in her mind, it bore no relation to the reality that Alice assembled on the far side of the shack, which faced Spider Woman and the trackless desert beyond.

It looked rather like a tripod on wheels. There was a bench on which to sit, and a steering mechanism formed by a bar attached to pulleys. And towering above it all was a blue silk sail that was already billowing and snapping with eagerness to taste the wind.

"Good heavens."

Alice dusted off her hands and jammed a wrench in a pocket of her pants. "I've had it out a few times. You need to be careful—if the wind gets ahead of you the whole thing can go top over teakettle."

"The sons of the squire next door taught me to sail a boat out of the harbor at home. I don't suppose this is anything like that?"

"Dunno—I've never seen the ocean."

"Never seen it?" She couldn't imagine going through life without having seen the ocean—so vast and changeable and full of wonders. It restored a sense of your place in the world, the ocean did, and kept you humble. "Oh, Alice."

"Well, when I get to San Francisco, I'll see it then, won't I?"

"I hope you do. You cannot go through life without doing so."

"I've managed so far, but maybe you're right. Come on over here, now, and I'll show you how to steer."

It was not a bit like a sailboat. In fact, managing the direction of the sail as well as the direction of travel was going to prove quite a challenge. Claire trundled across the ground, feeling at any moment as if the sail would catch a good stiff breeze and send her flying across half a mile before flipping her off and continuing on to New York without her.

"Lady!"

She jounced back at Lizzie's call and climbed down, halfway between exhilaration and humiliation. "Lizzie, wait till you—"

"Lady, they're coming!" Lizzie ran out to meet her. "A band of men, they're comin' this way from town. It's too far to see, but we have to hide."

Alice ran into the shack and a minute later came out, a fat bundle that might once have been a pillowcase in her arms.

"Claire, you have to go right now. That's pa coming, lit up and looking for a fight. I just heard shots."

"He's not going to fight you, is he?" Instinctively, she reached over her shoulder and touched the flared barrel of the lightning rifle.

"No, course not. But he made a law about fighting in town, so he can't break it. They come out here and raise a ruckus. I'm gonna lock the doors and put up the shutters, but you have to go right now."

"Maggie!"

The girl ran around the side of the shack, hatbox in her hands. Claire took it from her and felt around in the bottom, under Rosie's indignant protests. She drew out the smallest thing her fingers could find and pressed it into Alice's hand. "This is to thank you for everything."

Alice opened her fingers as if they held a snake. "But—but this is a diamond—what is it, exactly?"

"It's a watch pin. To hold a watch upon your blouse."

"Don't own a watch. Or a blouse. I can't take this. Where in the heck did your bird dig this up?"

"Some things must remain a mystery until we meet again. Show it to no one. Goodbye, Alice. Wish us luck."

"Luck," the girl said faintly. The sun burnished her unkempt hair, turning it nearly white, as she gazed at the object in her palm.

Claire grabbed the girls' hands and ran.

It became immediately apparent that five minutes of rehearsal was not going to be enough for a command performance.

"Lady, where are we supposed to sit?" Maggie seemed close to tears after the three of them had tried unsuccessfully to fit on the bench. "And wot about Rosie?"

It was difficult to design a conveyance with only thirty seconds to do it in. "Tie the hatbox to that crossbar there. Rosie will have to swing. Perhaps it will put her to sleep." Scuffling and indignant squawks emanated from within.

"She wants to see out," Maggie said.

"She will have to wait." Claire took a deep breath. *Hold on.* "This is less like a tripod and more like a Roman chariot. Lizzie, hop up next to Maggie. You will steer. I will stand on this bar behind you and manage the sail. Quickly, now. I hear shouting."

Before she'd even finished the word, a gunshot rang out. Lizzie yelped and jumped up, and Claire grasped the cords of the sail.

If one pulled the rightmost, the sail moved one way. The leftmost, the other. She had no idea what the middle one did, but first things first.

"Steer, Lizzie!"

"Where?"

Claire tightened the rope and the sail bellied out. They began to roll across the ground, bumping and jouncing.

"I don't care—away!"

The wind caught them just as Ned Mose burst around the corner of the shack and raised his gun.

Chapter 15

Both girls' shoulders hunched up to their ears in unconscious expectation of a bullet. Hers probably had as well, but the only thing that would get them out of range was speed, so Claire focused on the sail as if it were her salvation.

The velogig careened across the ground in the direction of Spider Woman, the sail bellying out like the breast of a frigate bird. The wind's speed might be constant, but its direction did not seem to be. Claire realized that as soon as they'd gone a hundred yards. She trimmed the sail and once again it filled. They flew toward the monolith as if they had wings, and both girls shrieked with either fear or exhilaration.

"Lizzie, to the right, or we shall drive straight into the rock."

"I dunno how!"

"Push your left hand out."

The velogig veered to the right and Claire distinctly felt the leftmost wheel leave the ground. "Gently, Lizzie."

"But you said—"

"It's all right. We are out of range of the bullets!" She laughed in sheer relief mixed with a healthy dose of terror.

The strange vehicle flew to the south, then Lizzie steered it around the worst of the rocks.

"Now to the north. We must get as far away as we can by nightfall. I wonder how many miles per day one can travel on this thing?"

"Where's north?" Lizzie held onto the steering bar like a drowning person, her knuckles stiff and white.

"To our left. A gentle arc, yes, that's it. The wind is coming from the south, so it will push us along nicely."

Lizzie pushed with her right hand even more, and the velogig's course curved in an arc until they were heading due north.

"'Ow do you know which way is north?" Maggie said through clenched teeth, one hand gripping a brass support and the other her sister's dress. "It all looks the same to me."

Claire adjusted the sail and they flew forward on the very wings of the wind. She would give anything to know their speed—but if the tears whipped from her eyes were any indication, it was faster than the landau had ever gone, and it topped out at forty miles per hour. If she only had her goggles!

"North is the only portion of the sky where the sun does not travel. We shall choose our landmarks each morning and simply do our best."

"'Ow far is it?"

Belatedly, Claire realized she might have asked more questions of Alice before their abrupt departure. "I'm not sure, but Miss Alice said there wasn't another landing field for two hundred miles, and the Rangers came from Santa Fe. So I would assume that is how far it is."

"Two 'undred miles," Maggie squeaked. "That's from London to Cornwall."

Dear me. It was, nearly. "Just pray there are no canyons to traverse. That will make it longer."

"Lady, I'm scared."

Claire risked a glance down and tried to smile with reassurance. "There is nothing to fear, darling. We are together, we have food and water, and Ned Mose is at least two miles behind us already."

But somehow Maggie did not look comforted. "'E's going to be awful angry with Miss Alice."

And there was the awful truth that Claire had been trying to evade even as they had evaded their pursuers. "I expect he is. But she is a lady of resources, too, and his own daughter. Lizzie, watch that mesa coming up. We must steer for that saddle-shaped valley in the middle of it."

"Bein' someone's daughter never 'elped us," Lizzie muttered, but the wind snatched away her words and Claire wondered if she'd actually heard them.

When life found some semblance of normalcy, she must bring it up again. In the meantime, she must concentrate on the movements of the air.

In her entire life she had never been quite so focused on the small shifts of wind direction that meant the difference between slowing to a bumpy creep and taking off like a sea bird from the surface of the sea. Around midday they stopped for some water and a few bites of the odd, hard strips of meat Alice had stuffed into the pillowcase.

"Wot is this?" Maggie chewed and chewed, and finally tore off a piece to give to Rosie, who swallowed it in one gulp. At least the bird had managed to find grass seeds under a bush, and was presently occupied in cracking a nut with her beak.

"I have no idea." Claire swallowed it half chewed. "But if Alice gave it to us, she must have believed it would be suitable."

"Tastes all right," Lizzie said. "It's better wiv water."

"Don't drink too much. We do not know how long it will take to get to Santa Fe and believe me, I have no wish to expire of dehydration out here."

Rosie made a chirruping sound and flattened herself under the bush. Far above, a bird with a wingspan of at least eight feet wheeled lazily against the sun.

"That's not good," Maggie observed. "She don't do that for doves and robins, nor crows neither."

"I'd be very glad of the sight of a robin right now," Claire said. "Come. Let's be on our way."

Lizzie had cut a hole in the hatbox for Rosie to poke her head through, but when they really got going, the hen hunkered down out of the wind. By sunset, Claire was wishing she could do the same. She patted her cheeks. Dry—chapped—she would be looking like the bottom of a dry lake before long.

"Lizzie, are those trees greener than any we've seen since Resolution?"

"Seems like." She pushed the bar, and the little craft made for the line of trees. "Let's go see if there's any water about."

There was not only water, there was a creek!

"I don't think I've ever seen anything so beautiful." Claire took off her boots and divested herself of her clothes. "I'm going to lie right in it."

If one could take a bath with no soap and while lying prone in two inches of water, then they managed it. Claire rinsed her underclothes, too, just for good measure.

Then they ate a little more of the bread and cheese, and gnawed on the meat strips.

It was not until the sun slipped below the huge tumble of rocks to the west that Claire realized their mistake. Night was falling and all their clothes were wet.

And cold.

And they had nothing—not even a pair of drawers—to change into.

"Oh, dear," she said. "I think we ought to have waited until the morning, when the hot wind would have dried us as we went."

"You mean we're to sleep starkers?" Maggie felt her dress, which, while not sopping, was still too wet to put on.

"I don't see a way around it, unless we—"

"The sail." Lizzie fingered the fabric. "We can wrap up in it, like bugs in a rug."

Claire considered the fastenings. It had gone together quickly. It would come apart just as quickly. "An excellent idea, Lizzie. The silk is treated, too, so no chilly breezes will be getting in."

Before the dark had fully fallen, they had bundled up in the sail, all together, with Rosie bedded down in the hatbox with the diamonds next to their heads.

"I have to say, I've never slept out in the open before," she murmured. "Have you?"

"Outside, inside, in squats," Lizzie said sleepily. "In a tree once. That were 'orrible. A wasps' nest not two feet from our 'eads, and a nasty waking it was."

"I fell out," Maggie added. "Nearly broke me leg. Sprained me ankle."

"Trees big enough to fall out of are one thing we don't need to worry over," Claire said. "Good night."

But the girls were already sound asleep under their stiff blue coverlet, stretched out on the ground. Claire lay watching, thinking, until the quarter moon rose over the horizon in the east, looking at least as big as any full moon ever had back in England.

What a vast country this was.

What an enormous, starry sky stretching to infinity.

And how very, very small and out of control she felt under it all. How very tired of being brave and positive and adult.

And it was only the first day.

She rolled over and tried to keep the tears from coming, but she could not say she succeeded.

୬୶

Claire woke with a start to the sound of shrieking panic right next to her head.

Clawing her way out of the blue sail, she rolled onto all fours, trying to clear the fog of sleep. "Rosie! Rosie, what is it?" She reached for the hatbox and froze.

A pair of eyes glowed in the gray light before dawn—eyes that had no business being so big or so close.

A low growl was her answer.

Rosie had succumbed to utter terror and the hatbox lay silent, a paw on top of it.

A large, feline paw. Larger than that of a house cat, but smaller than that of the lion she'd seen once at the Royal Menagerie.

Claire met the creature's eyes as it growled again, obviously as surprised to see her come alive as she was to meet it face to face.

It also made it plain that it had plans for Rosie, and she was not welcome to share.

"How dare you! Mopsies!" Maggie whimpered, and behind her, Claire felt a scuffle of movement. "Billy Bolt!"

The girls took off at a run, dragging the sail with them. The feline did not move. Instead, it snarled.

"I think not, you wretched thing." She snatched at the hatbox and wrenched it out from under the paw.

The cat screamed and leaped for Rosie. Claire dropped the box and grabbed it, holding it under its forelegs as she might a house cat.

"Oh, dear." Now that she had it, what was she to do with it? For heaven's sake, why hadn't she just thrown a rock at the horrid thing?

It screamed again, kicking with hind legs that had no business being that long. She felt the claws hook into her arms, dragging and tearing the flesh.

"Oh, no, you don't." She must get control of those lethal legs. The cat kicked and shrieked, but Claire gathered all four of its feet into her hands, holding it like a sack of candy. The infuriated beast wriggled and bucked, but it could not move. At last it hung there, glaring at her and panting with its exertions.

"Throw it!" Lizzie screamed from twenty feet away.

"What good would that do? It will just come back."

"Not before we get out of 'ere."

"We can't re-rig the sail until we can see. Lizzie, come here and pick up the lightning rifle."

"Lady, no, I can't—"

"Yes, you can, and you will. Now, before this creature decides to use its fangs on my hands. I can't hold it forever."

In tears, Lizzie fetched the rifle and pulled it from its holster.

"Activate the cell by pushing the lever forward. Good. Now give it a moment to build the charge and walk over here."

"I can't get close. What if it bites me?"

"It's a lot more like to bite 'er, Liz," Maggie told her. "Hustle yer bustle."

"It's not you who's never shot this thing!"

"Lizzie, it were goin' to eat our Rosie. And it still plans to, soon's it gets away. We gots to put an end to it."

Her breath one shudder after another, Lizzie approached.

"Now, take aim and fire."

"But—but—what if I 'it you?"

"You shall take care not to do so. Take a deep breath, aim, and pull the trigger."

"But—"

"Lizzie, do not fear. You are only five feet away. Even Lewis could hit a target at that range."

"Lewis would've been in Santa Fe by now, 'e'd be runnin' so fast."

"At your convenience, please, Lizzie," Claire said through gritted teeth as the cat wriggled and hissed. Any second now it was going to rear up and bite her hand, and she would have to let go.

Lizzie hefted the rifle, and it wobbled as she sighted down the barrel. Then she squeezed her eyes shut as she squeezed the trigger.

A bolt of lightning sizzled the air, caught the cat in the midsection, and ended its attempts on Rosie's life forever. Claire dropped it and turned away as the life writhed out of it, and gathered Lizzie close.

"Well done, darling. It's all right. It's over now."

"I killed it!" Lizzie wailed, dropping the rifle at their feet. "I didn't want to, Lady."

"I know. We never want to take another life. But it was the cat or Rosie. We are responsible for her safety. She is an innocent, and we must do what we must."

Lizzie drew back. "Lady, you got blood on me cammy."

There was almost enough light to see colors. "So I have. We will rinse it out again when the sun comes up, which will not be long now. Come. I'll wash off and bind up these scratches with a piece of my petticoat. And then we shall sit with Rosie on that rock and watch the sunrise."

And think of life, not death.

Chapter 16

With the resiliency of childhood, Lizzie seemed to recover by midday. The hot wind of their going dried her underclothes, and they were soon able to dress again completely. Though there was not a soul for a hundred miles or more, but Claire still felt naked and exposed in the vastness of the landscape.

As vulnerable as Rosie, with only the leather sides of the hatbox between her and death.

Hungry enough to regret that the cat had not been something more edible.

By late morning of the third day, they swallowed the last of the dried meat. The cheese and bread had gone the day before. Rosie killed a lizard and Maggie's speculative gaze caused Claire to say rather hastily, "They're not edible by people, dearest. We must have fortitude."

They had more water because of the creek, but while it went down like a blessing, it did nothing for the fact that her stomach appeared to be clinging to her backbone. It was all she could do to keep her temper every time the girls whined for something to eat or one more sip of water.

They were still heading north, weren't they? She was losing the ability to tell.

And surely they must have covered two hundred miles by now. In three days they could have walked halfway to Cornwall.

It would be all too terrifyingly easy to miss a city by ten miles, would it not? One could sail right by and never know that one had left safety and friends well behind—and they in turn would never know one had done so.

Why had they not seen the Rangers going overhead in their ship? She would have expected them on the first day, but not a whisper had they seen or heard.

In their miserable foodless camp, Claire tilted her head to the brazen sky, which reflected all the reds and oranges of the interminable mesas and rock piles in this godforsaken land.

Did no one care that they were going to die out here? Would no one search? Andrew—James—the Dunsmuirs—they were all probably sitting down to a huge dinner of roast beef and Yorkshire pudding and every vegetable imaginable while she was out here, sitting on a rock, staring death in the face for the umpteenth time in the past week.

One of these days it would come for her and the girls. Maybe not today. But tomorrow, certainly.

They were all lightheaded and weepy and she had never felt such pain in her stomach. Her tongue moved sluggishly, and she kept hearing bees where it was not possible for bees to be.

"I want to go 'ome," Maggie moaned. "I hate this place. Why aren't we there yet?"

Claire clenched her molars together to keep from snapping that if she knew where "there" was, it would go a long way toward actually finding it.

They could not die out here. It was insupportable and inconceivable … and inevitable, if they did not locate Santa Fe the next day.

How could she manage the sail with arms too weak to hold the cords? Maggie and Lizzie were already trading off the steering every hour, one resting while the other tried to concentrate on steering.

There was absolutely nothing she could do to help the situation except to go on … and trust to Providence.

In the morning, after waking from a dream of pastel-colored meringues raining from the sky, it seemed as though even Providence had forgotten them.

The wind died.

Claire stood with the cords wrapped around her hands, turning the sail this way and that to try to catch a breath of breeze.

"Wot's wrong wiv it?" Maggie's voice was so apathetic it sounded as though she asked for form's sake only. "Why ent we goin'?"

"There is no wind." Claire sat on the rail with a bump. "How can there be no wind? That has been the one constant of this place besides grit in one's eyes."

"Yer not doin' it right," Lizzie said. Her eyes were swollen to slits from sunburn. "Are you tryin' to get us killed?"

"I have been trying to save your miserable lives, you—" She bit back her temper, wondering why she even tried if that was what they thought of her.

"Miserable is it?" Lizzie flared. "I'll tell you this, we was a whole lot less miserable before you came. We was 'appy in London."

"What, picking rags and stealing bread? Yes, I'm sure you were."

"It's better'n bein' shot at and starvin' to death."

"We haven't starved. You're still talking, aren't you?" Claire took a deep breath. "Come. We will push the frame along until the wind comes up. We must make some progress today."

But the girls would not push. They would only sit on the bench and moan, and Claire could not hold the cords and push at the same time.

It was too much.

She sat in the dirt and a great sob came heaving up from her chest, but no tears stood in her eyes. Her body was too dehydrated to allow her that luxury. Wrapping her arms around her legs, she lowered her forehead to her knees and wept soundlessly.

"Lady."

She could not bear it. If Lizzie could think of nothing kind to say, she would just pretend the girl did not exist.

"Lady, I c'n hear something."

"It's just the buzzing in your ears, Lizzie. I have it, too."

"It ain't in my ears. It's in the sky."

"Yes, and it sounds like bees. I know."

"Lady! Look up!"

Atlas hefting the world up on his shoulders could have felt its weight no more than Claire. Wearily, she peered in the direction Lizzie's trembling finger indicated.

She sat up, then used the rail to drag herself to her feet.

"An airship!" They were saved!

Now she could hear the distant purring of the engine. She blinked, and rubbed her eyes free of grit. "Is that a double fuselage?"

The distinctive Y shape floated closer. Two gasbags, with a gondola suspended between them.

How many ships of that configuration flew these unrelenting skies?

"Girls! Conceal yourselves under something. It's the *Stalwart Lass*—Ned Mose has found us!"

 co∞

Maggie and Lizzie flung themselves at a pile of rocks, but there was not even a shadow to be found under them. Claire took refuge under a bush, which was rather like Rosie trying to hide behind a pebble—it offered no protection, either. They could do nothing about the velogig—there it sat in all its brass and silk glory, a rich man's plaything that was as immobile as a beacon advertising their location.

Even the slender hope that the pirates would think it had been abandoned and move on to find people on foot was dashed as the engine slowed and finally reversed.

They were going to moor.

If she and the girls were not shot on sight, at least there was the soup in the prison room to look forward to. And the nice sprigged-china ewer and basin with blessed cold water to drink. Why had she not been grateful for that ewer of water while she had it? If she had, she might have waited that half hour and none of the past four days would have happened.

If only ...

A lead weight slammed into the ground. In the absence of a mooring mast and any wind, it would act as an anchor long enough for the pirates to lower a basket. Because if she was to be required to shimmy up that rope, they may as well leave her to die. Claire put her head down on top of Rosie's hatbox as though it were a pillow.

One way or another, she really didn't care.

Rosie stuck her head out of the hole and bubbled a greeting.

Good grief, you silly bird. Those men will make a fine dinner of you. There's no need to sound so glad to see them.

"Lady!" a boy's voice called. It cracked—not a boy, then. Becoming a man. The one called Perry, perhaps?

"Lady Claire! Are you dead?"

She could swear she knew that voice.

With a Herculean effort, she lifted her head.

Rosie clucked again, and she heard a scream from the direction of the rocks. "Jake! Jake, is that you?"

A slim figure slid down the mooring rope and pounded across the dry soil. "Mags? Lizzie? All right?"

As if she were watching a flicker at the theatre, Claire saw the dead boy scoop Maggie up in his arms and hold her a moment over his head before he hugged her and grabbed Lizzie, swinging them both in a circle so that their limp legs flew out.

Hallucinations. Was this the precursor to death? It wasn't exactly her life flashing before her eyes, but close enough.

The apparition set the girls down and tilted his head up to the gondola floating above his head. "Alice, send down t'basket. The Lady's in a bad way."

In a moment a hatch opened in the stern, near the engine. A passenger basket was winched down and the ghost bundled the girls into it. It rose swiftly, to return empty, settling on the ground once more.

"Come on, then, Lady," the ghost said. "Cor, izzat Rosie? Ent you stew yet, old girl? Up wi' you, now."

There was only one reason a ghost came to fetch people. That was why they called it a *fetch*. Her Cornish nanny at Gwyn Place had been firm on that point. "Am I going to hell for my sins?" Claire's feet dragged as he pulled her over to the basket and bundled her in.

"Seems both of us 'ave been there an' back, eh? But they'll 'ave to wait a while to get us permanent-like."

And then all the buzzing bees coalesced into one giant swarm. The floor of the basket rose up and slapped her, and Claire went out like a lamp.

Chapter 17

Maggie's eyes unstuck long enough for her to see a perfect square of blue sky. She blinked, then raised a hand to rub them—not that it did much good. A blanket covered her. Wool, worked in odd patterns like stairsteps and lightning and the whirls water made when it went down a drain.

"Water," she croaked.

"Right 'ere, yer majesty." A mug was set to her lips and she drank and drank until it was taken away.

"More."

"In a bit. A little at a time, Alice says. That sunburn prob'ly smarts, but she put cactus goop all over it. She says it'll be better tomorrow."

The water was clearing her brain. "Jake?"

"Yes. Alive and well, no thanks to Ned Mose. I've a score to settle wiv 'im, an' no mistake."

"Lizzie?"

"Right next to you. Snug as two bugs, you are."

She had a moment to wonder why he was being so nice to her when he never was before, but then her eyes slid shut and she knew no more.

❧

The next time she woke, the square of blue was replaced by black, and a lamp burned in a niche in the wall. A wall made of mud. Was she in a mole's hole?

Maggie propped herself up on her elbows just as Lizzie pushed the door open with her bum and backed in carrying a tray. "You awake, Mags?"

"Water."

"Right 'ere, plus some soup. I already had some. It's good. *Poh-soh-lay*, they call it."

"Who?" She drank the whole mug of water and then tipped the pitcher up to her mouth and drank half of that, too. The soup was good. It went down almost as fast.

"The Navapai. Friends of Alice's." She lowered her voice. "I think they're real Wild West Injuns, like in the flickers."

"When did you ever see a flicker?"

Lizzie looked injured. "I might've snuck in once."

"Wivout me?"

"Maybe you were sick. Listen, d'you remember who rescued us?"

"Jake was here." Another thought occurred to her. "Where's the Lady?"

"Next door. I think summat went wrong in them cat scratches she got. She's been talking strange. Thinks Jake's a ghost."

"I think he is, too. He's nicer than in real life."

Lizzie giggled. "The Navapai are doctoring her. So's Alice. Can you get up?"

Maggie slid her feet out of bed. She was wearing her cammy and drawers and nothing else. "Where's our clothes?"

"Washed and drying. C'mon. Jake says to bring you."

"Where's Rosie?"

"Come *on*. I'll show you."

They emerged out of the mud house onto a flagstone terrace that dropped away into space on the far side. Maggie swayed and staggered back. "Is this Santa Fe?"

A voice came from across the terrace. "No. This is a Navapai village. Can't pronounce the name of it." Jake sat on a wide, low wall, his feet dangling over a couple of hundred feet of empty air. He could kick out one boot and practically nudge the leftmost fuselage of the *Stalwart Lass*, floating serenely at the end of her line. A skinny pinnacle of rock seemed to be her mooring mast.

Jake saw her looking at it. "A mast is a mast, eh?"

"Jake, what are you doing here? How did we get here? How did you get on the *Lass* and where are all those pirates?"

He grinned, that sly urchin's grin that immediately made her feel at home. "Probably ridin' shank's mare t'the nearest airfield and cursin' our names."

"Nearest airfield besides here is Texico City, and that's three days' flight from Resolution." Alice Chalmers stepped out onto the terrace. "How do you feel, Maggie?"

"Like that dried-up meat you gave us."

"That's called jerky, and it probably kept you alive long enough for us to find you. What were you doing all the way out there, thirty miles east? You were supposed to head north from Resolution. Santa Fe is hard to miss."

She waved a hand to the east, and Maggie took in the size of the city that lay in the distance. It seemed to go on for a mile, though maybe that was the clarity of the air, which made you able to see almost forever. Spires of rock and brass punctuated neat stretches of mud houses like the one behind them—only they were bigger, like layer cakes and building blocks all mixed up. Airships floated from mooring masts even in town.

"Does everybody have their own ship?" she asked in wonder.

"Most of those are the Ranger fleet, but some people do." Alice patted a stone bench and Maggie sank onto it with Lizzie. Not likely they'd join Jake on his wall, not with her head feeling as muzzy as it did.

"I dunno where we were," she said at last. "All I know is, we 'ad no wind and no hope of anyone, and next thing I knew there was Jake. Mind tellin' us 'ow you came to be not dead? Did Ned Mose really push you out of *Lady Lucy* in midair?"

Jake leaned back against a rock and stretched his legs out on the top of the wall. "He did. I thought I was a goner, for true.

But what 'e didn't know was that if 'e'd waited just a minute or so, we'd've been flying over land instead of water."

"He fell into the lake," Alice expanded helpfully.

"An' not just any old how, either," Jake said. "Remember jumpin' off the Clarendon footbridge that summer we found Willie?"

"I do. You pushed me off cos I wouldn't jump." Lizzie hadn't forgotten, that was clear.

"Did I? Anyways, wot we found is that if you jump in straight-like instead of floppin' around like a trout, it don't hurt when you hit. So there I was, fallin' out of the sky, out of me 'ead with fear. I remembered Clarendon footbridge and straightened meself out. Went into t'water like a spear and didn't get kilt."

Maggie could see it, plain as day. "And then what?"

"I swam hard as I could for shore and watched what direction the ships went in. Figured there'd be food I could steal to keep body an' soul together until I found you."

"What would you want to find us for?" Lizzie burst out, as if she'd had enough of being polite. "You turned us over to Ned Mose like we was cattle and I ent forgot it, Jake Fletcher. Nor am I like to, *ever.*"

At least he had the grace to look shamefaced. "Don't hold it against me, Lizzie."

"Where else am I supposed to 'old it? You nearly got us all killed."

"Nearly. Fact is, you would've *been* killed for sure. I were their first collar, you know. They woulda stuck me then an' there if I didn't go over to their side and show 'em where the family were and such."

"You never!" Lizzie stomped over to him and shook her finger in his face. He ought to grab hold of something, in Maggie's mind, in case she gave him a push, she was so angry. "I saw you. You were 'appy to 'and us over. Fact is, Jake, you go to whatever side you think is winnin', never mind who yer friends are." She paused, fists on hips, glaring. "Were."

"Don't be so hard on him, peaches," Alice put in from the rock. Maggie leaned against her side, and Alice slipped an arm around her. It felt nice. As nice as the hugs the Lady gave when she wasn't being leader of the gang.

"Why shouldn't I? I don't even know why you're 'ere."

"Because it was that or let pa kill me," she said simply.

Maggie stiffened and straightened up to stare at her. Alice coaxed her back against her side with a squeeze. Lizzie stood there, the wind properly taken out of her sails.

"Kill you?"

Alice nodded. "He caught me giving you help, see. So he locked me in a storage room in town till he was sober enough to shoot straight, and that's when—"

"—I broke in lookin' for food." Jake looked rather pleased with himself. "So between us, we took the engine out o' that locomotive tower and put 'er in the *Lass*, and—"

"—before pa woke the next morning, we set out to try and find you. Didn't see you in the logical places, so widened our search, all the while hoping pa and the boys wouldn't cobble together an engine and start out after us."

"There ent no airships left in that place, is there?" Maggie asked in spite of the fact that she felt so sleepy.

"Ranger ship was on its way, we knew that. Pa'd likely wreck it and use the fuselage."

"Did the Rangers come?" Even Lizzie had to admit that the prospect of being killed by your pa was heaps worse than going over to the other side to save your life. "We looked and looked but never saw 'em."

"Don't know," Jake said. "I expect me and one or two of Alice's friends here will go into town after a bit and do some scoutin'."

"I'm coming," Lizzie said at once. "You can't scout wivout at least one of us."

"Not lookin' like that, you ent." Jake's voice was firm. "You look like a tomato getting' ready to spoil, for true. Besides, someone has to stay and watch over the Lady."

Lizzie subsided, but Maggie could see plain as plain that watching over the Lady was just a job to fob her off while Jake and Alice got all the fun. She kept the smile off her aching face, though.

What Mr. Pleased-as-Punch didn't know wouldn't hurt him.

Chapter 18

"There 'as to be another way down."

Maggie gazed into the chimney of rock, down which spiraled steps cut out of the stone. The two Navapai boys who had gone along had lit lamps that flickered in niches every now and again, but other than that, only the glow left in the sky after sunset lit the stair.

"If there is, we ent got time to find it. C'mon, before we lose them." Lizzie started down as though she was tripping down the steps in the cottage in Vauxhall Gardens.

It was all an act. One misstep and in the morning, those big birds would be scraping her off the rocks hundreds of feet below. Maggie consigned her soul to Heaven and started down after her.

It didn't take near as long to get to the bottom as she thought. The stair wound inside for a bit, so that helped. The girls emerged at the base of the cliff feeling as though they'd managed to burgle the Tower of London, because on a difficulty scale of one to ten, that stair was definitely a ten.

In the distance they could see Jake and Alice and two Navapai boys, jogging along a road that looked white in the fading light. There was nothing for it but to jog along after them and hope they didn't look back.

They didn't—not until they'd reached the outskirts of Santa Fe. The girls' steps echoed off the mud walls of the houses, and before you could say Jack Robinson, Jake stepped out of a shadowy alley and grabbed them both by the scruff of the neck.

"Didn't I tell you two t'stay wi' the Lady?"

"You can't go on a mission wivout scouts, you silly gumpus." Lizzie wriggled until he set her down. "Ent you listened to Snouts ever?"

"Two days ago you almost died, and now yer givin' me guff?"

"Somebody has to," Maggie said. "Now, what's the plan?"

"Give it up, Jake," Alice said merrily, while the Navapai boys snickered. "There's no keeping these two out of the soup, so we may as well take them along. Maybe they can help."

Jake wagged his head. "Keep up and shut up, aye?" Maggie and Lizzie exchanged a triumphant glance. "Here's what we're doin'. Alice knows the mechanics at the airfield. We're takin' a steambus out there and doin' a reconnoiter for news of Ned Mose, and seein' if the *Lady Lucy* is here."

Hope surged in Maggie's chest. "You mean we c'n go home?"

His rapid pace checked, then resumed. "You can, likely. Don't see why they wouldn't take you an' the Lady on, now that yer not dead."

"Wot about you?" Maggie had to jog to keep up, but nary a complaint would pass her lips. "You c'n explain—'is lordship'll understand."

Jake kept his face turned away, faking like he was watching where they were going, like Alice wasn't in charge of this little parade. "I dunno. Ent much for me back 'ome except playin' second fiddle to Snouts. Might stay 'ere and scare up some work."

Maggie fell back to keep Lizzie company. It had never occurred to her that they wouldn't all go home together—and the sooner the better. Who would want to stay in this outlandish place all alone?

"Don't worry," Lizzie said in a low tone as they got on a steambus without paying any fare. "We're a flock. Of course we'll stay together. 'E's just talkin' up a show for them boys and Alice. I think 'e's sweet on 'er."

Maggie rolled her eyes. Alice was about a century older than Jake, and could probably do better in any case than a penniless runaway with a reputation as a turncoat.

They got off the bus outside the airfield, before anyone came to check for tickets, and followed Alice through a maze of hangars, piles of scrap metal, and wide acres where the airships floated at their masts. They approached a building where the plinkety-plunk of music told them airmen found entertainment, but Alice waved them off to the side behind a stack of what smelled like whisky barrels.

"No kids allowed inside, I'm afraid. Wait here while we take a look."

"Jake's a kid," Lizzie objected.

"He's over fourteen, and he's a boy, both of which you ain't," Alice told them. "I don't want you getting stole or mistook for a desert flower."

"What's a—"

"Never mind. Just stay here, all right? We won't be long."

They were long. They were interminably long. They were so long that Lizzie fell asleep behind the barrels, and when she woke up, she was in a fine temper.

"I ent stayin' here another moment." She craned up to look over at the door, where everyone in the city but Alice and Jake and those boys was going in and out and having a fine time while they were stuck here in the dark. "Come on. Who cares what them Rangers are up to? They don't want us. We c'n spot the *Lady Lucy* ourselves. They're probably sitting down to dinner and won't they be glad to see us?"

"Mad, more like." Maggie hurried behind her sister as they made for the biggest airfield, where the greatest number of ships was moored. "We didn't stay in our room, 'member. We didn't do as we was told." If they had, what then? Maybe the Lady would have found Rosie. Maybe not. But their hides would have been safe.

Was it better to keep your own hide safe, and not try to save those of your flock mates? Not likely. Even knowing what she knew now, she'd still have gone down that rope.

She wouldn't've nearly died in the desert, maybe.

But she wouldn't've met up with Miss Alice again, either, or known Jake was still alive.

All in all, the scale was about even.

Besides, they'd been in bed for two days. The goop Alice had slathered on her made it so her sunburn hardly hurt. And Snouts always said, if you didn't keep your hand in, you lost your skills.

Maggie had no intention of losing hers.

"There she is!" Lizzie pointed to the near side of the field, where the *Lady Lucy*'s distinctive golden fuselage rode gently next to a long, sleek craft with a shallow gondola set close underneath. It looked as if it were designed for speed records. "Come on. There's even a tower pushed up to it. We can walk right in."

Together, they ran across the field.

But someone was coming down the steps inside the tower. Running, more like. Light boots pounded on brass stairs.

Running people never meant good things, in Maggie's experience. She grabbed Lizzie's sleeve and dragged her behind the tower's wheels.

"Mopsies!" someone exclaimed, half a shout, half a whisper. "Mags—Liz—it's me, Tigg."

"Tigg!" Maggie had never hugged Tigg in all the time she'd known him, but that was before she'd almost died. They were a flock, and as far as she was concerned, flock mates hugged.

And the funny thing was, he hugged her right back.

"Cor, what a fuss you two caused, disappearin' like that. Where've you been?"

Lizzie just shook her head. "You wouldn't believe us if we told you. Was 'is nibs fit to be tied?"

"Yes. But 'er ladyship took it the worst. She cried. Thought you'd both been killed in the fall when we lifted."

Lizzie laughed. "Even Jake didn't get killed when he fell."

Tigg grabbed her. "What'd you say? Jake? Jake's alive?"

"Alive and havin' a wonderful time somewhere over there." Maggie waved a hand in the direction of the building with the music. She wasn't sure she could find it again if he asked her, but that didn't seem very important right now. "'E fell in the lake, just like off the Clarendon footbridge. Didn't 'arm a single 'air."

"C'mon, Mags, I'm starved." Lizzie pulled her toward the stairs. "Tigg, what's Cook got for grub? I ent had nowt but soup in two days."

He took a quick breath. "Don't go up there."

"Whyever not?" Lizzie stopped on the third step. "Did you eat it all?"

"No, but they're at dinner. And you don't want to join 'em, Liz. Not after what he done to the Lady."

"Who done?" Great snakes, the Dunsmuirs couldn't be eating with Ned Mose, could they? That was impossible.

"Lord James Selwyn, that's who." Tigg's face set in lines of implacable dislike. "That's why I'm out here instead of in there in me best bib and tucker. I ent sittin' across from that bounder if it were me last meal. Not after 'e stole our device an' kidnapped it here."

"How come we never 'eard of this?" Lizzie demanded. "The Lady never said a word."

"She never said nuffink to the Dunsmuirs, neither. Nobs don't run down other nobs, I guess, no matter what they done. And up till we left, she were going to be 'is wife, weren't she?"

"She ent goin' to be 'is wife now." Maggie knew that for true.

"Guess not." In the electrick lights on the tower, Tigg's face became bleak. "Not now she's dead."

Lizzie clutched his arm. "Cor, Tigg, didn't you know? She ent dead. She got swept off in that flash flood, but Alice pulled 'er out and she's right as rain now."

"Or mostly," Maggie corrected. "Had a run-in with some kind of cat creature so she's feeling poorly, but she ent dead at least."

Tigg looked from one to the other in astonishment. "The Lady's not dead? Somebody better tell the Dunsmuirs, then.

They already sent a pigeon to Gwyn Place, and Lord James is wearin' black like he 'ad a right to it."

Lizzie shook her head. "She might not want 'im to know. She might be quite 'appy wiv 'im thinkin' she's dead."

"Better ask her," Maggie agreed. "Soon's we get back."

"Back where?"

"The Navapai village, over there." Lizzie waved a hand in a general westerly direction. "Alice got the *Stalwart Lass* running again, and her and Jake flew it up here."

Tigg's eyebrows rose. "Who's this Alice, then?"

"Ned Mose's daughter, but he was goin' t'kill her for helpin' us, so she took off in the *Lass*." Lizzie tugged on his shirt sleeve when he didn't appear to be able to get mouth working properly at these astonishing revelations. "Sure you can't nip up t'the galley and nick summat for us?"

"All right," he said at last. "But stay out of sight. Lord James gets a peep at you two and the jig's up."

Back up the stairs his boots went, and Maggie pulled Lizzie down in the shadows behind the great wheels of the tower again. To keep her mind off the sad state of her stomach, she pictured his route—through the embarkation bay, then avoiding the open stair that led up to A deck, he'd nip along the corridor past the crew's quarters and the Chief Steward's cabin. The galley was the very next door. If Lord James had come to dinner, what would Cook be dishing up? Roast beef, maybe? Or pork? No fish, that was certain, unless there was a river within fifty miles. Her mouth watered at the thought of a nice roast beef, with Yorkshire puddings swimming in drippings—

"Mags!" Lizzie nudged her in the ribs with her elbow.

"Do you think Tigg's on 'is way back yet?"

"Sh! What's that over there? D'you see something moving?"

The vision of the beef and pudding evaporated as Maggie focused on a pile of crates stacked up near an airship that looked as though it had been through a war moored just off the *Lady Lucy*'s stern. Sure enough, a dark figure detached itself from the stack and darted across the flat ground into the shadow of the *Lady Lucy*'s fuselage.

Lizzie's hand closed around a broken brick. "He's headin' this way," she whispered, her lips barely moving.

Maggie whistled, the *unknown intruder approaching* whistle they'd used for years, just in case Tigg was on his way back and could hear.

In the distance, the call of a bird came in acknowledgement. Maggie sucked in a breath. "That were Jake."

The intruder gave no indication he'd heard, or if he had, that the sounds of night birds in a busy airfield were anything unusual. They could hear him breathing now, heavily, from all his running.

And overhead, the girls heard the sound of Tigg's boots on the first of the stairs.

"Thief," Lizzie breathed. "On three."

One ... two ...

Three! Both girls leaped at the black figure and Lizzie swung the brick so hard Maggie expected the man to drop like a stone.

Instead, an arm flashed out and caught her on the wrist, and the brick fell out of her fingers. "Dash it all," he said, "what do you mean, attacking me in this fashion, you little ruffians?"

With both hands, he pushed them off and Maggie landed so hard on her bottom that the breath was knocked clean out of her. When Tigg burst out of the entrance to the tower, a basket in his hands, she couldn't make a single sound to warn him.

Tigg's mouth dropped open.

"Mr. Malvern, sir!" he exclaimed when the man stepped into the light. "What in all the skies are you doing here?"

Chapter 19

Claire swam to the surface of an ocean filled with gibbering monsters and apparitions, all of which wanted her dead. Expecting at any moment for one of them to grab her by the ankles and pull her under once again, she opened her eyes to a warm darkness punctuated by gentle lamplight.

A cool cloth was applied to her forehead. "She wakes, and her spirit is with her," said a woman with dusky skin and calm dark eyes. "Are you feeling better?"

"Where am I?"

She put a mug to her lips and Claire drank. It tasted acidic and faintly like grass, but no matter. It was cold and wet and glorious.

"You are in the Navapai village west of Santa Fe. The girls who were with you are well. They have been out doing a reckoning with Alice and my sons and have brought back some folk who are anxious to see you."

Alice? Alice was here and not floating in the sky or back in her shack by Spider Woman? Claire roped her thoughts together. "Dunsmuirs?"

"No. Lie back. I have told them they cannot see you until you can sit up."

"I can sit up." She struggled up, allowing the woman to stuff a rolled-up wool blanket behind her back. "Forgive me for asking, but who are you? What happened to me? I had a dream that Alice and Jake came and rescued us—but that is impossible."

"I am Alaia, healer of this village, and it was no dream. Jake fell in Spider Woman's mirror and has lived to tell about it. He is now her son, and under her protection."

She rose, and Claire saw she wore a black dress belted with colorful woven wool in the same pattern as the blanket. She must be the weaver. Spinning threads like Spider Woman. She picked up a bowl of something that smelled delicious, and Claire leaned forward like a hound sniffing the wind.

"Thank you for caring for me, Miss—Mrs.—Alaia. The girls and I would surely have died without you."

"You are Alice's friends," the woman said simply. "And she is my friend and sister in spirit."

Claire took the bowl and tasted the soup. She couldn't remember ever tasting anything so delicious. The entire bowl went down in less time than it took to think about it.

Alaia nodded with satisfaction. "Now your friends may come in for a short time."

Claire touched her hair and realized it was down, and someone had brushed it. She was wearing a cotton shift and not much else, so she pulled the wool blanket up under her armpits.

And then the door opened and Tigg and the Mopsies poured in, followed by Jake. They fetched up in a wave on the bed, everyone except Jake climbing on in a great pile of hugs and relief and greeting.

Laughing, Claire kissed Tigg with such joy that he blushed and ducked his head. She settled the Mopsies on either side and extended her hand to Jake. When he took it hesitantly, she tugged on his arm so that he practically toppled over, and she hugged him fiercely as he knelt next to the bed.

"I am so glad you were not killed," she whispered. "If I never experience a moment as dreadful as you going out that hatch for the rest of eternity, it will be too soon."

He could not look at her. His face buried in her lap, he choked out, "I'm sorry, Lady. Sorry I turned coat. Sorry for everything. But they told me they'd kill you all and I—"

"Shh." Gently, she rubbed his heaving shoulders. "It is forgotten. We are all together again and we will not look back."

"We're a flock," Maggie put in from her cozy corner between Claire, the bolster, and the wall.

"Don't forget Mr. Malvern," Tigg said from his place next to her knees. "He's been awful anxious to see you."

Claire looked up and saw Andrew hovering in the doorway. For the space of ten seconds she could not speak. Instead, she drank in the wholly unexpected sight of him. Yes, he had told her he was in pursuit of James. But to see him here, in the flesh, in circumstances that anyone would call extraordinary ... she drank in the sight of him with shameless greed.

And speaking of extraordinary, what an astonishing rig he wore! Over the normalcy of his brocade vest and cravat and shirt was a dusty canvas coat, and he wore an airman's leather cap with the goggles pushed up on his forehead. A holster on his hip contained some kind of firearm, but she could not tell more than that.

Heavens. He looked positively wild. In a good way.

A very good way.

"Are you not glad to see me, Claire?"

And there was the Andrew she knew, a gentleman and a scientist to the core, complete with an endearing awkwardness around the fairer sex.

"I can think of no more welcome sight in the world, after that of Jake alive and well." She extended her hand and Andrew took it, folding himself onto the lightning designs of the rug next to Jake, who sniffled one last time and wiped his nose on his sleeve as he made room.

"I was awful anxious," Andrew said with a smile. "In what seems another life, I sent you a letter. Did you ever receive it?"

Claire nodded. He did not release her hand, and if he was content to do so, she was perfectly content to leave it there.

"A pigeon came about three days into the flight. But immediately after that, we ran into a dreadful storm, and—"

"Do not exert yourself. Tigg and the girls told me the whole story on the way here."

Claire looked over the little assembly. "Mopsies, if Alice was indeed here and not a dream, why do I not see her?"

"She's probably still at the airfield," Jake said. "She an' Alaia's boys were talkin' so long wiv these airmen friends o' hers that I thought I'd take a reconnoiter meself. When I didn't find t'Mopsies where we'd left 'em, I headed over to the *Lady Lucy*. Got there just in time to see Lizzie clock Mr. Malvern wiv a brick."

"Lizzie!" Claire looked down at her, shocked to the core.

"I thought 'e were an intruder," Lizzie said in her own defense. "An' I missed anyhow."

"What was in this letter you were talkin' about?" Tigg asked. "Mr. Malvern, I can't figure why you're here and not in the laboratory in London."

"All in good time." Andrew smiled and finally released Claire's hand. "It sounds like we owe this Alice a great debt for saving your lives."

"Jake, too," Lizzie said. "Tell 'em what you and Alice did, Jake."

Uncomfortable in the spotlight, Jake shifted and cleared his throat. "We put the locomotive tower's engine in the *Stalwart Lass* and came after the Lady and the girls."

"Wait—you did what?" Andrew leaned forward to look into Jake's eyes. "Two of you put a locomotive engine in an airship? How is that possible?"

"It weren't really a locomotive engine. It were an airship engine, but it runs the tower just fine. And we 'ad 'elp. Half a dozen automatons, easy. They're a lot stronger'n they look. They made a good crew, too, once we was in the air."

Goodness. A vision of a miniature army of automatons carrying bits of engine from one vessel to another played across Claire's mind. On one hand, what a triumph of engineering it must have been. On the other, they were automatons, bronze and faceless and mindless. And she had been unconscious and surrounded by them on the *Lass*. She swallowed.

"Where did the automatons come from?" Andrew asked with interest.

It was best he did not know their actual provenance. "Alice made them. She is a young lady of singular resources."

"I look forward to making her acquaintance. Very much so."

Hmph. Were her accomplishments as nothing? It was quite clearly time to change the subject.

"Now you must tell us your adventures," she said. "Including the parts about Lord James. I have a feeling our tales will dovetail rather neatly toward the end."

Andrew got to his feet and removed his canvas coat, while Claire and the Mopsies settled more comfortably against the bolster.

"As I said in my letter, the night of the exhibition at the Crystal Palace, James came to an agreement with a consortium of Texican railroad men and made off with the Selwyn Kinetick Carbonator. They had passage on a private merchant ship belonging to one of them, but I was able to leave the next morning on a Zeppelin vessel out of Hamburg going to New York. Once there, I made inquiries and learned that the Texican vessel was bound for Santa Fe, which is the capital of this territory."

Claire nodded, encouraging him to go on.

"When I arrived here, I realized that learning their intentions was paramount. They might choose to duplicate the Carbonator and build the devices here, or they might ship the Carbonator to some other location. They might even begin processing coal."

"Did you find out?" Tigg asked with the seriousness of a fellow scientist. He, after all, had as much invested in the Carbonator as any of them.

"I could not just hang about the railroad offices and eavesdrop, so I did the next best thing. I signed on as a laborer in the yard. They soon realized I had more skills than loading cars, so they moved me into the laboratory, where I had a fair task ahead of me to stay out of sight whenever James or one of the barons was on the premises. They'd all met me at the Crystal Palace, you see."

"Did you succeed?" Claire asked.

"I did. I found out that they plan to carbonate an entire trainload of coal and send a locomotive from here to San Francisco on the new Nevada Territory line as a kind of demonstration. They plan to sell a device like ours to the Royal Kingdom of Spain, you see. The Spaniards are building locomotives with the plan to run railways all the way down to South America."

"How will they get past the Texicans?" Claire asked. She had seen the charts. "The Territory covers nearly the entire southern half of the continent."

"Ah, but there are no railways directly to South America. The Spaniards are building lines down the west coast to evade the Texican tariffs, and you can bet the government in Texico City will not be happy about it."

"The money to be made will be astronomical," Claire murmured.

"And the carbonated coal is light, hard, and lasts a long time," Tigg said. "If you're aiming for speed, you can't stop to load your tender, can you?"

"What villains they are," Claire breathed. "Go behind the Texican government's back to supply the Spaniards, then claim innocence and rake in the money."

"With our device," Tigg said indignantly.

Claire's lips firmed. "I think not."

Andrew nodded, following her train of thought as though he had had the same one. "The Carbonator is heavily guarded, but there are brief periods when the guard changes and it could be possible to slip past. The power cell you and Dr. Craig developed is not so large that it could not be spirited out. And without the cell, of course, they have nothing."

"They're probably already working on more of 'em," Tigg said. "Wouldn't make sense to risk something happening to the one."

"You are quite correct. I have already seen the prototypes. Time is of the essence," Andrew agreed. "With assistance, I could repossess the cell as soon as tomorrow night."

Jake, who had not said a word during the tale, nodded now. "We could use a mission. Keep our 'ands in, like."

"You'll need scouts," Lizzie said.

"And someone who knows 'is way round bolts and suchlike," Tigg put in.

"I could not ask it of you all." Andrew seemed to have realized a moment too late that he was proposing that a group of children engage in criminal activity on foreign soil. "I will hazard the task alone."

"You would be foolish to do so," Claire told him. Her energy was rapidly seeping away.

Andrew's gaze became concerned. "We will discuss this in the morning. The moon is probably setting and you will be no use to anyone if you do not get some rest." He chivvied them out of the room.

"A moment, Andrew." When he returned alone to her side, she gathered her strength. "You will be careful on this enterprise?"

"I have had several days to reconnoiter the hangars and laboratory," he said. "Have no fear. You must concentrate on getting well." The assurance faded from his expression and he started to speak, then thought better of it. After a moment of struggle, he finally blurted, "Claire, I know it is none of my business, but considering James's behavior, I must ask you to reconsider your engagement to him." When she only stared, he rushed on, "I know what you are thinking. I am only the son of a policeman and a cook, and these things are done differently in Blood circles. But can you not—I cannot bear to think—" His voice stumbled into silence. "I apologize," he said finally, and had taken two steps toward the door before Claire found her voice.

"Andrew, I have not been engaged to James Selwyn since the night he stole the Carbonator."

He turned, stiffly. When his gaze found her face, his eyes were blazing. "You have not?"

She struggled to sit higher against the bolster. "He removed my name from the patent that night, so as not to shock Ross Stephenson. He said he would reinstate it as a wedding gift. And at that moment I realized he would never do it—he would use it as a carrot for years to come, and expect me to follow it as obediently as a brood mare. I broke it off that same moment."

"You are not engaged to him," he repeated. He took a step closer. "You are a free woman."

"As free as you."

Another step. "I have not been free since the moment you knocked on the door of my laboratory." The sound of voices came from outside the door. "Claire, would you—"

The door flew open and Alice burst into the room like a whirlwind. Her hair was a wild tangle, and there appeared to be pieces of those tumbling weeds stuck in it. One sleeve of her cotton shirt had been torn out, and her knuckles were scraped raw. She had either been dragged some distance by a vehicle, or had been in a fight.

"Claire, you're awake! I'll tell you, you gave me quite a scare. Listen, you'll never guess who I—oh, I'm sorry. You have company."

Claire released a long breath and with it, any hope of knowing what the conclusion to Andrew's question might have been.

"Alice. We've all been worried about you. I'm glad you're back. But are you all right?"

"Not near as worried as I've been about you." She paused. "I'm fine. Just a little dustup. Are you going to introduce me?"

Exhausted as she was, the situation was too interesting to ignore. "Do you not know?"

Alice looked puzzled. And awkward. And a trifle embarrassed. "Um. No." Gamely, she held out a hand to Andrew. "I'm Alice Chalmers. Sorry about the mess."

Andrew looked equally puzzled, but it was quite likely about Claire's behavior. She could not resist. "Cast this face as a daguerreotype, perhaps. And surround it with print—an article on the properties of coal. Give it a byline, one that says—"

Alice gasped, and covered her mouth with filthy fingers. "It can't be," she whispered.

Andrew had clearly had enough of being sported with, particularly so soon after … whatever he had been going to say. He bowed. "Do forgive Lady Claire, Alice. She is not in full control of her faculties just now."

"Not in—!"

Andrew ignored her and spoke to Alice. "I am Andrew Malvern, and I am very pleased to make your acquaintance. I do hope you fared better than the other person."

"Andrew Malvern," Alice whispered. "*The* Andrew Malvern, of the Royal Society of Engineers?"

Andrew peered at her, as though doubting the strength of her mind. "The very one. Have you read one of my monographs?"

Alice grasped her hair in both hands, yanked some dried vegetation out of it, then clapped one palm to her mouth. She dashed to the window, and in the next moment, was violently sick onto the terrace outside.

Chapter 20

Claire woke in the cool dawn feeling much better than she had in days. Whatever the herbs or chemicals in the drink Alaia plied her with every hour, they certainly worked. She touched her face. Even the sunburn had cooled to the point where she did not feel her skin would crack and bleed should she smile.

Alice stirred on the pallet next to the bed, and sat up with a groan. She clutched both sides of her head as though it were a melon ready to burst open. "Please tell me I didn't toss my innards in front of Andrew Malvern last night."

"Not directly in front of him. You made it to the window in time. Are you ill, dear?" Alice looked utterly miserable. Claire reached for the mug half full of the healing liquid, and offered it to her.

Alice drank it down. "No, not ill." She wiped her mouth with her sleeve, having gone to sleep fully clothed. "It's the mescala. Never, ever drink that stuff, Claire. It's poison."

"Is it some form of liquor?"

Alice nodded miserably. "We met a couple of the pilots who fly the Ranger airships, and in the party were some airmen from the Canadas. Me and Alaia's boys thought we might get some good information, and I guess we did, but then they started in on the mescala. One thing led to another and we … well, one of them said something Luis didn't like, and then Alvaro went to his defense, and I couldn't just stand there and do nothing, so …" She sighed. "It was a mill, plain and simple. So of course that had to be the night I meet Andrew Malvern." She buried her face against her knees. "I want to die."

"Have some more of Alaia's cordial. It's in that lovely pottery jug with the spider pattern."

"Not about that." Her voice was muffled. "About being the ugliest, most harum-scarum idiot that ever made a man run for the nearest ship."

"Oh, Alice." Claire touched her hair, and the girl actually flinched. "Come and sit by me."

Reluctantly, Alice hefted herself up on the bed and they both leaned their backs against the wall. Claire tucked the blanket around their legs. "Look. From here we can see the sun rise."

"I wouldn't be getting too excited about the sun just yet. You need to stay out of it until your skin heals some more."

"I know. But what I was really pointing out is that today is another day, fresh and new, with no mistakes in it yet for either of us."

Alice would not look at her. "What must he think of me?"

"He will think that you are the one who saved our lives. Who engineered the *Stalwart Lass* so she could fly again. He knows about your automatons, and I must say, he is impressed."

"He won't be so impressed with the sorry reality."

"Why does it matter so much?" Claire asked gently. "He is a stranger to you, and once our aims here are accomplished, he will likely be going back to London."

"It's stupid, I know. But I admire him so much, and—and—oh, never mind."

Admire? This was not the despondency of unrequited admiration. Claire was not sure exactly what it was, but she was determined to see her spirits revived. She could not bear to see her friend so cast down, after all she had risked for them.

"I suppose you'll be going back to London with him?" Alice asked, gazing at the clouds through the window, which were streaked with red and orange that might have seeped from the mesas themselves.

"No." She would not be eighteen for another three weeks, and she was taking no chances. James might be a mere two miles away, but the laws of the Empire did not apply here in the Texican Territory. He could force her to do nothing. "My original plan was to meet friends in the Canadas—in Edmonton—and visit the diamond mines. I am already a week late, so I must let them know I am alive, and find my way there somehow."

At last Alice slid a glance her way. "We could go in the *Stalwart Lass*."

"Alice, you cannot steal your father's airship and go gallivanting about the continent." Claire's face felt almost natural as her eyebrows rose. The skin was tight, but at least it did not feel as though it would peel right off.

Alice pleated the patterned blanket between her fingers. "Pa was pretty mad about me helping you. It was either leave town or get shot, so I left. I don't expect I'll ever go back."

"I'm so sorry." She hesitated, then plunged on. "My father removed himself from me. He—he shot himself rather than face the poverty he had himself created."

Alice's lips trembled around the edges. "I'm sorry to hear it, Claire. But Ned Mose—he ain't really my pa anyhow. He's just living with my ma. My real pa went off to seek his fortune and—removed himself, like you say. Maybe now I can pick up his trail." Life came back into her voice. "One of those airmen from last night—an old-timer—said he remembered a man with one blind eye working on one of his crews in the Canadas. My pa was a mechanic—he lost his eye to one of his early machines. I suppose that's where I get it. Mechanics, I mean. Not blind eyes."

"Then we must go together, as soon as our work here is done."

"What exactly are you all up to? I'd have thought you'd be off on the *Lady Lucy*."

"Tigg said he'd found the girls and Mr. Malvern ready to board her. It would not surprise me if she lifts soon—I imagine Lady Dunsmuir will be anxious to put this country behind her. I wonder if the Dunsmuirs know yet that I am alive?"

And that Rosie still had their diamonds in her possession. She must get up and see about returning them, if indeed they were planning to leave soon.

"We'll ask him. Come on. My stomach could use some of Alaia's *poh-soh-lay*. It's guaranteed to bring even the dead back to life."

Claire threw the blanket back. "Let us hope not. I will settle for breakfast."

৩৯৵৶

"The *Lady Lucy?* This morning?" Tigg could not have looked more dismayed if Claire had said she was going to leap off the cliff stair. "Lady, are you mad? Lord James could be aboard. 'E came to dinner last night like some fine gentleman and hood-winked 'is lordship well and truly."

Claire spooned up the last of her *poh-soh-lay* and Alaia filled the bowl before she even swallowed. A flat wheel of unleavened bread lay in the center of the table, nearly all consumed. It had arrived bubbling with cheese and a paste made of beans and layers of tomato, corn, and small green chiles. Claire could not imagine what such a thing might taste like, but she was a believer now. A lady might not be permitted to take a second helping, but in the Texican Territory, ladies had to adapt.

Before Tigg could become any more upset on her behalf, Alice gave him a companionable nudge with her shoulder. "Truth is, youngster, this James person owes her one. She saved his life the other night."

Claire nodded at her to go on. If she wanted to speak of her stepfather's criminal behavior, then it was her place to do so, and Claire would not claim the story.

Andrew stopped shoveling in his flatbread, which he had rolled into a tube, the better to preserve its ingredients. "You saved James's life? After what he did?"

"The man who skyjacked the *Lady Lucy* and all aboard was the man I've called my pa for the past dozen years," Alice said.

"It's no secret he's a sky pirate and a heartless man, but if not for him, the town of Resolution probably wouldn't exist."

"He was holding us all for ransom, but unfortunately, I am not worth very much," Claire said. "He had no idea what to do with me, but in the meantime, James had found out what had happened to the *Lady Lucy*, and was on his way to pay my ransom."

Andrew nearly choked on his breakfast, and Maggie handed him a mug of the grass-scented liquid.

"Pa—Ned—decided that he'd take both ransom and ship if he wrecked her. Without witnesses, he'd have nothing but profit." Alice glanced at Claire, who took up the tale.

"I had been washed downstream by the flash flood, and Alice pulled me out. So when Mose and his crew went to set out the lamps to lure the ship in, I climbed up on a pinnacle of rock—"

"Spider Woman," Alaia said, passing behind her to fill Andrew's clay mug. "She had not finished spinning the thread of this man's life."

"Yes," Claire said after a moment. "I flagged the ship with a lamp like the railway men do, and it changed course at the very last moment."

"I heard about that," Andrew said. "The airmen at one of the public houses—"

"Honkytonks," Alice put in, then blushed scarlet.

Claire smothered a smile. One would not correct one's idol in public if one had thought about it beforehand.

"Honkytonks, yes." Andrew nodded at her, and she blushed even more deeply. Even her hair seemed to be turning scarlet.

Andrew went on, "The word was that the ship must have been in poor repair to have lost a piece off her bow."

"Scraping along Spider Woman would have torn the canvas right off." Valiantly, Alice attempted to recover. "It's sandstone, you know—it'll take your skin off soon as look at it."

"James may not know it yet, but he owes me a debt. And when I go this morning to return the diamonds, if I should meet him I will tell him so."

"And then you can have the bobbies come an' arrest him for thieving," Tigg muttered. "'E 'as to pay for making off wiv our device."

"You will do no such thing," Andrew said firmly, but whether to Claire or Tigg, she was not sure. "James must not know that I am here, or that you know what he has done. It is clear that the Dunsmuirs do not, or they would never have received him."

"I did not tell them," Claire said. "I allowed them to think he had business here, and that he was pursuing me with the hope that ..." Her voice trailed away. If he had been willing to pay her ransom, perhaps he really did still hope.

"You were wise, then. He has duped them the way he duped Ross Stephenson and most of London society." He gazed around the table with seriousness. "When we have Doctor Craig's cell safely in our hands again, that will be punishment enough. You may believe that the only reason he had funds enough to pay Lady Claire's ransom was because the Texicans have already paid him off. Without the cell, he will have them to deal with."

"If it's Stanford Fremont's boys he's dealing with, he won't last long," Alice told them. "Those boys shoot first and ask questions later, and they don't tolerate anyone taking advantage of them."

Claire got to her feet—there was no table, but the sleeping pallets acted as seating and were arranged around a flat stone that served as one. If she was to enjoy any more meals like this one, she would need to let out the strings of her corset. Of course, four days of next to no food had made it rather loose, anyway.

"Who is coming with me?"

Jake got up, and Tigg as well.

"I don't like this, Claire," Andrew said. "Look what happened the last time you were alone with him."

"I believe I stole his coach and relieved him of nine hundred pounds," she said crisply before she thought.

Andrew goggled at her. "That was you? You sent that money in a tube?"

It was too late now to deny it. "I did. So you see, I am as guilty of thievery as he is." She lifted her chin. "If you wish to break off our acquaintance, I shall quite understand."

With a shake of his head, he conceded. "I wouldn't have the opportunity to put right his crime were it not for that nine hundred pounds. And since my plans for tonight include thievery on a grand scale, I can hardly point fingers at you."

"Do all the toffs in London have thievery on their minds?" Alice asked, looking from one to the other.

"You bet yer boots they do," Lizzie said with certainty.

Chapter 21

The Dunsmuirs' joy at learning Claire was not among the angels knew no bounds. Lady Dunsmuir fell on her neck rejoicing, and even the earl clasped her hands in both of his, tears standing in his eyes.

"Never for a moment would we have left you if we had known you were alive," he said, his voice breaking. "But the flood was so fierce it did not seem that anything could survive it."

"It's the Lady," Willie informed his father, as though fire, flood, or act of God was irrelevant where she was concerned. He clasped her legs through her skirts and gazed up at her with such happiness that Claire couldn't help but kneel to hug him.

His parents, of course, thought he referred to her title. "It is, indeed, darling," the countess said. "And I have never seen a more welcome sight."

"Then allow me to offer you another." Claire handed her one of Alaia's mats, rolled into a tube. She and Alice had scrubbed away all evidence of the diamonds' misadventures in the hatbox, where Rosie had used them for a cushion, and when the mat unfurled on the mahogany dining table, their full beauty glittered in the lamplight.

Lady Dunsmuir gasped. "But how—where—oh Claire, we thought they were lost forever! Even when Will told us they were safe, I did not believe him. I am sorry, my darling, but I did not see how it could be true."

Claire smiled at Willie, and Tigg rubbed the top of his head with rough affection. "Willie, the girls, and Tigg put them into a hatbox with Rosie, attached a small dirigible, and launched them into the air the same moment that—" She stopped and glanced at Jake, who had just emerged from the earl's hard clasp looking rather ruffled.

"The same moment as I went into the lake," he finished. "Wish I'd seen 'em. Rosie wouldn't've had to spend a night shut up in a box elsewhere."

"Jake, my dear boy." Captain Hollys appeared, breathing rather heavily, as though he'd run all the way from the gondola. "One of the middies just told me he'd seen you board." He shook his hand, pumping it so hard Jake's jaw flexed in an effort not to wince. "I am so very glad to see with my own eyes that you are safe and unharmed."

"Thank you, sir." The boy swallowed, then stood straighter. "I want to apologize to you all. I done so to the Lady, but I want you folk—I mean to say—" His lips trembled and his voice broke. "I wouldn't 'ave done it if they 'adn't threatened to kill you, starting wiv the youngest. Turned me coat, I mean. I were sorry then and I'm sorry now." He stumbled to a halt.

"My dear fellow." The earl shook his hand a second time. "One doesn't come back from the dead to apologize. Consider it forgotten, and we will go on as we began—as friends."

Jake's face crumpled, and it was only with a heroic effort—and a glance at Tigg, who would never let him live it down if he wept like a girl—that he blinked his tears back and clasped the earl's hand in return.

Lady Dunsmuir gasped. "John! We must send a pigeon at once to Gwyn Place. Poor Flora—she must hear this happy news at once, before she undergoes the dreadful trial of a funeral."

In the air hung the word *again*, which Davina was too delicate to say.

Claire put a soothing hand on her black silk sleeve. Black—could she be wearing mourning for Claire herself? "Do not distress yourself. We have already done so, with a message in my own hand so she knows the happy truth."

Her ladyship beamed with relief and did not seem to wonder where Claire had obtained her information. "You must fetch the girls—why are they not with you?—and bring them to dinner. We will be lifting in the morning, and were having something of a send-off. It was to be rather a sober affair, but now we shall have a real celebration. Claire, you will never guess who our other guest is."

"The Prince Consort?" she asked, as though she could not possibly already know.

"Lord James Selwyn!"

Tigg sucked in a breath through his nose, and the earl did not miss the cautioning hand Jake laid on his shoulder. "Are you young men acquainted with his lordship?" he asked.

"Aye," Tigg said with admirable brevity.

Lady Dunsmuir looked from them to Claire. "Now I know that you are no longer engaged, of course, but he has crossed two continents to see you, in the midst of his business affairs. I cannot help but think—"

"Dear Davina." Claire did her best to remember how one acted with blushing modesty. "Really, you must not suppose that he … that there is any danger of …"

"That he's still carryin' the torch," Tigg put in with an edge to his tone.

"Yes." Oh dear, she must not laugh. Not when Davina had put her fingers to her lips in distress at the thought that she might have embarrassed Claire.

"Oh Claire, surely you are mistaken. Why on earth is he wearing mourning for you if he harbors no tender feeling?"

"I cannot imagine. I would be grateful if you would send the message informing him that I am alive and well, so that he is prepared to celebrate rather than mourn. And do not think of trying to mend what is broken. My mind is made up, but that does not mean we cannot be civil to one another."

Tigg and Jake stared at her as if she were speaking the language of the Navapai, no doubt wondering why she was actively inviting the blackguard into their company. After kissing Davina and telling her she could not wait another moment to retrieve her clothes and change, she pulled Tigg and Jake into the cabin that had been hers and closed the door.

"Lady, what are you thinking?" Jake's gaze was wary, but she could tell he expected her to have a reason behind her mad behavior.

"Just this. If Lord James is here indulging in the earl's good wine, he will not be at the laboratory tonight when Mr. Malvern goes in. I am going to contrive to have one or two of the barons invited to dinner, if I can, to lessen the chances of his discovery even further."

"Lady, are you sure?" Tigg's face creased with doubt. "I wouldn't want to be within a mile of 'im, meself. What if 'e convinces you to be Lady Selwyn again?"

"I can safely assure you that will never happen." She chivvied them into the corridor. "Now, Jake, I want you to go find Mr. Malvern and tell him my plans. I will make your excuses to the Dunsmuirs. Tigg, off to your cabin for a scrub and a change. I'm not ashamed to appear anywhere in my raiding rig, but I must say I will be glad to see a waist other than this one."

Her lovely blue evening gown was gone, confiscated by Ned Mose—no doubt to bestow on Alice's mother. Claire could not regret that, though it did mean she must appear at dinner in a plain navy skirt with an embroidered white waist more suitable for work in a laboratory than at an earl's table.

She twisted the St. Ives pearls around her neck—hidden safely under Maggie's clothes this whole time—and touched her grandmother's emerald ring with affection. Both pieces went a long way to restoring her confidence.

She was not feeling a dearth of confidence at the prospect of sitting across a dinner table from James. Rather, she needed the pearls to remind herself of who she was—the Lady of Devices, who did not tolerate attacks upon herself or her own. It would take all her self-control not to fling the roast at James's head for his confounded thievery.

James had removed the black armband, but his face still carried traces of strain in the pinched look around his eyes and a physique that had lost weight in the weeks since she had last seen him.

Claire doubted, however, that these touching proofs could be attributed to his belief in her demise.

"Claire," he breathed as he came toward her, hand outstretched, in the lounge of the *Lady Lucy*. "I cannot tell you how happy I am to see you alive and well."

"And I you." She stepped back when it appeared he might take her in his arms, and he bent to kiss her hand as if he had meant to all along. "Thank you for being willing to pay ransom on my behalf."

Lady Dunsmuir gasped. "Claire, that is hardly a topic to bring up in polite company."

James smiled at his hostess. "If I have learned nothing else in my business affairs here in the Texican Territory, it is that while the country is beautiful, life here can be unexpectedly brutal, with no regard for polite company. For instance, the airship that carried me south to come to Lady Claire's assistance barely missed a rock formation that would have wrecked it. Who would have predicted such a thing?"

How convenient it was that they seemed to be in a mood for truth. "It missed the formation—called Spider Woman—because your navigator has quick reflexes. I was up in those rocks signaling with a lantern to turn the ship aside. It was about to be wrecked on purpose by Ned Mose and his gang of sky pirates."

How satisfying it was to render him completely speechless for once—he who had an answer for everything.

Mr. Stanford Fremont, the most powerful railroad baron in the Texican consortium, nudged James with an elbow. "Saved your life, eh? Maybe there's a little spark in that cold fire yet."

James flushed while Claire gazed at the man, marveling at his effrontery. He had only just met her—how very rude of him to make such personal remarks about a stranger!

"I would have done the same had you been on the ship, sir," she said coolly.

The insult sailed over his leonine head. "I like a woman with spirit. How did she come to be so intrepid, so young?" He rocked back on his heels, his thumbs hooked in the velvet lapels of his dinner jacket.

"I do not call an unwillingness to see a good ship and crew die *intrepid*, sir. Any of us possessed of a lamp and the ability to climb rocks would have done the same." She turned from him with a polite smile and addressed James. "You have not introduced the others in your party. I should like to make their acquaintance."

He gathered himself with difficulty. "Certainly. Lady Claire Trevelyan, may I present Garrison Polk, who owns the Silver Nevada Railway, and Lieutenant Robert van Ness, commander of the detachment of Texican Rangers here in Santa Fe."

She offered her hand graciously to each man. As Lieutenant van Ness bowed over it, he clicked his heels as precisely as any Prussian soldier. "I am honored to make your acquaintance, Lady Claire," he said in accents that confirmed he had not been born on this side of the Atlantic. "Let me assure you the Rangers are doing everything in their power to bring Ned Mose and his crew of miscreants to justice."

"I hope you find him," she replied. "It should not be too difficult—his airship has, I believe, been stolen and he is grounded for the time being."

"There are more ways to get out of Resolution than by air," the lieutenant growled. "But rest assured we know all of them. It is only a matter of time."

Lady Dunsmuir came forward and laid a hand on James's arm. "Dinner is served, gentlemen. James, will you escort me in?"

The villain, patting Davina's hand on his arm as though she were a child too innocent to see what kind of man he was. Claire set her teeth and thought longingly of the lightning rifle, under her pallet in Alaia's home.

Never mind. By this time tomorrow they would all be in the air heading for the Canadas, with the rifle once more in her possession and the Carbonator's cell safely tucked under canvas in her steam landau in the hold.

And then James's perfidies would all catch up to him with a vengeance. Her only regret was that she would not be here to see it.

Tigg had taken his supper with Willie earlier, but as Lord Dunsmuir cut the roast beef and Davina passed her a plate, as though they dined *en famille*, her ladyship returned to her previous line of thought.

"Are the girls quite safe, Claire? I must say it surprises me to see you separated."

"I hope you told them in no uncertain terms that their behavior in leaving us was unconscionable," John put in. "When we realized what they'd done, I nearly stopped breathing."

"What had they done?" James inquired. "I've long been of the opinion that those children belong in a school or institution of some kind that will impose a little healthy discipline on them."

Claire's knife clanked on china as she cut her beef with a little more energy than necessary. "They would not be separated from me," she said mildly, to cover it up. "They refused to believe I was dead, and came to find me though it might have meant their lives." Her lashes flicked up. "It is difficult to instill such loyalty in an institution, would you not agree?"

Stanford Fremont gave a bark of laughter. "She's got you there, James."

The man's familiarity was beginning to get on Claire's nerves.

"But where are they, Claire?" The countess was honestly concerned. "And how did you get from Resolution to Santa Fe? I cannot puzzle it out."

She smiled. "This land may be brutal, but it harbors people who are willing to help when one is in need. Friends brought us here, and the girls are with them."

Technically, the girls were with Andrew, acting as his scouts, but he was a friend, was he not?

"I am glad to hear it, though I must say, finding a friend in that dreadful little town is quite an accomplishment." The countess shuddered.

"They will be aboard in time for lift tomorrow, Claire, I hope?" John asked.

"Of course. You may depend upon it."

"And that extraordinary hen?"

Lieutenant van Ness leaned forward. "I beg your pardon, sir? Did you say *hen?*"

"I did. When was the last time you took ship with poultry in your party?" Lord Dunsmuir's question, Claire was quite sure, was merely rhetorical. "But this bird travels with Lady Claire, and woe betide anyone who mistakes her for a meal."

"Does she ride your shoulder, as the parrots do in Nouveau France?" Lieutenant van Ness's eyes twinkled with honest humor, and Claire found herself liking him. What a pity he kept such deplorable company.

"She will if she is forced to, but for the most part, she travels in my hatbox. I lost the hat, alas, somewhere over the eastern part of the Territory."

"I should like to see this bird. I never would have believed a chicken could possess a spirit of adventure." Smiling, the lieutenant addressed himself to his dinner.

Claire did as well, it being the first solid food other than *poh-soh-lay* and the flat bread that she had eaten since she had been ill.

Oh, if only she knew what was happening at the laboratory! But it was miles from here—at the south end of the city, where the railyards were—so she would not have news until Andrew, the girls, and Alaia's sons returned.

Those boys would fit right in at the Vauxhall Gardens cottage, she was certain. They could hardly contain their anticipation at the prospect of another adventure, and had gone with James before their mother could prevent them.

"So if I might inquire, Lord Dunsmuir, what are your plans from here?" James asked, forking fluffy mashed potatoes and gravy into his mouth with appreciation. Perhaps he did not care for the local cuisine as much as others might—and his haggard appearance was due less to emotion than to simple reluctance to eat unfamiliar food.

And then a particular intensity in his eyes caused a *frisson* of alarm down her back. She did not want James knowing their destination. Who knew what he might be capable of, frustrated and infuriated without the means to power the Carbonator?

She opened her mouth to deflect the conversation to safer waters, but the earl forestalled her. "As I said, we lift in the morning, to continue our voyage to Edmonton."

"Edmonton," James murmured. "And the Canadas, I understand, are part of the Empire, under the dominion and laws of our glorious Queen?"

Claire could not imagine why he would state the obvious—he must simply be making dinner conversation for the benefit of their Texican guests.

"Yes, we have a home and many friends there," Lady Dunsmuir put in. "I am looking forward to introducing Claire to society—I am sure she will be the toast of the town."

"It seems a certainty," Lieutenant van Ness said gallantly. "What a pity you are lifting so soon—I would be pleased to show you what rough society we have here."

"It cannot be so rough if you are a representative of it," Claire told him with a smile. "Did you spend much time in the court of the Kaiser, sir?"

He smiled while Fremont guffawed. "There's no putting one over on this young lady, is there?"

Claire suddenly realized why she did not like the man—was it necessary to refer to her in the third person at every opportunity? Did he never make a remark to a woman directly?

"Lady Claire has a good ear," the lieutenant said. "As it happens, I was in the service of Count von Zeppelin himself."

"And is he as remarkable an engineer of airships as I have heard?" Claire asked, unable to tamp her eagerness down to polite dinnertime levels. "When I left, I was particularly interested in the new B-30 model, built for military communications and transport at high speeds."

Fremont guffawed again. He might be rich as Croesus, but he sounded like the donkey in the farm across the river from Gwyn Place.

Lieutenant van Ness did her the courtesy of answering quite seriously. "In fact, a prototype model is at the airfield here. If it were not so late, I would have been honored to give you a tour."

"I saw it on our way in. What is its top speed?"

"Really, Claire," murmured Davina.

"Under steam power, and with a tailwind, it has reached speeds of nearly fifty knots—well in excess of the fastest train in England—"

"—the *Flying Dutchman*," he and Claire said simultaneously.

James glanced at Fremont with a smile of which an automaton might have been proud. "I feel as though I am at a meeting of the Royal Society of Engineers."

"Why, thank you, James," Claire said. "Our voyage may have delayed my plan to attend the university to study engineering, but it has not weakened my intention."

"Claire, shall we leave the gentlemen to their port and cigars?" Lady Dunsmuir rose gracefully, and Claire had no choice but to follow or appear hopelessly forward and discourteous. "We will have coffee and dessert in the lounge."

She settled next to Davina on a soft couch near an expanse of glass that would have given them a view of the prototype airship had it not been dark and the drapes drawn.

"Lieutenant van Ness seemed quite taken with you." Davina offered her a Sevres porcelain cup bearing the Dunsmuir crest picked out in gold. "It is almost a shame we are leaving so soon. But I cannot be altogether sorry." She lowered her voice. "It is only by chance and misfortune that we are here at all, of course. I have asked John to convey my wishes to Captain Hollys that we make for Edmonton with all possible speed. The sooner we are in the Canadas, the happier I will be."

"It has not all been misfortune," Claire said softly, stirring cream into her coffee. "I have met some wonderful people." Without Alice and Alaia, her life would have been the poorer. As it was, she did not know how she was going to say goodbye to Alice, knowing it was unlikely she should ever see her again.

"I am glad to hear it, but weighed in the balance against these few are people like Ned Mose, and Jake's near death, and now poor dear James's own brush with mortality." Davina tasted her coffee and looked up. "He came all that way to ransom you. Are you sure that, whatever your reasons for breaking your engagement, they are valid now?"

"Quite sure." Claire sipped her own coffee.

"But in the face of such devotion—his face when he came in and saw you—"

"Davina, it pains me to speak of him. There are things you do not know."

"There always are," the countess said with a sigh. "It is a great pity. He would be a fine match."

"Socially, perhaps, but in no other way, shape, or form." It was long past time to change the subject. "I am glad we are leaving sooner rather than later. Tell me, do you think this climate is healthy for Will? I hope he is not developing a cough from the aridity and the dust?"

This sent Davina into a lengthy commentary on the health of her beloved boy, and Claire nodded and smiled in all the right places. Not for worlds would she hurt Davina's feelings after she had been so good to her and the children, but some topics were so distasteful that the less time spent with those words upon the tongue, the better.

When the gentlemen came in and settled on the couches for their dessert, there was no more talk of eligible men. Instead, the talk turned to what Claire supposed was inevitable—railroads and the prospects for more of them.

She was content to occupy her couch, back straight, an interested smile upon her lips, while all the time she counted hours and steps and miles, wondering where Andrew and the girls were and whether they had accomplished their mission. In fact, within half an hour she was quite ready to bid her host and hostess goodbye for the evening, and make her way back to the village to wait for news of them.

She had just put her plate down after finishing a dessert that resembled pumpkin pie but certainly was not, when there was a thump on the decks below, and the sound of raised voices.

Claire and Davina both glanced toward the door, and the lieutenant half rose. "Is there some trouble below?"

A shout was his answer, and Lord Dunsmuir and the Chief Steward started for the door at the same time. A scuffle could be heard on the gangway, and then a muffled curse in a voice Claire could swear sounded familiar.

James had risen to his feet as well. "Is that—?"

Three or four men in black coats much like those Claire had seen Andrew wearing in his laboratory appeared in the doorway. "Mr. Fremont, sir!" one of them called.

Between them they held a man who was covered in dust and bruises, his hair flung over his face. His canvas coat appeared to have been dragged along the ground—possibly with him still inside it.

His canvas coat.

Claire started to her feet, but James beat her to it. "Andrew?" he said in tones of utter astonishment. "Stanford, ask your men to release him at once. I know this man."

"What is the meaning of this?" Stanford Fremont demanded. "Can't you see we are at dinner with Lord and Lady Dunsmuir?"

The biggest of them gave Andrew a shove, and he stumbled to his knees. "We thought you'd want to talk to him yourselves, sirs," he said, "seeing as he was trying to steal the power cell right out of the Carbonator. Caught him red-handed, we did, and you know the penalty for thieving here. The only question is, do we shoot him now or wait until dawn?"

Chapter 22

Lizzie kicked the man in the black laboratory coat with all her strength. He howled and his grip loosened for a split second, just long enough for her to tear loose and pound up the gangway. "Lady!" she shrieked. "Help!"

Maggie seized her opportunity, kicked the man in his other shin, and took off after her sister, screeching loud enough to raise the dead.

They burst into the lounge together, only to realize a moment too late that there were more men in black coats—the room was crawling with them—and there, looking like death warmed over, was his nibs himself, the Lady's former fiancé.

Oh woe, the plan was all at sixes and sevens, and now what were they to do?

Maggie dove for the Lady's skirt and clutched it, sobbing in terror that was half real. "Lady, that man grabbed us and they was 'orrible to us and oh, Mr. Malvern is in such trouble!"

The Lady sank to her knees and gathered Maggie and Lizzie into her arms just as the bloke that had tried to hold them ran into the room, red-faced and swearing.

"There!" he shouted. "Mr. Fremont, sir, those two little she-demons were in on it with him. You just leave them to me, sir, and I'll show 'em how to mend their manners. I'll shoot 'em myself."

"You will do no such thing." The freezing tones that could quell even Lizzie on a rampage made a shiver tiptoe down Maggie's back as the Lady rose to her feet. "What is the meaning of this?"

The man gawked at her, then at the big man with the mane of hair groomed so perfectly that it could have been carved like the angels in Westminster Abbey. "Mr. Fremont, sir?"

"Answer the young lady—Baxter, is it? I'd like to know myself why you're wrangling children when you're supposed to be working in my laboratory."

"They ain't children. They's devils. I got bruises coming the size of apples, sir."

"I dislike repeating myself," the Lady said, enunciating so clearly the consonants cut the air. "Why are you manhandling my wards?"

Maggie straightened, but didn't leave off her hold of the Lady, instead slipping both arms around her waist. A comforting hand came down upon her shoulder, and the Lady drew Lizzie close as well.

"Your ... wards?" Baxter didn't look as if he knew whether he was coming or going. "I dunno nothing about that. All I know is that when we captured Malvern here breaking out the power cell, we found these two in the yard outside. Ain't no reason for kids to be there, so they have to be together."

"I believe the children are acquainted with Mr. Malvern, as am I," Lord James said. "I cannot help but think there has been a dreadful misunderstanding."

"Not much to misunderstand," another man said. His moustaches were the size of mice. Maggie stared, wondering if he ever lost his food on its way to his mouth. "This man Malvern was caught thieving, and it looks like these girls were with him. The penalty for thieving in the territories, like I said, is death by a single shot. So I'll ask again—are we doing it now, or at dawn, so he has the services of a padre before he meets his Maker?"

"They," Baxter said, feeling his calf. "Those little demons are going with him. I'll do it myself."

"You will do no such thing," her ladyship said in scandalized tones. "They are only children. And Mr. Malvern is a very good friend of ours, to whom we owe a great debt. I am sure it is as Lord James said—a misunderstanding."

"Andrew, would you like to explain?" his lordship said. "What were you doing at the laboratory? What are you doing here in the Americas at all? The last I saw you, you were coming to an agreement with Ross Stephenson about that device you exhibited at the Crystal Palace."

Mr. Fremont laughed a big laugh that didn't sound a bit as if he thought something was funny. "You're behind the times, Dunsmuir." He slapped his lordship on the back, and when Lord Dunsmuir turned slowly, his eyebrows rising, Mr. Fremont went on oblivious to the fact that his lordship didn't appreciate the familiarity. "That deal's dead in the water. Selwyn here went with the horse that's going to win this race."

Horses? Maybe the man had had a knock on the noggin. He wasn't making a bit of sense.

Mr. Fremont waved an expansive arm. "I understood from James that Malvern had signed off on the whole shebang. Isn't that right, James?"

"Whether he did or he did not is immaterial," his nibs said, smooth as butter. "The fact remains that I own the Carbonator and can do with it as I wish."

"That is *not* the case." Andrew struggled in the grip of the black coats. Mr. Fremont waggled a hand at them and they let him go. He tugged his beaten canvas coat into place while his face reddened with temper. "I am joint owner of that device, and you people stole it out from under me. Ross Stephenson paid earnest money in good faith and James, you reneged on that deal. This entire enterprise is a dishonorable mess from start to finish."

"Is that so?" With two fingers, Fremont dug in the pocket of his fine jacket and pulled out a chased-silver cigarette case. Maggie would bet Lizzie's fingers had twitched at the sight of it. He lit a cigarillo and blew a stream of smoke in Mr. Malvern's face.

Ooh, if that weren't as rude as rude could be!

"So, what, were you planning to take back what you consider your own?"

"It is half mine." He glanced at the Lady. "More than half. Lady Claire is invested in it as well. It cannot be sold—or moved—or duplicated—without our consent. I do not speak for her, but I certainly do not consent."

"Really." Lord James accepted a nasty, stinking cigarillo from Mr. Fremont. "And whose name is on the patent application, might I ask?"

"Yours and mine, of course," Mr. Malvern said.

"Are you quite sure? I believe at this moment it is in Fremont's offices with only mine on it, to be filed in the Santa Fe Office of Engineering as soon as we have the manufacturing process in place."

The Lady's fingers were digging into her shoulder, and Maggie squirmed.

"So you redacted his name as well, James?" she asked. "I am fascinated at the way you treat your friends."

"The real application is in my laboratory," Mr. Malvern snapped. "I don't know what counterfeit you plan to file, but it is not the real patent. That can only be filed in London, with the approval of the Royal Society of Engineers."

"Spoken like a true subject of an irrelevant Empire." Mr. Fremont waved this away as though he were bored to death with the whole subject. "The fact is, you broke into my laboratory with larcenous intent, and assaulted my men in the defense of my property, as Murphy here says. Out here we deal with thieves ourselves. Baxter, Murphy, take Mr. Malvern here to the city lockup and see he has a padre."

"Mr. Fremont, I must protest." The earl stepped in front of the man called Murphy, who had grabbed Mr. Malvern's arm in a grip he couldn't shake. "This man is a subject of the Crown. He cannot be shot. He cannot even be detained without benefit of a hearing by a magistrate. He did no harm. He was most likely examining this device to see that it had come to no grief."

"He had the cowling off and had the power cell half discon- nected," another man put in. "That's more than an examination. Five more minutes and who knows what damage he would have done. Lucky thing Murphy here forgot to take his smokes with him during shift change, and came back to get them."

Murphy dragged Mr. Malvern, kicking and struggling, to the gangway. They all seemed to have forgotten Maggie and Lizzie.

"This is outrageous!" the Lady cried. "You cannot do this! Lieutenant van Ness, do something!"

"Fremont, Lord James—surely this bears looking into," said the man in the slate-blue uniform with the little gold birds on his collar points. "It isn't the Texican way to execute a man before we have all the facts. Especially not a citizen of the Empire."

Mr. Fremont's eyes narrowed, and Maggie pressed closer to the Lady. She'd seen a snake in the Tower Zoo once that had looked just like that. The poor rat they'd put in the cage with it for its dinner hadn't had a ghost of a chance.

Lord James stubbed out his cigarillo in a crystal dish that Maggie knew her ladyship meant for candies. "Let us be calm," he said. "Perhaps I can see a way out of this difficulty."

"I knew you would." Fremont made to clap him on the back, too, but James stepped out of the way. "Let's hear it."

"Since Stanford and I are joint partners in this venture, I be- lieve I can speak for him as well, when I suggest an exchange."

"An exchange?" his lordship said. "A man's life for—what?"

"For a woman's." Lord James smiled at the Lady, who simply stared at him while all the color drained out of her face. "I pro- pose—" He smiled wider at the word. "—that Lady Claire retract the statements she made to me when last we saw one another in London, and reinstate our engagement. Instead of fabricating the Selwyn Kinetick Carbonator immediately, I further propose we continue with our manufacture of enough carbonated coal for a demonstration run to San Francisco, where we will conclude our arrangements with the Royal Kingdom of Spain, and then Claire and I will take ship for Her Majesty's namesake city, Victoria, in the Canadas."

"No," the Lady whispered, but only Lizzie and Maggie were close enough hear her.

"The Canadas being a dominion of the Empire, all Her Majesty's laws apply there, including the age of majority. Lady Claire and I will be married in Victoria, and spend our honeymoon traveling from there to Edmonton, as she had originally planned."

The Lady forced her fingers to release Maggie's and Lizzie's shoulders, and Maggie let out a breath of relief.

"What are you saying, Selwyn?" Fremont boomed. "That I set this man free in exchange for this young lady's hand? What kind of a bargain is that?"

"A fair one, I think." His nibs didn't take his eyes off the Lady for one second. "She and the Carbonator go with us on the demonstration run, safe from the depredations of my former partner, who, I'm afraid, will have to find his own way home— unless he runs afoul of the Rangers."

"This is outrageous," Lord Dunsmuir said. "You can't treat Claire this way. Or Andrew. Or any of us."

"She already said yes to me once," Lord James pointed out. "And in any case, my affairs are none of your business."

His lordship rode right over this insulting observation. "But Claire is under my protection and—"

"Yes, I've seen how effective your protection has been," Lord James said. "So far she has been skyjacked, washed away in a flood, and left for dead. I believe I can keep her at least a little safer than that."

Maggie would never have believed Lord Dunsmuir capable of violence, but she believed it now. Shaking with rage, he turned from Lord James to the Lady.

"Claire? What do you say to this plan?"

Maggie could distinctly feel her trembling, but whether it was from rage or fear, she did not know.

"If I agree to go with you," she said in a voice that only shook a little, "Andrew will go free?"

"Yes."

"And what of the children?"

Lord James's dispassionate gaze swept lower, and Maggie shrank back against the Lady's skirts. "I'm afraid there is no provision on the train for children."

What?

Lizzie's fists clenched. "We go where the Lady goes."

The carpet might have spoken up and said so for all the interest he showed. "The children may stay here with the Dunsmuirs, or find a ship back to London, or set out across the desert in a pram, for all I care. But they will not be coming with us."

"But we're a flock!" Maggie cried. She looked up into the Lady's face. "You can't go wiv 'im and not take us!"

The Lady knelt so that they three were face to face, and spoke so only they could hear. "Would you have Mr. Malvern be executed instead? Because you know perfectly well there is no magistrate or law or any other thing in this wild place that will save him, if they are determined to do it."

"I don't care!"

"But I do," she said softly, and behind her, even through her distress, Maggie saw Mr. Malvern's face sag into lines of despair. "It is in my power to save his life. It may be the only thing I will ever be able to do for him."

"But what about us?" she wailed. "You promised we'd always be together! That wiv that piece of paper, no one could separate us!"

"We will be together, back in England," she said. "I will find a way to contrive it."

"He'll never let you go back." Lizzie's cheeks were wet, and her nose was running. "He'll take you away and we'll never see you again. You know he will."

The Lady shook her head. "Impossible."

"You said this would never happen." Maggie clutched at a straw. "You said you'd never marry him. You have to do what you said!"

"Children oughta be seen and not heard," Fremont remarked to no one in particular, and Maggie burst into tears.

"All right, all right." Mr. Fremont turned to the lieutenant. "Until the happy couple are on their way, maybe the lockup is too severe for a man my new friends are in debt to." He bowed to the Dunsmuirs. "Mr. Malvern will be comfortable in the peace and quiet of a pinnacle cell." Baxter and Murphy's eyes widened, and Maggie's stomach turned over. "I don't want to cause an international incident, now, do I?" He laughed his big laugh.

Maggie sat on the floor like she was only Willie's age, and gave herself up to tears of utter hopelessness.

"I do not know what a pinnacle cell is, but I think Mr. Malvern would be much more comfortable here, among his friends," Lady Dunsmuir said over the sound of her weeping. "May he not spend the night aboard the *Lady Lucy*?"

The big man smiled and directed his reply to his lordship. "Well now, that would be a real fine plan, but I don't want to put you good folks out." He held up a hand as Lord Dunsmuir began to protest that it would be no trouble at all. "No, no, I'll take responsibility for him. It would be a terrible shame if some … misunderstanding … occurred and the *Lady Lucy* continued on her voyage with my prisoner aboard, wouldn't it? My sense of justice would oblige me to ask the lieutenant here to mobilize his Rangers in that speedy vessel moored next door. In the chase, it would be a terrible thing for your family to be put at risk of being shot down."

"Sir, you speak in fabrications and impossibilities," his lordship said through stiff lips. "I don't know which is worse—the fact that you and Selwyn both are ruthless blackguards, or the fact that I did not recognize it until now."

"Lieutenant, please," the Lady pleaded, turning to him. "Surely you can see that this is unacceptable."

The man in the uniform took her hand in both of his, but his eyes had gone hollow. Maggie could see that it required an effort of will for the Lady not to pull away. "Your friend will come to no harm on a pinnacle cell. He'll be far more comfortable there than at the lockups, I'll guarantee you that, and we will release him once the demonstration party and the *Lady Lucy* are away."

"Claire, this is absurd," Mr. Malvern said desperately. "You cannot even think of this. Please. I got myself into this—I will get myself out without you sacrificing yourself for me."

Murphy batted him across the face with one beefy hand. "Shut up, you. Save your noise for the vultures."

The Lady's lips trembled as she asked Mr. Fremont, "What exactly is a pinnacle cell?"

"Why, simply one of those spires of rock that protrude out of the ground here and there about our city. They are seven hundred feet high, and once a man is imprisoned on the top of one, he cannot escape—not unless he wishes to save the executioner the cost of a bullet."

The Lady's face could not pale any further. It turned gray. "And will you guarantee his safety?"

"I will," the lieutenant said. "Justice is swift here, but it is justice. No harm will come to him while he's in our custody."

How could he make a promise like that? It seemed to Maggie that all a man would have to do was roll over in his sleep, and so much for their harmless custody.

The lieutenant signaled Murphy to take his hands off Mr. Malvern. "If you will accompany me, sir, I will escort you off the ship."

Maggie had never seen a look quite like the one exchanged between the Lady and Mr. Malvern. One part fear, one part apology ... and two parts despair.

The party disembarked and her ladyship retired to her room in tears. His lordship followed her, so angry he could hardly speak.

Lord James approached the Lady and she held up a hand. "No closer, James, or I will spit in your face. How dare you?"

"It seems you dare quite a lot for my former partner. It is very touching. I look forward to the day when I inspire such emotion."

Maggie caught Lizzie's eye and cut her eyes toward the serving pantry. As the Lady faced his nibs, they drifted toward it a step at a time.

"I saved your life."

"And now I am saving his. One would think you would be grateful."

"I'm afraid you inspire no such tender emotions. I cannot fathom why you do not find another woman who cannot see through your falsity and who does not hate you with every fiber of her being."

He smiled at her, though it did not extend to his eyes. "When are you going to understand that you are mine, Claire? You promised yourself to me, and Selwyns do not release what is theirs."

"I am not yours. I will never be. I will throw myself from that train first."

"Then I will have to keep a careful eye on you. Beginning now. You will accompany me back to my hotel, where I will have a room prepared for you. An inside room, preferably without windows. And in the morning, after I see the *Lady Lucy* lift, we will be on our way to San Francisco. I am sure you will waste no time in boarding the train, so that dear Andrew may have his freedom."

The Lady's jaw flexed as she ground her teeth. "May I collect my things from my cabin?"

"Certainly. I shall ascertain that it has no porthole, and then I shall wait outside the door."

"And may I return to my friends to collect my belongings there?"

"How very careless of you to leave your property behind. I am afraid not. There will be no time." He indicated that she should precede him down the corridor.

No one paid the least attention to Maggie and Lizzie. Which is why it was so easy to slip out of the serving pantry, down the gangway, and out into the night.

Chapter 23

They hadn't gone two steps when a thin, wiry shadow detached itself from behind the wheel housings of the embarkation tower.

"Mopsies."

"Jake!" The last they'd seen of him, he'd been telling Mr. Malvern what the Lady was up to. Then they'd heard a sound and he'd dived behind a huge machine with arms as big as a building, evidently used for moving things on and off trains. "Where are Luis and Alvaro?"

"Hightailed it back to the village. Ent nothin' they could do to help, and getting' caught wouldn't do us any good. Wot 'appened?"

Catching him up as they went, they ran deeper into the shadows until they were on the edge of the airfield near where the steambus would stop.

"D'you mean t' tell me the Lady is goin' off with that blackguard? To San Francisco? Is she mad?"

"She's tryin' to save Mr. Malvern's life," Maggie panted, "but that devil's goin' to hurt her somehow, I know it."

"Simply lookin' across the breakfast table at 'im would 'urt," Lizzie observed.

"We 'ave to stop it," Jake said, but this was so obvious that neither girl bothered to answer. "Hey. Where's our Tigg?"

"On *Lady Lucy*, I think." But Maggie did not know. "Liz? You see 'im?"

"He was supposed to go wiv the Lady. If 'e's anywhere, 'e's in the engine room."

Jake stopped dead. "You silly gumpies. They're goin' t' lift tomorrow, ent they? We can't leave wivout knowin' for sure where 'e is."

In the distance, the steambus huffed and chuffed its way toward them. Lizzie planted her fists on her hips.

"He's a fair sight better off than we are. The Lady's sendin' 'erself to the noose wiv that rascal, Mr. Malvern's to be trapped on a pinnacle 'e's like to roll off of before daybreak, we're standing in the road miles from anywhere, and where's Tigg? Prob'ly tucked up nice and safe in 'is bunk, wiv a good breakfast waitin' for 'im come morning."

The conveyance spewed steam everywhere as it pulled up next to them, and they clambered aboard. Jake grumbled and grumped, but really, Lizzie had the right of it. Someday soon they would all be together again, but if anyone had to leave with the Dunsmuirs on their lovely ship, Tigg would be the happiest to do so.

They, on the other hand, had to think of something, and quick.

They would have got to the village sooner if their steambus hadn't had a ticket collector on it. They were forced to jump down two stops ahead of the end of the line, which meant they had to ride shank's mare for more than a mile. It was another two miles out to the village, and then the sick-inducing spiral rock stair ... by the time Maggie staggered onto the flat top of the mesa, she was gasping for breath and every muscle felt as though it was made of iron.

Lizzie and Jake hadn't fared much better. They rested for a moment at the top of the stair, neither one inclined to rib the other about their powers of endurance. In fact, when Lizzie finally spoke, it wasn't about the climb at all. "D'you think she'll really go through wiv it?"

Jake chucked a rock into the whispering darkness. Several long moments later, they heard a distant *clack*. "I think she'll fob 'im off wi' what 'e wants to 'ear, and then choose 'er moment to scarper."

"He's going to lock 'er in a room. We ought to spring 'er like we sprung Doctor Craig out of Bedlam."

"The lightning rifle," Maggie said suddenly. "She didn't take it to dinner. Said it weren't proper. That's why she wanted to come back 'ere."

"He said no." Lizzie chucked her own rock. "We gonna try to get it to 'er again? It worked last time."

"That train's going to be crawlin' wiv black coats," Jake said. "If 'e's got 'er locked in a room, then under guard when she gets on the train, we won't stand a snowball's chance."

"We could get on the train now. Tonight." That was our Lizzie. Always thinking.

"What train?" That was our Jake, always finding the holes in a perfectly sound plan. Which was good, Maggie supposed, but it did tend to be demoralizing. "There must be a dozen trains in Stanford Fremont's railyard alone. We got no way to know if they're goin' on one o' his, or on a proper one, where you pay a fare and all."

The problem seemed insurmountable.

"Maggie? Lizzie?" Alice's voice floated out of the darkness between the square mud buildings. No matter that she looked like a miner or a stevedore half the time, Maggie liked her voice. It was like honey with toast crumbs in it, and just as sweet.

Alice!

"Alice will know what to do." Maggie scrambled to her feet. Her legs felt wobbly, but at least they'd got moving again.

"Aye, best person to fox a villain is another villain." Goodness. Jake actually sounded like he might be smiling.

"Our Alice ent no villain, even if she's a villain's daughter," Maggie told him. "She saved our lives, out there on that blasted velogig in the middle of the desert."

"I know, I were there, remember? An' I might've had a bit to do with savin' yer cantankerous hide."

He *was* smiling. Maggie took heart.

In the little mud cube that was Alaia's home, the boys were back and she was feeding them prodigious amounts of black beans and cheese and those little green chiles that she fried on a flat piece of iron. Maggie still could not fathom how they could eat the little beggars with apparent enjoyment while tears and sweat streamed down their faces.

Alaia had them seated and was dishing up grub in a matter of moments.

"I hope you plan to tell me what happened," Alice said urgently, "or you'll hear a scream that'll reach clear over to Santa Fe. Claire gets all gussied up to go have a fancy dinner with the man she's not engaged to, and she doesn't come back. Mr. Malvern goes to steal the power cell and he doesn't come back. What in tarnation is going on?"

So they told her, in fits and gulps between great mouthfuls of food. Raiding was hungry work, particularly when you failed miserably at it and came home empty-handed and hopeless.

Alice stopped eating right about the time Maggie said *pinnacle cell.*

She put her bit of flatbread down, as if she'd lost her appetite. "They're going to put him on a pinnacle?"

Maggie nodded. "That Ranger lieutenant said 'e'd be safe, but 'ow can he when all 'e 'as to do is roll over to be killed?"

"And people called my pa inhuman. At least he never used Spider Woman for such a thing." She took a breath and looked away from her flatbread as if it made her ill. "Mr. Malvern'll have to kick aside the previous prisoner. I hope he's got a strong stomach."

Maggie stopped chewing.

"What do you mean?" Lizzie demanded. "Don't one person get a pinnacle to himself?"

"One live person does," Alice said grimly. "They don't bother to clear off the dead ones."

It took a moment for the macabre picture to sink in.

"That Ranger man," Lizzie said. "He promised Mr. Malvern would be let go soon's the Lady were on the train an' *Lady Lucy* were in the sky."

"He may have promised that," Alice conceded. "He may even have meant it. But that's what they do with the really bad criminals. The lucky ones get a single shot. But the ones they really want to punish—murderers, kidnappers, extortioners, and the like—they put them in a pinnacle cell. They sit up there and you ain't ever heard anything more pathetic than those men up under the broiling sun, callin' for mercy."

"What if you tried to help one?" Jake asked.

"You'd be shot, same as if you tried to spring someone out of lockup."

"But if they can get 'em up there, they can get 'em down again," Lizzie objected. "We'll just steal whatever device they use and—"

"—and you'd be stuck up there with him," Alice finished. "They use a balloon with a puncture in it. It has just enough lift to get 'em up there, but if they stay in it, it'll outgas. The fall kills 'em. Some stay in the basket, of course. The optimistic ones, they climb out, hoping for mercy or help." Sadness and hopelessness pulled at her mouth, turning its corners down.

And suddenly Maggie, who left the losing of tempers up to Lizzie as a general rule, lost hers with a vengeance.

"So you're just gonna leave Mr. Malvern on his pinnacle to die?" she demanded, pushing away what was left of her food. "Yer just gonna give up and wait for the vultures to come and finish 'im off like they nearly did us?"

"Of course not. Sit down, you little fireball. We have to think of something that's not gonna get us shot."

"Think!" Maggie waved madly at the little mud house and beyond. "We got everything we need—we don't need to think. We need to act, before everyone in our flock either dies or gets scattered so's we can't ever find 'em!"

"And what would you suggest, Little Miss Ingenuity?"

Maggie didn't know what *engine-ooity* was, but she knew a solution when it was floating right outside. "You silly gumpus, we got the *Stalwart Lass!* And we got eighteen different kinds o' nasty capsacious chile peppers right here and—" She flung an arm out and Jake ducked. "—in Jake's brain we got the recipe for gaseous capsaicin."

With his quick pickpocket's fingers, Jake was already gathering up the raw chiles on the flat table stone. Lizzie pitched in to help him.

On the other side of the table, Alaia nodded with approval. "Spider Woman's spirit moves with the power of the wind, and we must obey or lose that which we value most."

Maggie saw the moment the penny dropped and Alice figured out exactly how to save Mr. Malvern's life.

Her smile was so big, it was almost as if the sun had risen, right there in the room.

Chapter 24

The hotel, as it turn out, possessed no rooms without windows, but it did have the next best thing. James gazed with some satisfaction at the elegant whorls of ironwork covering the windows, securely anchored with iron bolts to the sandstone outside.

"It's to keep them thieving Indians from ransacking the rooms," Stanford Fremont said, chewing the end of his cigarillo and rocking back on his boot heels. "I trust your lady will be comfortable?"

Claire did not dignify this with a reply. She was firmly on the side of the Indians, and the moment she had even the slenderest chance, she would be ransacking these rooms herself for a tool or implement with which to get out.

She seated herself on a chair upholstered in moss-green velvet and inclined her head at her male visitors in a way that clearly indicated she wished them to leave.

Stanford Fremont winked at James. "I'll leave you two to say your good nights. I'll be in the bar downstairs if you'd like a nightcap, James." Claire could hear his booming laughter all the way down the stairs to the lobby.

Gazing at a wall sconce of chased glass, she prepared to wait in silence until James decided he wanted that nightcap.

"I know you are angry with me." He strolled to the mantel and rested an elbow on it, though the grate was cold and the night too warm for a fire. "But I want you to believe I am acting for the best."

She could sit here until she froze him out, or if she must tolerate his presence, perhaps the wiser course would be to attempt to discover something useful.

"Whose 'best' do you mean?"

"Why, our own, of course. I have nothing against Andrew. I have no idea what he's doing here, apart from some harebrained plot to sabotage the Carbonator. Is he really so angry that I chose to partner with Fremont instead of Ross Stephenson that he would harm his own device to prevent us using it?"

"I rather think that if he is indeed angry, it is because you fled the country without telling him of your plans, or including him in them."

"Oh, I would have. There simply wasn't time. The Texicans are an impatient lot, as you may have noticed. They make up their minds quickly, and their justice is equally swift."

"Some justice."

"This is a lawless land, Claire. They don't call it the Wild West for nothing. If one is to hold onto one's possessions, one must act decisively to prevent others from taking undue advantage."

There was no point in discussing Andrew with him. She must be sensitive to the direction of the wind and direct the conversational course as she would the velogig.

"Does Mr. Fremont hold extensive possessions in these Territories?"

"Indeed he does. I saw at once that his vision for the Carbonator extended far beyond that of Ross Stephenson. Why, one could fit all of England into one tiny corner of the Texican Territory, and Stanford Fremont owns a good chunk of it. The potential for profit is much greater here—especially when one looks west, to the Royal Kingdom of Spain."

"And the Selwyn holdings could use an infusion of that … potential."

"They can indeed. Selwyn Place is practically falling down around my ears, and there are improvements I wish to make to the farms and machinery that are simply too costly without an investment like this one to produce an income stream."

Claire wondered how many years of mismanagement it had taken for an estate as old as Selwyn Place to fall into such disrepair.

"Mr. Fremont seems like a most sagacious businessman," she observed. "I am sure the Texican government relies heavily on men of vision to bring the country forward in true progress."

"I thought you didn't like him."

She lifted a shoulder in a shrug. "Perhaps not at first. But it seems he may play some part in my future, so I am willing to reassess his qualities."

James laughed. "And now you are playing a part, my dear. This ladylike compliance is most unlike you."

Perhaps she had, as they said at cards, overplayed her hand.

"Making observations about the character of others is hardly compliance," she replied. "I am still most upset with you for removing me from my friends."

"Ah, but I don't want to lose you. You are a young lady of resources, and I have learned to my chagrin not to underestimate you." He met her gaze in the mirror. "It is one of the qualities I most admire in you."

"I cannot see why, when it has played against you nearly every time."

"I live in hope that some day you will look upon me with a softer eye. In the meantime, I enjoy your spirit—and take appropriate precautions."

If she dwelled on that for more than a moment, she would lose her temper—and she was determined to expend no more emotion on him. Besides, the sooner he left the room, the sooner she could search it for a weapon. She had her ivory hair pick, of course, but short of stabbing him through the eye with it, it was not very useful at present. She had not saved his life only to murder him now.

As if he were a stage savant, he said, "You saved me from a dreadful death in an airship wreck, Claire, at some risk to your own life. Surely you must harbor some feeling for me deep in your heart?"

At last she met his gaze directly, not through the medium of the mirror. "If I did in the beginning, I am afraid you hope for too much now. James, you cannot belittle me in public, steal my future, and imprison me without annihilating those feelings you desire so much."

He shook his head. "If I did any of those things, it was only to fit you for the place you will hold in society. You must trust me to know such things better than you—I have nearly ten years more experience in the world."

She could have retorted that the depth of her experience more than made up for the length of his, but she did not. Instead, she folded her hands on her blue merino skirt. "Speaking of experience, what are your plans upon our arrival in San Francisco?"

He crossed to the other chair, hitched up the knees of his trousers, and sat. She smothered her disappointment and impatience and gazed at him with placid interest.

"The things I have been hearing about that city would amaze you, Claire. It is built on seven hills, like Rome, and there is a World Exhibition planned there next year by El Rey himself, ruler of the Royal Kingdom of Spain and the Californias. They say it will rival anything Her Majesty or the French have ever built."

"Rival the Crystal Palace? Or the tower designed by Monsieur Eiffel to moor *Persephone*? This El Rey must be very ambitious."

"Stanford has seen the plans, and he says they are very ambitious indeed. In fact, that is part of our partnership here in the Territories. If the Selwyn Kinetick Carbonator proves to be all I believe it is, we will not only have an exhibit hall that can hold the chamber, but an entire moving train inside it to demonstrate the coal's longevity as well."

"Heavens."

"You may well look astonished. And of course, to manufacture chambers and other devices based on its power cell will make us some of the richest men in the world. There is no end to what we might accomplish."

"It is the cell, then, that is the key." She made a rueful moue of her lips. "And here I thought it was my movable truss."

He chuckled and reached over to pat her hand. She marveled at her own self-control in not leaping to her feet and swatting him.

"The truss is a necessary component, and as my wife, I will make sure you are properly credited with it on the patent we file here."

When she looked away, he misread her. "I see that you are tired, and no wonder. Your skin still bears the depredations of sun and wind. You will enjoy the journey to San Francisco, I know—especially since there is no way to expose your skin to the weather unless you stand on the viewing platform at the back of the train. By the time we reach the coast, your complexion will be back to its usual loveliness."

She had never aspired to loveliness, preferring intelligence instead. However, she allowed her shoulders to droop, and offered him a wan smile.

"Until the morning, then." He rose, tipped his beaver hat to her and would have leaned over to kiss her, but she got up and moved her valise to the chair he had occupied. At the door, he said, "Our train leaves at dawn. I will have the maid wake you."

"Thank you, James. Good night."

"Good night, Claire."

The door closed behind him.

The lock turned over.

She leaped for the window, tugging at the iron scrollwork, looking for a weakness. Finding none, she tried the hearth next, flinging a towel down and lying on her back to peer up the flue, but it was merely a stovepipe masquerading as a chimney. Frustrated, she went into the water closet, but short of turning into a trout and swimming down the hole, there was no escape there either.

She tapped the walls, but no hidden doors revealed themselves. She lifted the carpet, but the floors were solid, with not even a crack between the heavy planks of dark, adzed wood.

Fuming, she sat at last upon the bed. It was clear there was no hope of escape tonight. She would have to do so on the way to the train, then. Or on the train itself. Trains had plenty of windows and doors through which to slip.

Since she could not do what she must, she would do what she could.

She took the longest, hottest bath of her life, washed her hair with creamy, scented soap, and washed all the clothes and underthings she had with her. There was a heated drying rail—wonder of wonders—in this godforsaken outpost, so everything would be dry by morning.

Then, clothed, clean, and with her mind honed to sharpness by fear and loss, she would escape at the very first opportunity.

Because she would not get a second.

Chapter 25

Maggie woke to the gentle touch of Alaia's hand upon her cheek.

"It is nearly dawn," she said. "Gather up your things, for Spider Woman will pass her shuttle many times in your life's pattern before I see you again."

"She will? How do you know? But we will see you again, won't we?" Lizzie always came wide awake, with none of the sleepy stretching and curling Maggie did.

"I feel that we will, little daughters of the air."

Maggie smiled and stretched up her arms for a hug. "I like that. Thank you for everything."

Alaia smelled of wood smoke and warm grass and the capsaicin they had extracted from the chiles the night before, and her lips on Maggie's forehead were soft as she gave her a mother's kiss. "Come. I have given your little hen enough corn for many days, and she is safe in her box. Alice is waiting."

The sky was a clear bell of ink over their heads, cold with the promise of frost before too many days passed. But on the hems of it burned a gray light that was rapidly strengthening to a shine of pure pewter.

Maggie hefted the lightning rifle, rolled in a wool rug with a lightning pattern woven into it—Alaia possessed a sense of humor—and the weaver's clever fingers passed a wide knotted sash around her that hugged the bundle close against her back.

"Remember, daughter. Should you need a rope, merely tug these knots. The thread is thin, but I have woven metal into it. It will not break."

Lizzie picked up a rucksack filled with food, Maggie collected Rosie's hatbox—the hen's head poking out and tracking their movements with interest—and they followed Alaia outside, where Jake was waiting for them.

"'Ow we getting to the ship?"

Her bow tethered to the pinnacle of stone that was her mooring mast, the *Stalwart Lass* rode serenely on the updraft not twenty yards off, but in between was a drop at least as high as the top of Big Ben.

"I 'ope yer recovered from last night," Jake said, adjusting his own rucksack of food. "We got to go down the stone stair on this side and up inside that pinnacle. See the hatchway?"

Maggie groaned, gave Alaia a final kiss, waved to her boys, who lounged against the door eating their breakfasts, and plunged down the stair.

When she emerged at the top of the pinnacle opposite, legs aching and lungs aching, Alice was waiting on the gangway, utterly heedless of the drop directly below her feet. "Careful, now. That's it, don't look down. And right through here. Well done, Maggie."

The gondola of the *Lass* was much smaller than that of *Lady Lucy*. It held the wheel and the instruments, and a speaking horn protruded from one wall, but there were no control panels, and no gears to signal changes in engine speed to the stern, because the engine was right behind it. A person only need shout to give a command.

Alice closed the hatch. Jake chucked his rucksack on the floor and took up a station next to the navigation charts and the huge viewing glass as if he belonged there.

"Nine, full reverse," Alice said, and Maggie jumped nearly a foot as behind her, a gleaming brass automaton took hold of the gear levers and began to work them.

"Seven and eight, stand by to close vents." Two more automatons moved stiffly to obey.

"Cor," Lizzie breathed. "That's 'ow they flew the ship wiv only two in the crew. The rest of 'em's them automatons."

"What should we do, Alice?"

Alice spun the wheel, and the *Stalwart Lass* floated up and over the mesa, where down below, Luis and Alvaro waved their flatbread in farewell.

"It's going to take us a few minutes to find out what pinnacle they're holding him on," she said. "We don't have much light to see by, but that means they won't see much of us, either." She straightened the ship's course, and through the viewing glass—pocked with bullet holes—Maggie could see the city dead ahead, lights beginning to come on in some of its windows.

"I want you girls to go with Four and Six here, and station yourselves in the bombing bays, one in each fuselage. I can give you some orders through the speaking horn, but it'll be up to you to keep them from shooting at us."

"Aye, Cap'n."

Alice grinned. "I suppose I am, aren't I? I kinda like the sound of it." She handed each of them a big burlap sack that clinked in a most ominous way. "Off with you, now. We'll be overhead in a few minutes and I don't want to give them a lot of warning. Leave Rosie there, on that hatch. And don't forget to use the safety lines up top."

The racket that old engine was making, Maggie didn't see much hope of approaching undiscovered. But she and Lizzie had a job to do, and if she'd learned anything since Snouts had allowed them into the gang, it was that each person had their part. If you didn't do your part, it put everyone else in danger.

And this raid was touch and go to start with.

She and Lizzie emerged from the top hatch and when the automaton called Four began the climb up the ladder into the starboard fuselage—this one seemed to be an earlier model, and its legs were articulated backward, like those under their walking coop—she clipped a waving safety line to her belt and handed one to Lizzie. The wind whipped at their braided hair and sawed through their dresses. "Good shooting," Lizzie shouted, and Maggie nodded the same back. Then she followed Four—who had not bothered with a safety line—up the ladder and into the bombing bay.

It held no bombs, which was something of a disappointment. But Four braced himself—itself?—against a strut and Maggie looked down past the rack where bombs might have been, down … down into whistling, empty air.

The ground floated past seven hundred feet below her boots, covered in the square reddish-brown buildings all laid out in neat, dusty rows, like cakes in an abandoned bakery-shop window.

And then they drifted over the first pinnacle cell.

Maggie gasped and clapped a hand to her mouth, rearing back from the bay and fetching up next to Four, who might as well have been a metal strut himself for all the response he made. The coffee she had bolted down just before they'd lifted rose in her throat, and she swallowed hard.

A skeleton, dry and bleached and horribly human, lay on the flat top of the pinnacle, the bones of one arm extending out and the little bones of its fingers hanging off the edge, as if the poor sod had tried to wave someone down in his last moments.

Maggie gulped cold air. She must not faint. She must not throw up. She must do her part.

"All right up there?" came Alice's voice through the horn.

"Aye," Maggie managed. A squawk in the depths of the horn, she assumed, had come from Lizzie.

"Say a prayer for the poor devil. It helps."

Doing her part would help more. It would be downright satisfying, in fact. Maggie ordered her stomach to behave, and took up her position next to Four.

When the next pinnacle passed under her boots, she nearly averted her gaze, and then realized the man was still alive. He lay face down, one hand beating the rock in a steady rhythm. The light had strengthened now so that she could see color—the dark red pool of drying blood beneath that pounding hand.

Oh dear. *Courage*, she heard the Lady say in her memory. *Courage and good cheer, Maggie.*

Well, she could not manage the one, but she could certainly try for the other. "Courage," she said in bracing tones to Four.

He did not respond.

Right, then. She was on her own.

The clattering drone of the *Lass*'s steam engine changed pitch, and Maggie knew beyond doubt that Alice had seen Mr. Malvern's pinnacle.

"Look sharp, ladies," came her voice. "We've been spotted. Seems like they were expecting some kind of rescue—though maybe not from this angle."

Maggie doubted they expected anything like them at all—how could there be another airship flown by a girl who'd probably not even seen twenty summers, a boy who'd come back from the dead, a pair of nearly eleven-year-olds, half a dozen automatons, and a hen in a hatbox?

Below, a shot rang out, and she flinched, expecting the bullet to tear through the fuselage and strike her where she stood. But it did not hit the ship at all. Instead, Alice's laugh came rat-a-tat through the horn.

"They're gonna have to break out something more serious than a sixgun with a three-hundred-yard range if they want to scare us."

"I dunno, it worked up 'ere," Maggie muttered.

Never mind. Concentrate. Do your part.

And then she sucked in a breath of air that chilled her lungs, but the sight was so grand that she hardly felt it.

Mr. Malvern!

He clung to the top of what was surely the smallest pinnacle of them all. If the other poor blokes had had enough flat space to spread themselves out, then they had it good. Mr. Malvern had only enough to sit on with his feet drawn up. It was cruel—inhuman. A man could not sleep, nor stretch, nor do anything but sit or stand—and once unconsciousness finally claimed him, nothing would keep him from slipping off the side and falling to his death.

"This is 'ow you keep yer word, eh, Mr. Gold Birds?" she snarled. "Guarantee 'is safety, will you?" The only thing she'd guarantee was that the Lady would blast him to bits if she ever saw him again.

"Girls!" came Alice's voice, urgently. "We got company to port—look sharp, Lizzie!"

Down below, an enormous engine with as many arms as a spider or an octopus lumbered into view at the base of the pinnacle. Maggie recognized it at once—Jake had hidden behind it not eight hours before. In the open chamber at the top of it stood at least eight men—one to operate each arm—every one with his eyes trained upward.

An arm ratcheted back and Maggie's eyes widened as she realized what was in the bucket at the end of it. In the next moment, the arm gave a great heave and flung a boulder as big as Alaia's house straight at them.

It struck the pinnacle fifty feet below where Mr. Malvern clung, and Maggie heard him cry out as the spire of stone shuddered and cracked.

Below, men began to scream.

A flash in the air—the tinkle of glass far below—more screams.

Three of the engine's arms fell idle, whatever their purpose had been abandoned as their operators shrieked under the assault of the gaseous capsaicin, and attempted to scramble free.

"Well done, Lizzie!" she shouted, though she had no idea if her twin could hear her.

"My stars, that's a nasty trick," came Alice's voice. "I guess that makes us vicious rabble—or a criminal gang, maybe. Look sharp, girls, it's got five arms left. Jake, stand by to lower the basket."

This time Maggie did not wait for an arm to reveal its weaponry. She threw down the glass globe full of its crippling liquid, and the aim that had not failed her with stone and brick did not fail her now. An arm with a giant grappling hook—one from which an entire cargo car might have hung on a mighty chain—halted in midair, touching the pinnacle as softly as a woman touching a child's cheek.

The gondola obscured Maggie's view of the *Lass*'s basket, but from the encouraging sound of Mr. Malvern's shouting, he was able to see what they were about.

Boom!

Maggie staggered. "We're hit!" she shrieked to Four, who still did not reply.

"No, we're not. Steady on, girls. Seems they've got a few Canton chemists roped into this. That was an exploding rocket. Maggie, watch it—one more of those and we'll be landing on this pinnacle ourselves."

The Canton chemists looked like dolls from this height, but even so Maggie could see the chains looped from one to another.

"I'm sorry!" she shouted to the poor devils before she lofted another globe, and winced when, moments later, it shattered all over the cannon they were using to launch them. Men spilled over like ninepins, writhing. She shouted another apology as if they could actually hear her, and threw another one as a second crew ran into to replace the first.

The great engine, dragging four of its arms, backed up.

"They're giving up!" she yelled.

"Maggie! Fire!"

"But they're—"

And then she saw what they meant to do. The engine growled and seemed to gather itself—and then it picked up a train car with two of its arms.

It had cracked the spire of basalt the first time. One more strike and it would shatter, raining rock down upon the poor suffering Cantons chained to that cannon, and burying Mr. Malvern in the wreckage.

"Lizzie!" she shrieked. "One—two—three!"

She flung the last globe and saw another fly from the opposite bay. Winking in the sun, they fell, and shattered dead in the center of the chamber where four of the men cranked the levers and gears with mad precision.

Gaseous capsaicin formed a green cloud of agony, and Maggie shouted, "I'm out! If 'e's not in the basket now 'e's a goner!"

Not five seconds later, Alice hollered, "Winch, Jake, fast as you can! Seven, Eight—*up ship!*"

Someone had roused the poor Cantons, who were now tracking their course with the mouth of their cannon tilted skyward. Sandbags rained down among them and they dove for cover.

The *Stalwart Lass* fell straight up into the sunrise ... and freedom.

Chapter 26

Mr. Stanford Fremont, as might be expected, owned the train on which they were to travel. It departed from the railyard at whose laboratory Andrew had been apprehended shortly after dawn, steaming due west away from the rising sun.

Claire had not had a single opportunity to give James or the infernal black coats the slip. During every moment, he accompanied her, and when she required the use of the ladies' powder room, he produced a female black coat to attend her there as well.

"No offense, ma'am," the woman said. "But I got orders to wait in here with you."

"None taken." If she were pleasant and civil and utterly lady-like, perhaps they might let down their guard for just the second she needed to run. "We all have our obligations."

"Thank you, ma'am. I appreciate your forbearance."

"Are you to accompany me all the way to San Francisco?" she inquired as she washed her hands at the shining copper sink in the waiting lounge before they boarded.

"Yes, ma'am." The woman tucked a strand of hair into her Gibson coiffure, a new style that seemed enormously popular among the Texicans—perhaps for its sheer bouffance. "With what they're paying me to watch—er, attend you, I can send my kids, Kate and Jeremy, to the city school for a year."

"Well, then, I assure you I shall be as little trouble as possible."

They issued out onto the platform, where the train waited, steam hissing out of the wheels and pistons of the locomotive, and porters bustling this way and that to load luggage. Down at the very end, a small crane hefted the crate containing the Selwyn Kinetick Carbonator into the caboose.

The woman gazed at her, her brows slightly knit. "You ain't a bit like Mr. Fremont said."

Claire hardly dared ask, but the temptation was too great. "What did he say?"

"He said you're a great heiress and you're leading Lord Selwyn—"

"Lord James. Lord Selwyn would be his father."

"—Lord James a merry dance. You've broken his heart so many times that he's finally had to carry you off before your enraged father can stop the wedding."

A laugh bubbled up out of Claire before she could remember she was supposed to be civil and ladylike. "My father would need to be enraged indeed to climb out of his grave to do so."

The woman's eyes widened.

"It is quite true that I am here against my will, and you are obligated to see that I stay. However, I am neither an heiress nor Lord James's fiancée, much as he would like to think so."

"But the carrying off part? That's true?"

"Quite true." Down the platform, James and Fremont were coming toward them.

"Why, those rascals," the woman said in scandalized tones. "It's one thing to assist in an elopement, but it's quite another to aid in a kidnapping. What am I to do?"

They were almost in earshot now.

"I shall not hold it against you." Claire held out a hand. "I am Lady Claire Trevelyan, of River Cottage, Vauxhall Gardens, London."

"Tessie Short, of Sand Street, Santa Fe."

"Do give the impression you are restraining me," Claire suggested.

Tessie's workworn hand slid around her wrist. She had a grip like iron, which under any other circumstances would have given Claire pause. But the frown had not left her forehead, which was a good sign.

A lady of integrity, then.

The stuff of which allies were made.

James's gaze took in Tessie's hand, though they stood close together to screen it from passersby. "That will be all, Mrs. Short, thank you," he said, and offered his arm to Claire.

"Welcome aboard the Silver Queen," Fremont said proudly, and led them up a set of steps into the most luxuriously appointed lounge car Claire had ever seen. Even the train on which Ross Stephenson had tested the carbonated coal did not look like this.

Velvet covered every possible surface, even the walls, which were chased in a hunting pattern of horses and hounds. What was not velvet was mahogany and teak, and on top of every surface were metals: copper, tin, brass—inlaid in the wood, forming the trim, decorating every possible corner and curve, ceiling, wainscoting, and window.

One could go utterly mad trying to force the senses to take it all in.

Beyond the lounge car was a dining car, and beyond that, a smoking car saturated in the smell of the cigarillos Fremont favored. A library was a welcome respite—books covered every wall and surface there, too, but somehow the mind did not shudder away from those as it did the chaos of the lounge.

Disappointment settled heavily upon her when she reached to take down a volume and discovered the entire bookcase to be a false front.

"This one's real," he said heartily, indicating the glass-fronted shelves that ran under the window frame. "Feel free to read what you like—as long as you like books on engineering!" Another hearty laugh with his head thrown back, which meant he missed the keen glance Claire bestowed on the titles as they passed.

One shelf of the sane and rational. An oasis in a wilderness of ostentation and sheer vanity.

There were a number of sleeping compartments beyond the entire car designated as Fremont's sole domain. Claire and Mrs. Short were to be housed in the second to last car, immediately before the caboose, which suited Claire admirably. The farther she was from that lounge, the better she would feel—though the sleeping compartment, alas, had its share of velvet as well.

"We'll expect you for breakfast in fifteen minutes," Fremont told her and James in the corridor outside. "Feel free to wash up if you like—there's hot and cold running water in every car. Only the best, eh, Selwyn?"

Laughing his donkey laugh, he went away down the corridor, swaying slightly with the motion of the train.

Claire inclined her head to James and stepped into her compartment, closing the door firmly behind her.

The outside lock clicked.

She stood there a moment, fuming. No, a display of temper and pounding upon the gleaming panels would net her nothing except a closer watch. For the moment, she must channel her emotion into examining her situation.

The window was large and surrounded by a cowling that did not look like that of the windows on the other cars. In a moment she saw why. The window had once tilted open, but it did so no longer. It had been soldered in place, and the decorative brass trim fitted over it.

Heavens. Someone must have been up late cutting off this means of escape.

Well, the other windows had not been augmented in such a manner. She would simply find one she could use.

Breakfast was very welcome, though she would have preferred a tray in her compartment or at the very least, the library. Biscuits had been heaped with creamy gravy laden with crumbled sausage, and there were mountains of eggs and potatoes and fried tomatoes and squash.

Eggs. She felt a pang of anxiety.

Rosie. The girls. Tigg and Jake. What had become of them when she did not return? She had been so upset at James's perfidy and threats and Andrew's arrest that she could not even remember seeing the twins after he had been taken away.

She was the worst guardian in the world, losing children left and right, leaving them scattered across the landscape, just as Maggie had said.

She could only hope that the Dunsmuirs would have collected them all and taken them away to safety in the Canadas. This hope must sustain her as she made her way there herself.

It might take months, but she would find a way.

Her appetite faded, but she forced herself to keep putting forkfuls of food in her mouth at regular intervals. She had gone hungry once and did not care to repeat the experience. If a person intended to escape, she had better do it on a full stomach.

"So, Lady Claire, what do you think of my train?"

Stanford Fremont leaned back in his chair, his thick workman's fingers toying with the delicate handle of his porcelain coffee cup. At the table behind him, Claire noticed, Tessie was drinking hers from a plain white mug, as were the other black coats taking breakfast with them.

Hmph. Her own cup was porcelain, too—and he was speaking directly to her. How she had risen in the world!

"It is quite a marvel," she said with sincerity. "I have never seen anything like it. Have you clocked its speed?"

"You must have been talking to James." He grinned at her. "We have indeed. One hundred miles per hour on the flat—and there's plenty of flat between here and San Francisco. Once we come down out of the mountains east of the Great Salt Lake, I expect she'll clock closer to a hundred and twenty."

"Goodness. Will that be a world record?"

"I expect so." He looked so satisfied and pleased with himself that Claire wanted to fling her coffee in his face.

But of course she did not. That would get her thrown into her compartment, and what good would that do?

"So the trip to San Francisco, then, will take how long?"

"With the carbonated coal, we won't need to stop as much. I expect we'll make it in twenty-four hours."

That was not much time. And at a speed of a hundred miles per hour? Even if she did contrive to lose Tessie's surveillance and get out a window or a door, to leap from a train at that speed or even half of it meant immediate death.

"And the stops we do make? Are there towns along the route?"

Towns where she could send a pigeon or a tube or whatever passed for communication in this sprawling land?

"Sure," he said, "though, you understand, there won't be time for sightseeing."

You will not be allowed off the train, she heard quite clearly.

"I shall be quite content to observe from these lovely windows," she said, and addressed herself to the fruit cup which appeared before her.

Outside, a plume of steam whipped past in the wind of their going. The window was open a sliver at the top, and she could smell it, over and above the smell of the grass and sagebrush that stretched to the horizon, punctuated by the red mesas and spires of rock that seemed to be unique to this part of the Territories.

Something didn't seem quite right.

The steam and the hot oil and the working iron of the locomotive—these smells were familiar to her. Even the smell of carbonated coal was familiar, after eighty miles of it only a few weeks ago. But there was something else. Something ... different.

She could not identify it, but it would bother her until she did. Perhaps one of those engineering books would hold the answer.

She laid her damask napkin upon the table. "With your permission, James, I should like to go into the library."

"Certainly. I shall join you there."

Fremont jerked his chin as Tessie looked up. She had not finished her breakfast, but she laid down fork and knife and stood.

Flanked by her two captors, Claire left the dining car feeling frustrated and anxious, her fine breakfast sitting uneasily in her stomach.

In the library, she perused volume after volume on subjects as varied as steam locomotion, metallurgy, and manufacturing, but she found nothing that might explain that peculiar smell. How odd that James had not noticed it. Was it something utterly mundane and she was being—as Lizzie might say—a worrywart over nothing?

It must be. There were any number of scientists and railroad men aboard, not to mention the owner of the railroad. If something had been out of kilter, they would have known.

By afternoon, they had steamed out of the desert, and stopped for the night in a thick forest, where they took on coal and the black coats set the Carbonator to work. When Claire woke the next morning, they were passing through a country of undulating grassland broken by pinnacles of stone and thundering herds of what Tessie told her was a creature called the buffalo. Claire had never seen any animal so huge and majestic— they reminded one of cattle in some ways, and in others were utterly unlike them. She watched leaping herds of antelope with fascination and something akin to joy, and, as they came down out of the mountains toward the enormous salt pan stretching for miles below them, on the side of the track Claire saw her first bear.

Of course, steaming past it on a downhill grade at nearly eighty miles per hour, she did not get much more than a glimpse.

Her hopes of escape faded utterly. Even if she did manage to get off the train, where would she go? She had not seen a single airship overhead, and according to Fremont's endless conversation on the subject, this was the only rail line running west between the Canadas and Texico City. There were more under construction, of course, Mr. Polk's Silver Nevada line, after which their train was named, being a case in point, but Claire could not see how she could get off this train without being picked up by another of Stanford Fremont's trains shortly thereafter.

And finding her way in one of these wild frontier towns, alone, without money or food, and without her lightning rifle, was unthinkable.

Every mile took her further and further from Santa Fe, which was beginning to feel like an old friend in comparison.

She must pin her hopes of escape on San Francisco.

"Tell me about our destination, Mr. Fremont," she said over drinks that afternoon. "Is it a large city, there on its seven hills?"

"Larger than Santa Fe, but not so spread out." He was already on his second brandy, while Claire's thimble of cordial sat nearly untouched. "The Viceroy of El Rey has his seat there, as does the Spaniard governor, so the society is quite, er, elevated. See, the Californias are divided up into these enormous ranchos, thousands and thousands of acres each. The owners are called Californios and each rancho has a market town. Everyone works for the Californio and owes their loyalty to that man's family."

"It sounds very … feudal."

"Oh, there's feuds, all right. Some of these rich landowners can get into a quarrel at the drop of a hat, and then they raid each other until their tempers cool. But with all the money they control, they like their good time. San Francisco has its own opera house. Did you know that Madame Louisa Tetrazzini herself sang there this spring? Thousands of people flooded the streets to see her, and she actually sang an aria from the steps of the opera house just to please 'em." He chuckled. "With them hot Spaniard tempers, I s'pose there would've been a riot if she hadn't."

Claire had heard Madame Tetrazzini once, in London. If ever a woman could create heaven simply by opening her mouth, it was she. No doubt her song had soothed the savage breasts of the surging crowds and she had been allowed to proceed into the building.

The steam puffed past outside the window, and Claire could smell it again. Only, it was stronger now, since they had descended onto the dry saltpan. More … burned.

"Mr. Fremont, I must ask you something."

"Sure, I can get you an audience with the Viceroy. He's the closest you'll probably ever come to a king."

"I have danced with the Prince Consort, thank you, and that is quite sufficient for me. No, what I would like to know is, by what process is the carbonated coal being used? Because I must say, the quality of the smoke and steam—the smell of it, sir—is disconcerting."

He chomped on the end of his cigarillo for a moment. "The steam smells?"

"It does. And not quite right, either."

He gazed at her as if he didn't understand. "James, has this girl got a bee in her bonnet? The steam smells? What is she on about?"

"Dear, perhaps you might wish to lie down. Mrs. Short will accompany you to your compartment."

"I do not wish to lie down, James, I wish to know what has changed in the carbonation process to make its product smell as though something is burning."

"Nothing's burning, missy, that ain't supposed to be."

"It doesn't smell right," she repeated stubbornly. Missy, indeed. "When the carbonated coal was used in Ross Stephenson's tender, it smelled normal. That is to say, it smelled like steam and iron and gear oil, as these things do. It did not smell like metal heating past the point of safe operation."

Fremont gaped at her, and then he guffawed. "Look who's been reading my engineering treatises! James, this one's a keeper."

"I am not to be kept, and I should appreciate it if you would refer to me as *your ladyship*, or *Lady Claire*, not *missy*."

In the overstuffed chair a few feet away, Claire distinctly heard Tessie draw in a breath.

"You don't say." Stanford Fremont's eyes narrowed. "Don't take that tone with me, missy. Where I come from—"

"Yes, I know. Children should be seen and not heard. But I am not a child."

"You are not an adult yet, either," James reminded her silkily. "Do remember your manners, Claire. Mr. Fremont is a kind and generous host. Here, let me refill your drink."

"No, thank you." Claire rose and shook out her skirts. "I believe I shall take your suggestion, James, and retire for an hour."

Head high, she glided from the lounge car, Tessie scrambling in her wake. The car was immediately behind the tender, and as she passed from it to the dining car beyond, the burning smell—hot metal and acid and something that triggered a memory of a house fire she had witnessed in Cornwall—was nearly overpowering.

How could they think that was normal? If she were the engineer, she would be stopping the train this instant to investigate.

Hurrying now, she gained the sleeping compartment, and then changed her mind. With Tessie still making her way through the sleeping car, Claire stepped into the caboose, past the Carbonator in its tied-down crate, and out onto the viewing platform at the back.

The hot wind snatched at her skirts and whipped them out in front of her, and she pressed a hand to her chignon to keep it in place. The railroad track scrolled into the endless distance until the mountains swallowed it up. On either side of the track, the salt pan stretched for miles in all directions, the sun beating down upon it, bouncing up off it, and baking every living thing at temperatures that must be well over one hundred.

The heat was devastating. But she could not go back in.

If she did, she would weep with frustrated rage, and much as she liked Tessie Short, she did not want to do so in front of her in case the woman was obliged to report upon it.

"Claire?" Tessie called from the doorway of the sleeping car. "I don't think Lord James will want you out th—"

The train jerked and knocked Tessie off her feet.

Claire was flung back into the doorway of the viewing platform, and before she could catch her breath, an explosion concussed her eardrums.

A fireball blossomed into the sky as under it, the train leaped the tracks, flinging cars this way and that as though a fractious giant had swatted them.

The doorway disappeared as earth and sky cartwheeled past.

Plowing up earth and salt and broken rail ties, the caboose scraped to a halt with a groan of dying metal.

The only thing that moved was the thick column of black smoke, rising into the burning sky.

Chapter 27

Andrew Malvern's knees buckled under him. Jake wedged a shoulder under his armpit, passed an arm about his waist, and heaved him up, and together, they staggered into the navigation gondola. Maggie and Lizzie followed, in case at any moment Mr. Malvern should tip over and collapse.

"Good show," he gasped. "I'm all right. Thank you. Dear God in heaven, thank you."

He tottered to the navigator's chair and clutched the map rack to hold himself upright, then gazed about at them.

Alice Chalmers looked as though the Angel Gabriel had come to give her a personal escort to heaven. "That was a close one," she said, almost shyly, from her post at the wheel—though why she stayed there Maggie could not imagine. She was not looking at their course at all. "I'm glad we were able to help."

Good grief, a daring rescue and a near brush with death, and she sounded like she was at a church jumble sale, presiding over the teapot. What was wrong with her?

He glanced from one to another. "Where is Tigg? And Claire? Are they with the engine?"

At the mention of the Lady's name, some of the brightness in Alice's face dimmed. "We think Tigg is aboard *Lady Lucy*, but we don't know for sure. And Claire left on Fremont's train this morning. At least, the girls believe she did. She never came back with them last night."

"Why not?" Mr. Malvern tried to stand, but his knees wobbled and he sat rather suddenly. "What happened?"

"Lord James took 'er to an 'otel," Maggie said. "'E wouldn't let us go wiv 'er—told us we could shove off and cross the desert in a pram for all he cared!"

"Nasty old boot," Lizzie put in. "Said 'e would lock 'er in a room with no windows and they'd be off to San Francisco this morning."

"San Francisco!" The color drained from his face. "We must pursue them!"

Alice left the wheel with a leap. "Mr. Malvern, you aren't recovered from your ordeal. Jake, take him to the crew's quarters in the starboard fuselage and find a bed for him. He'll need some—Lizzie, what's the matter?"

Lizzie had plastered herself against the viewing window. "Alice, we 'ave to go back to the airfield."

"Over my dead body. If we're going anywhere, it's the Canadas or San Francisco or—"

"No! Go back! That's Tigg down there, runnin' like mad. Don't you see 'im?"

Alice leaned far over the wheel, and Maggie dove between her legs to peer out the very bottom of the viewing port. Far below, a tiny dark figure ran and dodged between the craft moored on the field, waving his arms and jumping over barrels and crates. Even as they watched, he slowed, and Maggie could see the moment when hopelessness overcame him and he realized he was going to be left behind.

"Why in tarnation ain't he on *Lady Lucy*?" Alice demanded of no one in particular. She spun the wheel and the *Stalwart Lass* put her hip to the wind and came about in a great gliding circle.

With a leaping wave, Tigg took off for the eastern edge of the airfield, where the flattened, tended ground gave way to hillocks and dry watercourses and sagebrush once again.

Lady Lucy had lifted and gone, for her great golden fuselage was nowhere to be seen. But between Tigg and the edge of the airfield lay the Rangers' B-30, and to Maggie's eyes, there was far too much activity on her.

She had not been trained as a scout for nothing.

"Alice, that Ranger ship is awake and I don't like the look of it. I bet that lieutenant who pretended to be so nice to the Lady knows we just sprung 'is prisoner."

"Our engine ent gonna outrun that thing," Jake said. He had not removed Mr. Malvern, and the latter was again struggling to his feet.

"We must not leave Tigg."

"Ain't no question about leaving him," Alice said through stiff lips, as if he'd offended her. "Question is, how we gonna evade the Rangers when that ship lifts and comes after us? Nine, give me some reverse. Jake, get your skinny behind back to that basket. This is gonna be fast."

Maggie and Lizzie ran after Jake to the aft hatch. He grasped the crank and began to lower the basket, but their speed was so much faster than it had been at the pinnacle that it blew straight out behind like a wind sock. "One of you, get in!" Jake shouted. "Your weight will take it straight down."

Lizzie shrieked in an agony of indecision, torn between fear for Tigg and her own terror of heights. Without another thought, Maggie leaped into the basket, and before she could fairly get her feet into the bottom, Jake was winching her down so fast the crank was a blur.

The wind snatched the basket and swung it like a pendulum, but it did not blow back. Lower and lower they circled, and below them, Tigg's running figure disappeared beneath a garish scarlet fuselage that would look like a setting sun if it flew. He emerged on the other side, and now he only had to get past the B-30.

Maggie could feel the *Lass* adjust her course to meet him, out on the far side of the B-30 in the desert. Tigg could draw a trajectory with his eyes as well as the next man, and he changed his direction to the same heading.

Talk about touch and go.

She was close enough to the ground—ten or twelve feet—to see him clearly, now, and waved encouragingly. His coffee-colored face split in a white grin, and then he bent all his energy to the task of getting to that point in the sagebrush where basket would meet body and they could do the Billy Bolt to end all bolts.

Even over the roar of the wind, Maggie heard the shouts of the Rangers as they realized what the *Lass* was about. If before they had meant to pursue them, now it seemed that they were simply going to shoot them out of the sky, for here came a contingent of blue uniforms dragging another one of them rocket cannon—this one long and slender and no doubt possessed of the kind of aim that could take a ship out in one shot.

"Tigg!" she screamed. "Run!"

As if he had merely been standing there sipping a lemonade before, Tigg poured on the speed and in seconds he was running beneath the basket.

"Jake!" she shrieked upward. "More line!"

But he could not hear her, forty feet above, and Tigg was tiring, his hands grasping at the basket bottom fruitlessly, trying to get a grip.

Oh, if only she had a rope!

A rope!

Scrabbling with numb fingers, she pulled at the knots of Alaia's woven sash. She had left the lightning rifle in the gondola, for it was heavy, but hadn't removed the sash. She tied one end to the winch line just above the join that spread four cables to the corners of the basket, and whipped the other out over the side.

"Tigg! Grab hold!"

The ground raced below her, and on the edge of her vision she saw the Rangers push the cannon into position and ram something down its throat.

With a mighty leap like his very best dive from the Clarendon footbridge, Tigg grabbed the end of the rope.

Immediately the basket began to rise—the *Lass* fell up into the sky—and the rocket launched from the cannon with an explosion that slapped Maggie's ears.

Tigg kicked, hanging onto the sash with both hands and trying to find purchase on the side of the basket as Maggie grabbed him around the waist to pull him in.

The rocket struck the basket with the force of a runaway steambus, tearing the bottom and sides out of it as it blasted out the other side, trailing fire, into the sky.

Maggie screamed, dangling by nothing more than her grip on Tigg's waist as he hung onto her sash with both hands, his fingers piercing the knotwork.

"Hang on, Mags!" he shouted.

Weeping with terror and the cruel wind that needled tears from her eyes, she buried her face in the front of his dirty shirt and prayed.

Someone must have been listening, for the next thing she knew, hands were pulling her and someone had her in a hug so hard she could barely breathe and the wind finally stopped and when her eyes opened at last, gummy with grit and streaming with tears, there was Jake on his knees on the engine-room floor, hugging her to his chest like she were his own long lost sister, sobbing as if his heart would break.

ৡৎ

One of the children was sitting on her feet.

How dreadfully annoying. The weight kept her from turning over, from throwing off the sheets—she could hardly breathe. What were they about, the rascals? Why, she was just going to—

Claire opened her eyes.

Her cheek pressed into bare dirt that was loose and crumbly, as if it had been dug up. It smelled burned. Everything smelled burned, even the air, which had a peculiar cast to it. Not the clean, sharp light she had grown used to of late, but a smoky, rotten kind of light.

She lifted her head.

Blinked.

Her mouth fell open as she remembered what had happened—*what* had happened, but not why, or how.

And her feet? She reared up and attempted to turn over. Ah, there was the problem. The slatted side of a heavy crate lay across her legs.

Toes? Yes, they wiggled.

Knees? Both bent.

It had not broken her legs, thank goodness. As she moved, pain stabbed into her side, as vicious as a blow from the Cudgel, back in London. She gasped and tears started into her eyes.

Oh, dear.

Gritting her teeth, she shoved the planking off her legs, and slowly, breathing as shallowly as possible, climbed to her feet. She had never had a broken rib before, but Papa had, having fallen from a horse in Cornwall. Now she understood his bad temper. Well, she had no choice but to hope her corset would act as a binding, in the absence of anything else.

She stood, marveling that she could even breathe. The world had been transformed, and she could no longer see any familiar thing.

Yes, the sun still beat down on her bare head.

Yes, the saltpan crunched under her boots, its crystals winking and glittering.

The twin threads of the railway still extended back into the mountains, but where she stood, it was broken and twisted, dragged into tortured bends by the train cars' derailment. As she gazed at them, trying to get her bearings, a car groaned with the agony of twisting metal and fell on its side with an earth-shaking *boom*.

Dust sifted into the sky and was carried north by the wind.

Did any remain alive?

Tessie! Tessie Short had been immediately behind her in the sleeping car. There was the caboose, upside down. It must have thrown her as it flipped, for it now lay on its roof, its metal wheels helpless without the track to which they were mated.

There.

Limping, wheezing with the pain, Claire stumbled to what had been the sleeping car. It lay on its side, which meant she had to duck through the twisted door. At any moment it might collapse upon her, but if Tessie was alive, she must get her out.

A shoe, a stocking, a skirt. Tessie lay as though asleep on the partition, her back against the ceiling. She gazed, astonished, at something past Claire's shoulder, her head tilted at a peculiar angle.

"Tessie? Can you hear me?"

Claire touched her wrist, then her neck.

No pulse.

Her face crumpled, and the tears that had been so close trickled down her cheek. "Oh, Tessie. If it hadn't been for me, you would have been safe in Santa Fe with your children." Gently, she closed the open eyes. "I'm so sorry," she whispered.

The partition in her own compartment had popped off its moorings and now lay askew and crushed. There was her valise, lying on the window.

Or rather, on the dirt under it, for the window lay in pieces everywhere. She picked it up. She had not unpacked it, since if one planned to escape, one had to be ready to snatch it up and do so at a moment's notice.

This was not quite the escape she'd had in mind.

She must find out whether any others had lived.

Once again sliding through the sideways door, she set the valise on the ground and approached the other cars. There had been no one in the library, nor the dining room, either. James and Fremont had been in the lounge, and she assumed that aside from Tessie, the other staff had been forward taking their meal.

The lounge car, being immediately behind the tender, had not fared so well as the caboose. Half of it was utterly gone, as was the tender. In fact, the explosion had torn the locomotive to pieces, leaving only the great smokestack and half the cowcatcher in recognizable form, lying on the other side of the track at some distance from the mangled body.

She walked forward, skirting pieces of flung mahogany, now reduced to kindling, in which brass and copper glinted. What could possibly have caused such a disaster?

Clearly it had been centered in the tender. The great furnace full of the carbonated coal would have—

The carbonated coal.

Her mind could not grasp it, but there was the evidence that something very dreadful, very unforeseen, had caused the carbonated coal to explode in the steam engine. She staggered back, unwilling to look on destruction of such magnitude any longer.

The lounge car. Could any have survived?

In the wind, hundreds of Texican bills—dollars, they were called—blew in whirlwinds with the dust, sifting and blowing out of what was left of the end wall of the lounge car. Mr. Fremont, it appeared, had had a safe there. And then she received the dreadful answer to her question, which would repeat itself in her nightmares for many years to come.

She did not know how long it was, but some time later she came to herself, on her hands and knees in the dirt fifty feet from the destruction, retching up the rest of the contents of her stomach.

The pain finally drove her to her feet. Wiping her mouth on her torn and filthy sleeve, she staggered to the caboose, her mind reeling at the possibility that of all the people on Stanford Fremont's train, she might be the only survivor.

She had been furthest from the destruction, flung through an open door when the brakeman had thrown the switch to slow the train, and thrown out again when the caboose had been wrenched off its couplings.

Pure chance. And luck. And perhaps the grace of God.

The hot wind whistled across the saltpan, pressing her blouse against her back and doing absolutely nothing to cool her burning skin.

Claire walked back to her valise, removing her blouse as she went. The St. Ives pearls still lay under her chemise, the raja's emerald on her finger—and that only because her fingers were still a little swollen from her ordeal in the velogig. She put on a fresh waist. Then she wrapped the torn blouse over her head like a fieldwoman's scarf, winding the sleeves about her throat.

As protection from the furnace of the sun, it wasn't much, but it would have to do.

Feeling hollow, as though her soul had been torn away and twisted like the iron of the train, she forced herself to consider her prospects.

The sun was on its way down, lengthening the shadows of the tumbled train cars like beseeching fingers across the white waste of salt.

The last town she could remember seeing had been some miles before the bear, and that had been on the downhill side of the mountains.

She had no idea where the next town might be. It could be San Francisco, for all she knew, with any number of miles of the Kingdom of Spain to get through before that.

She had no food and no water, for the dining car had been crushed between the library and the exploding lounge.

She did not even have the means to bury the dead, for the saltpan was hard and unyielding, and with her broken rib, she could not dig even if there had been anything but broken spars to use as a shovel.

Tessie. James.

Tears welled in her eyes. She had hated him, yes. She would willingly have gone the rest of her life without seeing him ever again. But to die like this? His body left unclaimed and unmourned, merely unidentified bits and pieces that the vultures even now circling lower and lower would soon discover?

She gave a single sob. She could not even identify enough in the carnage to conceal it from the birds and predators.

She could do nothing.

With what they're paying me to attend you I can send my kids, Kate and Jeremy, to the city school for a year.

She did not want to go back to the remains of the lounge car. She did not want to look at what lay there. But she owed Tessie a debt, and if she survived, she had only one way to repay it.

When she was finished her sad task, shuddering, she picked up her valise and made her way back to the caboose. Here lay the culprit, the root of all this destruction, smashed and flung out of the broken car. The heavy iron and glass of the chamber was twisted and broken now, the power cell—

The power cell!

It had nearly cost Andrew his life. It had certainly cost James his. But would it take hers, too—or would it mean a new life somewhere if she were able to find her way to civilization before she collapsed?

The cowling was bent, but if she lifted this panel, no, pushed it—tore it off—*there*. The power cell lay within its housing, its fine brass windings unharmed. The glass globe within was smashed to pieces, but that could be replaced. It was the gears and works that were important.

Working quickly, she released all the cables and hoses that still survived, and pulled the cell from its damaged prison. Dr. Craig had told her this was her inheritance. It was heavy, that was true. But it was also hers, to do with as she would.

She dropped it into the valise, too, fastened it closed, and bent to hook its two leather handles over her shoulders. Her broken rib stabbed, and she gasped in pain as she straightened.

The gleaming ribbon of undamaged track stretched out into the distance, giving her a direction, at least.

Claire set her teeth, hefted the valise on her back, and took in the wreck one last time. It was foolish to hope that something would move. And sure enough, nothing did ... except the wind, moaning through the wreckage, humming against the broken metal like a dirge.

She set her face toward the east and gasped in fright.

Something did move. Like a cloud, but not a cloud.

An airship.

A ship with a double fuselage, its gondola hanging between them in the shape of a Y. She had only seen one ship designed like that in all the time she had been in this country.

Her heart lifted, a sob catching in her throat.

Claire began to run.

Epilogue

TO: TEXICAN TERRITORIAL BANK, SANTA FE
FROM: ROYAL RENO BANK, RENO
           ROYAL KINGDOM OF SPAIN AND THE CALIFORNIAS

TRANSFERRED HEREWITH IS THE SUM OF FIFTY THOUSAND DOLLARS PAYABLE TO MASTER JEREMY AND MISS KATE SHORT, SAND STREET, SANTA FE STOP CONDOLENCES ON LOSS OF YOUR MOTHER STOP SHE WAS A GOOD WOMAN STOP

END

Coming soon

Don't miss book four in the Magnificent Devices series—
Brilliant Devices will be released in early 2013!

www.shelleyadina.com

Find Shelley on Facebook: www.facebook.com/shelley.adina or on Twitter @shelleyadina.

To learn about Shelley's Amish women's fiction written as Adina Senft, visit www.adinasenft.com. And don't miss her blog, *A City Girl's Guide to Plain Living*, at www.adinasenft.com/blog!

Available now

The Magnificent Devices series
> *Lady of Devices* (2011)
> *Her Own Devices* (2011)

The Moonshell Bay series (contemporary romance)
> *Caught You Looking* (2011)

Other
> *Immortal Faith* (2011, paranormal YA)
> *Peep, the Hundred-Decibel Hummer*
> (2012, children's picture book)

The All About Us series (contemporary YA)
> *It's All About Us* (2008)
> *The Fruit of My Lipstick* (2008)
> *Be Strong and Curvaceous* (2009)
> *Who Made You a Princess?* (2009)
> *Tidings of Great Boys* (2009)
> *The Chic Shall Inherit the Earth* (2010)

3075159R00135

Made in the USA
San Bernardino, CA
02 July 2013